God, it's me, Andrew." I whispered.

I hadn't prayed in so long I thought that maybe He didn't recognize my voice. Everything was happening so fast—I had to figure a way to keep myself from going crazy. Whatever worked for Mom has to work for me, too.

"I'm having some hard times here. So much is coming at me at once and I know you are there for me but I'm just so scared. I don't know what's going to happen or what I'm supposed to do. I need some help, please. Whatever you want me to do, God, please help me. I can't do this by myself."

"Keeps the hair on the back of your neck standing until the last page."

~ Judy Candis, author of *All Things Hidden*

Heaven Sent

Montré
Bible

West Bloomfield, Michigan

WARNER BOOKS

NEW YORK   BOSTON

Published by Warner Books with Walk Worthy Press™

Warner Books

Time Warner Book Group
1271 Avenue of the Americas, New York, NY 10020

Walk Worthy Press
33290 West Fourteen Mile Road, #482, West Bloomfield, MI 48322

Visit our Web sites at www.twbookmark.com and www.walkworthypress.net.

Printed in the United States of America

First Edition: April 2005

10 9 8 7 6 5 4 3 2 1

Library of Congress Cataloging-in-Publication Data

Bible, Montré
     Heaven sent / Montré Bible.—1st Warner Books ed.
        p. cm.
     ISBN 0-446-69529-7
   1. Fathers and sons—Fiction. 2. Supernatural—Fiction. 3. Young men—Fiction. 4. Twins—Fiction. I. Title.
     PS3602.I25H43 2005
     813'.6—dc22

                                                     2004017800

Book design and text composition by Nancy Singer Olaguera
Cover design by Erin Sharpe

For Rosa,
without whom
this could not be.

Heaven Sent

"**H**urry! Get in the car!" *She yells at the top of her lungs. She is running so frantically that she doesn't notice the blood running down her leg. She doesn't have time to notice. All she can see in the pitch-black darkness are the taillights of the car ahead of her. She runs with the wind, and even the broken branches on the stony trail don't seem to trip her up. The young man in the car starts it up and she jumps in. He cranks the engine, and before she can even close the door he is off. Dark whispering shadows consume the forest behind them.*

"It's moving faster!" she yells.

He takes a glance at her leg. "You're bleeding."

"Drive faster!" She doesn't care about herself. She turns to the backseat at the little innocent eyes staring back at her.

"I'm trying!" he yells back. She knows they can't run for long. They've run for far too long already. She reaches to the backseat and tries to comfort the crying baby.

"I won't let him get you," she says through her tears, but her eyes grow even larger as the darkness behind them is now practically on the car. She can hear the whispers cackling through the window and scratching the surface. A look of panic and then anger fills her eyes. The car jumps as if something is trying to pick it up from behind.

"What's happening?" he yells.

"Don't stop! I won't let him get . . ." The back window shatters and the darkness grabs the baby.

She reaches out while releasing a spine-chilling scream. "Andrew!!!"

"Andrew!"

I jumped up from my sleep. Mrs. Gardner was standing over my desk giving me that stern look. I flipped through my book attempting to find the correct chapter the rest of the class was reading. A couple of people in class chuckled. I was embarrassed for falling asleep and my heart was still beating hard. These crazy dreams have to stop. They have been really interfering with my school performance, and if I have them I'm still tired when I wake up.

I looked up at the clock. This class was way too long. I couldn't wait until I was finally through with school. There has to be more to life than people frantically going to school, getting a job, falling in love, getting married, and having children, only to teach them the same routine. There has to be more. Throughout my life I have tried to find some logical explanation for this mindless rut.

Trying to find my life's purpose, I'd sit for hours daydreaming that I was part of some adventure, ya know, the type of stuff you see on TV. I hoped that one moment I would find out that I was from Krypton or somewhere. Okay, maybe I read too many comic books and just maybe I daydream too much while I'm supposed to be paying attention in my history class. But dang, Mrs. Gardner had to be the worst teacher in the world. Why do people with horrible speech skills become stuff like history teachers? History lessons need to be upbeat and fun for people my age not to fall asleep.

I sat there listening to her ramble in her quiet monotone voice about something or other. I really, honestly, was trying to pay attention but the rain hitting the window next to my seat was more interesting.

Next to me, Tonya Jeffries was putting on makeup. I watched her for a second. How much makeup was she gonna put on? She was already beautiful to me. Too bad she was going with that butthead Leonard Freeman. I think if she wasn't with him she would be dating me. Well she'd be dating me if I actually tried to talk to her. She was fine to every guy in school, but every time she spoke to me she talked to me like I was her brother or cousin or something. Matter of fact, that was her title for me, "cuzzin." I guess it was because we all attended the same church.

"Tonya, this ain't cosmetology class," I joked with her. She was liable to create a permanent line with that eyeliner pencil if she did one more stroke.

"Boy, you crazy." She smiled. "Hey, Andrew, let me borrow your notes after class—okay, cuzzin?"

I nodded in agreement. Okay, my name is Andrew and I am a sucker with a capital S. Look, up in the sky, it's Suckerman! I wasn't even taking notes. If paying attention actually paid money, this teacher would be in debt. I guess I could give her yesterday's notes. She didn't pay attention in class ever. Maybe one day Tonya would realize that the true love of her life was the man who helped her keep her passing grades in this history class.

Just look at her, was there any flaw in this woman at all? She had a Janet Jackson smile and the skin of a goddess. Her hair was incredibly long and brown and completely all hers, no extensions at all. Did I mention how deeply hypnotic her eyes were with their diamond-like sparkle and their cinnamon color? I loved the way she pulled the hair behind her left ear and how the remaining would fall ever so slightly over her right eye. Her lips were coated with a thin layer of gloss, giving them that wet sensuous look that made me just want to kiss them so-so softly.

I turned around and looked at my reflection in the misty window—I wasn't a bad-looking brotha either. I wasn't your typical-looking seventeen-year-old. My face was smooth, unlike most kids my age, no facial hair at all except for my sideburns. I had just had my birthday a month ago, so I thought it was because everyone else in my senior class was older than me. My hair was curly and thick but I had never put any type of hair chemical on it at all.

People asked me often if I was mixed with something else. Nope. Both Mama and Daddy, Andrea and Anthony Turner, were as Black as can be. Mama, however, could be mixed; for a black woman she had a bright complexion and she was adopted, so she didn't know her real parents.

Daddy had left us a long time ago, and I hadn't heard from him since I was a little boy. Sometimes he would drop by late at night and talk to Mama and leave the same night. He was a preacher, and some people rumored that he went crazy. I guess that's why I don't get into my Bible a lot. I mean, I'm a Christian, but not as much as I could be. If God couldn't protect my father from insanity, then why should I even bother with getting deep into religion? Besides, the Bible just appeared to be a bunch of stories that had nothing to do with the life I was living; in a nutshell, I just didn't see the point.

I stared at myself. I wondered if I looked like my daddy. Maybe I got his ears. I knew I was taller than him. I didn't like being tall. I had a manly body with a baby face. I had these dark, defined brows that accented my every word. My eyes were a light brown, almost green, but really brown—okay, hazel. Physically, I could be quite a pimp . . . oh yeah, I could see it now, my harem of women walking behind me as I went to class. Hey, Andrew! I love you, Andrew! they would say as I strolled down the halls.

Pop that fantasy. Let's come back to reality in Mrs. Gardner's history class. What was my problem? Why didn't I have a girlfriend or, for that fact, Tonya? Oh yeah, I didn't know how to talk. When a girl came around I was bound to say something really dumb, and girls at this school seemed to be very attracted to verbal communication. There was a class on everything but pickup lines. Now that would be a cool class. I would take it, twice maybe.

So I had to settle for "friends," the closest I would get to any female. Now Tonya was fixing her hair, her long brown hair. She was seriously primping. How she did all this beauty preparation without the teacher saying anything was beyond me. I was deep in the friend zone with Tonya. Once a guy falls into the friend zone there is no way out. Girls make sure of that. This zone has a door with a handle on only one side. Once you walk in, you don't walk out. You can't. It's a zone where a female will talk to you, cry to you, hug you, almost undress in front of you until she remembers that you are a guy. You have access to her mind but no access to her heart. In a nutshell, this zone is hell; complete, utter hell.

If this was hell, was Tonya Satan? No, nothing that beautiful could be Satan. But I think I remember in church the preacher saying that Satan was beautiful, the most beautiful angel in heaven; that is, before he got exiled and took a third of the angels and fell to earth. How many exactly were a third of the angels in heaven? And where are all these angels now? All these crazy thoughts were spinning in my head like a whirlwind; it made me wonder if my father had gone nuts because he thought too much. The bell finally rang a sound better than what any angel could sing in my opinion. I grabbed my books and stuffed them in my bag.

"Cuzzin, you forget about me?" Tonya asked, still at her desk, her arms out as if she were a helpless damsel in one of those romance novels beckoning my strong arms to pick her up and embrace her ever so gently.

"I could never forget about you . . ."

"You said I could use your notes!" she interrupted me. Okay, scratch that last thought.

I pulled some notes out of my folder. "Um, Tonya, you know it's raining and you worked all that time on your hair."

"I knoooow," she whined. "Hey, can you be a sweetheart and let me borrow your umbrella?"

"But uhh, I gotta catch the bus, and Leonard takes you home."

"I know, but I gotta walk to the car, pleeeeease." Her eyes were piercing my very heart. The friend zone had caught me in its horrible web. I was a pitiful fly waiting to be sucked of all life by the black widow. God forbid she gets wet.

"Okay, here." I handed it to her. "Just make sure you bring it back to me tomorrow."

"Thanks, you're an angel." She rubbed my face with the palm of her hand before she left. Oh, she is good, playing me like a fiddle and I keep giving her the sheet music. "An angel," she called me. Like an angel without wings is how I'm falling for Tonya. No, I'm in hell, just pure hell. I looked up at the clock. Oh no, the bus! I ran past Tonya and the herd of other students blocking the way in the hall.

"Scuze me! Sorry!" I hurtled past one student after another like an NFL football player, knocking over innocent bystanders in the process. I clung hard to my open book bag to make sure the books didn't fall out and busted through the front door of the school building.

I almost slipped when I got outside. The rain was pouring down so hard that my curly mini-Afro was soon slick and straight down on my head. I squinted to see if I could find my bus. But all I could see through the shower was the distant taillights driving off, and I could smell the exhaust trailing behind. I was gonna have to walk home. I zipped up my jacket to keep my sweater from getting any more soaked and pulled up my hood. I wiped my face with the sleeve of my jacket and tucked my hands within the sleeves like gloves.

"Dang it, Tonya . . ." I said to myself, wishing she wasn't so beautiful. I looked around to make sure no one heard me make that comment out loud. I thought to myself all too much, to the point where I wasn't sure if I was thinking or actually speaking at times. Here in the small town of Heaven, Texas (population 8,281), gossip spread around faster than e-mail, and the last thing I needed was people passing around that I liked Tonya. Not that it really mattered, but I just didn't want people in my business. Maybe a little gossip would help my popularity. It probably wouldn't be a surprise to many people though.

The rain was fierce. I thought maybe I should jog but it only made the rain hit me harder.

"Okay, just walk and look down," I told myself. I could see that my light brown shoes went from a freckled look to a completely dark brown. Water was soaking the bottom of my pant legs, so I kneeled down real quick to roll them up.

I was four blocks from home; I was going to be late for work again. Man, sometimes it's better to stay in bed. A passing car splashed a tidal wave onto my back while I was rolling my cuffs that caused me to launch a feminine screech, a screech I might have held in if I was still in the company of my friends. The water was cold and dirty and rolled down the back of my jacket and backpack. I flapped my arms to remove the excess water, which was a slightly redundant act since it was still raining. I growled slightly and crossed my arms, continuing my voyage through the streets. When I reached the intersection, I saw an old man standing in the rain and trying to collect money from cars passing by. This man must be really poor to endure such weather.

"Hey, old man, you need to find shelter," I said, touching his shoulder. He grimaced at me. His face was unshaven and his skin was dark and blotchy. His hair was dreaded in the most unusual fashion, locked with all types of lint and particles of dirt. His wrinkles told his age much like the rings of a tree tell theirs. But his eyes were most amazing. They seemed to be glazed over and appeared to have rings themselves. The whites were almost yellow. His eyes were dark brown but appeared to have a bluish haze like a glaze reflecting the sky, and if you didn't look closely you would think they were blue. For a minute I wondered if the man was blind, but he made eye contact with me. What type of life must one live to develop eyes like this man's?

"Help me out, brotha, anything you can spare, a dime . . . a nickel . . ." His voice was high and crackled. I told him I'd give him something and guided him out of the rain underneath the gas station covering.

"What's your name?"

"My name is Frank . . . I just need a little change, that's all, I ain't tryin' to hurt nobody," he continued.

"I know, I know, I want you out of this rain. No point on giving you anything if you get sick, now is it?" He laughed with me. I took off my backpack and jacket and wrapped him in my jacket. I went into my back pocket and removed a folded ten-dollar bill.

"Okay, Frank, promise me something."

"Okay, what? I just need a lil change . . ."

"I know." I smiled slightly, unsure if he was coherent.

I grabbed his hands and looked him in the eyes. "Promise me that you won't use this money for alcohol. Take this money and use it for the shelter and go there now."

His head looked left and then right and whined to me. "I ain't tryin' to hurt nobody . . . I just need some change . . ."

"Frank, promise me."

"Okay, brotha, I promise."

"Okay, Frank, God is our witness. I won't be able to see you but He can."

Frank looked down and looked away. "I'm trying . . . I'm trying to get my life right. I used to preach, I used to be a preacher. I know this. I don't know what happened. I need to pray, I know I do. I know I do." I looked at him and my heart almost stopped. For a minute I imagined that my dad was standing before me. What if my dad was on the street somewhere drowning his soul in alcohol? The rain got harder and the cold breeze was giving me chills. My heart felt for Frank. For an instant I saw what Frank was. *I saw him as a preacher, married.*

I grabbed his shoulder and directed his attention back to me. He looked at me with his sad glazed eyes. "Why don't you go home, Frank? Go back to church?"

"I can't go back . . . They wouldn't let me back in." *I fig-ured that Frank came from a very conservative church. He wouldn't be allowed to return in his present state. But that wasn't the only thing, I could feel Frank's overwhelming pride.* I was peeking into his soul like he was a book.

"Well, Frank, you shouldn't care about those people, this is about you and God. I'm sure it's not His divine plan for you to live your days out here begging."

"I know . . . I need to get right," he repeated.

I looked him dead in the eyes and wanted to shoot the passion from within my heart into his. Suddenly I had an idea—it gripped me and I knew it was the right thing to do and the only thing I could really give him that mattered.

"Then get right, Frank. I'll pray with you if you like." He nodded, and I grabbed his dark, hard hands. His fingertips were the only rough part of his hands. The rest was smooth but plastic feeling, not soft. His hands were very dirty and long, and normally I would have been reluctant to touch them. But it wasn't about me; it was about helping Frank reconnect. As I prayed I looked up, and Frank began to cry. This was evidently a prayer that Frank needed, and con-necting with God wasn't hard for him. I remembered that someone had told me those who seem farthest from God are the ones God wants the most. It touched my own heart and even increased my own faith watching Frank cry. He opened his eyes after my prayer and his eyes seemed a bit clearer and he stared me directly in the eyes. I smiled at him and hugged him.

"You're a good man. You have a good heart," Frank told me.

"You're good too, Frank, now go home." I watched as Frank pulled a bottle of whiskey from his pocket and poured it out. Not only had Frank connected with God in that instant; *we* had connected. I watched him walk off slowly down the street. The rain roared down in buckets, but all that didn't even matter to me. I continued to walk home and it seemed that all these things were part of a divine plan, even my missing that bus. Maybe I was meant to meet and connect with Frank. Now whatever else happened was up to Frank. I truly believed in God and that somehow I was part of some bigger picture and experiences that only reinforced that belief. It may not be destined for me to ever see Frank again, but it encouraged me that my life—my bad day—was used to turn his bad day into a good one. Then at that moment, my bad day wasn't so bad after all.

The rain didn't seem to be easing up at all and I began to get really cold with the mixture of the wind and rain blowing against the direction I was walking. Running would only make things worse.

"Oh crap, I hope my books don't get wet." My backpack was soaked and I was sure the water was seeping through the material. I moved my backpack to the front and cradled it like a child, hoping to protect the probably already soaked books. I couldn't open my eyes entirely before a shower of water was hitting my entire face. If I looked up, I was sure that I might drown. Now that would be an interesting headline for the evening news . . . KID DROWNS IN RAIN. No, that would be embarrassing. Well I couldn't be real embarrassed if I were dead.

I was trying to avoid the cars that were passing by as they created tidal waves from the flooding streets. Some of these cars didn't know the meaning of slowing down when the rain got heavier. Another car passed by and slowed down; I could tell only because the brake lights glowed so brightly in the blinding veil of rain. Beaming-white lights joined the red brake lights. Was the car backing up? Yes! I stopped walking and squinted to see who was attempting to rescue me, or was this some cruel joke merely to tease me? Folks in school did that often. Some would see you walking and would honk at you and wave and keep driving. Others would even drive past, knowing that you would be going to the same place as them and when you got there they would be like, "Hey I saw you walking but I was in a rush, so you know . . ." and I would want to say no, I don't know. I don't understand how you can drive past a suffering person you knew was going in your direction. But not this person; no, this person was taking time to rescue me from this storm . . . I hoped.

"Andrew?" the voice inside the car yelled out. "Man, get in this car!" The car was close enough that I recognized it. It was a rusty, burgundy Cadillac. The windows were tinted. Inside, the voice was not only familiar, but also extremely ghetto.

"Big Mack?"

"Drew, if you don't get in this car, boy, I'm gonna pull off fo' real."

Big Mack was my best friend. We called him Big Mack not because he was big—he was only five feet four inches—but because his real name was Mackenzie. He had to be the most ghetto white boy I knew, but he was super cool. There was nothing Mackenzie wouldn't do for me. We had gone to school together since elementary. He kept his hair short in a buzz-cut style and always kept a nicely trimmed goatee. His ears were pierced, and this boy loved to sing. To me, he looked slightly Latino. Actually, most people questioned what color he was, because when he wore a baseball cap down on his head with his tanned skin he almost looked black. I laughed to myself at the thought.

"Boy, quit laughing and being goofy and get in this car,

damn!" He rolled up his window. I ran to the other side of the car, splashing through the puddles in the process. I grabbed the handle but it didn't give. Tried again, still didn't open. Okay, now I was getting impatient. I knocked on the window.

"Hold up!" a muffled voiced yelled from inside. I held my peace and looked around to make sure no oncoming cars were going to hit me. I was soaked and cold. I looked like I had just been swimming with all my clothes on. The door clicked and from the inside the door was pushed open.

"I forgot your car was raggedy," I laughed. Mackenzie threw some newspapers down on the seats.

"Just sit yo' raggedy a** down on those newspapers. I don't want you getting my seats all wet."

"Dude, why do you always gotta cuss me out?"

"Well *dude*," he mocked my slang, "I forgot you're Mr. Preacher boy." I sat down and threw my backpack in the backseat.

"Big Mack, I am not nor will I ever be a preacher. I know some stuff but that's about it. I'm not trying to end up like my dad. I just find life easier the closer I am to God."

"You believe what people say about your daddy is true? Man, come on! There's gotta be more to it than that. People used to say ya' daddy would freak out about demons being everywhere and angels . . ."

"Can we just . . . not talk about him. I know what people say. All I know is that he's insane and he's gone somewhere. My mom won't tell me any more."

"Yeah, well, life for me is fine without church, thank you very much. I'm not too sure if I believe all that demon stuff. Shoo', you talk so much about God to folks anyways, you might as well grow up and be a preacha'."

"What are you talking about?" I looked away. Did I really

talk about God all the time? Was preaching based solely on ordination or was it something as genetic as singing? I had seen whole families who were gifted. Mackenzie, his mother, his father, and even his baby sister could sing like angels. Was the ability to understand and bring others closer to God a gift of mine? Was I, by some universal law or some cosmic cataclysm, chosen to be God's agent on earth to thwart the evil plan of Satan and bring people into the divine plan of God . . . had I been reading too many comic books?

Mackenzie swerved a little bit on the road.

"Maybe you should slow down." I clicked my seatbelt on, almost forgetting that my compadre was a crazy driver. He handled his car as if it were a horse trying to break loose from its reins. What was the DMV thinking when they gave this guy a license?

"You seem tense, Drew, relax, enjoy the ride."

"I would relax more if you learn to drive." Mackenzie turned his head and stared at me for a good two seconds. Three seconds, four, five, six.

"Hey, can you look at the road and not at me!" That was beginning to freak me out and he knew it.

"Apologize and admit that I can drive." Mackenzie definitely had the dice and wasn't going to give up till I gave in to his little game.

"Fine! *Okay!* You drive so wonderfully!" I stared at him as he continued to drive with his head pointed in my direction.

"And . . ."

"And . . . I'm sorry! Dang, Mackenzie! Look at the road." He slowly turned his head back toward the road and continued to drive, smirking a bit and even speeding up some. I'm sure he thought it was cool to freak me out.

"So uh, how's your mom doing?"

I froze. I didn't want to tell him. I knew he was my friend and was concerned, but my mother hadn't been herself lately for about a month.

"Why? Is your mother asking about her?" This time I looked away through the rainy glass window. Mackenzie bit his lip, holding back his own tongue.

"Naw, I'm just concerned, that's all. I'm ya' boy and gotta look out for ya." He patted my shoulder and I patted his hand to acknowledge his concern. Then a cold chill ran down my spine. And for that moment I imagined his mother coming over to our house. What could she have seen? *My mother opening the door, half dressed, eyes all red. What would my mother say? I couldn't hear these things. But I know Big Mack's mom would have thought my mother was crazy. That would make her think my mother was taking drugs or something. But she wasn't; no, not at all, she was just sick.*

"Your mom thinks my mom is crazy doesn't she?" I asked, still looking out the window. He looked shocked—I could faintly see his reflection in the window.

"Well, she went to your house the other day because she was worried because she hadn't seen her in some time. Your mom has locked herself away, man, is that cool? I'm just checking to see if you all right, ya' know." He confirmed everything that had just hit my mind. It scared me a bit. It was almost like déjà vu. I looked at him with a straight face.

"I'm cool, if me or my mom need help, you'll know. I'll come to you, Mack."

"Well, man, I'm here if you need a brotha." I laughed at his "brotha" comment but, to me, Mack was a brother—the brother I never had. Being an only child was probably the hardest thing for me. Some kids get used to it but that wasn't my case. I was the type of kid who always wanted somebody else there. I mean it seems that every game is made for at least two people. The only solo game I could think of was solitaire, and I didn't even know how to play that. I remember asking my mom when she was going to remarry and have another child. She'd just smile and look at me with her sad eyes and tell me that I was all she needed. But I always wondered what it would be like to have a real brother, someone whom I could share secrets with, fight with, and laugh with. Mackenzie was the next best thing.

Mackenzie and I had met when we were in the fourth grade. He was way chubbier back then and definitely a girl repellent because of his overall attitude. But we all were. If there was a girl near she got her hair pulled or some dirt thrown in her face, just because.

"Wake up, man, and get out of my car." Mackenzie shoved my shoulder, bringing me out of my daydream. Lately, it seemed as if my imagination could take me into another realm. I took "my imagination carried me away" literally.

"Dang, I'm sorry I wasn't paying attention, I was . . ."

"Daydreaming—I know, I know. Who is it this time . . . or are you still sprung on Tonya?" I looked at Mackenzie and tried to pretend as if his comment did not faze me. Oh yeah—I wanted to blush and grin, but I didn't want him to know that. One way of being cool was never letting anyone see you sweat—or was that a deodorant commercial slogan? Whatever, that was my motto now.

"Whatever, dude." I grabbed my backpack from the backseat. "Hey, if it's raining in the morning, can you pick me up?"

"No problem. Matter of fact, check the weather report tonight, then call me so I'll know if I need to get up early."

"Cool, will do, peace out, Mack." I slammed the door shut and threw up the peace sign and watched him speed backward out the driveway. Mackenzie never slows down in the rain.

Here I am playing the game of Jeopardy:

Can I have greatest DMV bloopers for 500?

Answer: People get in accidents trying to avoid accidents with this person.

Question: Who is Mackenzie Larue?

Correct!

chapter 2

The rain was settling down as I rummaged through my pockets for my keys. Why did the jingle of keys seem to trigger an automatic response from my bladder? I danced back and forth grabbing my keys and inserting them into the lock. The jiggling swayed the unlocked door open. I quickly threw my backpack to the side and ran for the bathroom at the end of the hall.

After quickly relieving myself it dawned on me the door was unlocked. Was I crazy!? Someone could have broken in and here I am running through the house with only my bladder on my mind! I left the bathroom trying to be silent, as if I didn't make enough noise running through the house the first time. Maybe Mom came home early from work. I walked quietly through the hall to my mom's room. I peeked in her door and, yep, there she was asleep.

"Mom, I'm home," I whispered, checking to see if she was in a deep sleep. I looked closer and could see she was sweating. She was getting worse. I touched her forehead; her skin felt cold and clammy, and it gave me shivers.

I imagined that her boss was probably concerned about her health and sent her home for the day. But I knew my mom—she probably didn't want to go. Her eyes popped open.

"What are you doing?" She glared at me so diabolically.

"What? I'm just feeling your forehead, Mom, you're sick."

"No, you're doing more, stop it. Stop it right now! I will not let them get you too!"

I stared at her, confused.

"Let who get me, Mom? Never mind . . . you're not well. I'll get you some water. Go back to sleep." I stood up to leave, but she grabbed my arm tightly and I was shocked at her strength. I would have fallen over but I managed to gain my balance. She looked at me; her face was distraught, as if she had seen something horrible.

"I don't want to lose you, baby, you mean so much to me; you know that, don't you?" Tears flowed down her face and into her mouth.

"Yes, Mama, I know. Don't worry, you just had a nightmare."

"I don't want you to get hurt, but—but I don't know what to do now." She sounded so helpless and frail—nothing like her normal self. The mother I knew growing up was so strong—almost like a soldier. She was the mother and the father in the house, and she absolutely never allowed anything to bother her. We had moved several times through Texas until I was in the fourth grade, and then we settled here in the small town of Heaven. I think she liked that it was small. *She had avoided the bigger cities like Houston and Dallas. I think maybe because my father lived somewhere there.* She never told me that but I just felt it sometimes.

"Stop it! You want them to come!? Stop it, d**n it! Stop!" I stood shocked that she cursed, never before had I heard her do that. She screamed, sweat pouring down her face. She sat up, and her blanket fell from her shoulders. Her gown was drenched in sweat and she stared up at the wall in front of her. She was inhaling each breath like it required all her strength. I could smell how stagnant her breath was. She just stared blankly at the walls and then back at me. I noticed the dark circles under her sunken eyes. A single tear appeared, followed by one of my own. She kept staring up at the wall and it forced me to look, but I saw nothing. I used to see babies direct their attention like that, it would make me feel that they could see something I couldn't.

"Mom, lie back down, please." I tried to direct her back down but she pushed me back with such a force that I landed against the wall next to the bed. I shook off the pain and I watched as she grabbed the lamp next to her bed and threw it at the wall. I stayed in the corner and began to pray. "Jesus, help us, I need you, help us, Jesus." Her eyes snapped at me, and my heart jumped from the harsh look.

"Lord, help me please."

Her eyes softened and her whole visage changed. Her eyes closed and she fell into her pillow with an exhausted crash. Was she sleeping now? Did she pass out? I crawled back over to the bed. I covered her with the blanket and opened a window. The air smelled like rain, and the curtains waved gently across my face. It appeared the storm was calming down. I slowly backed out of the room, watching her slumber. My face was wet with my own tears. My God, what was happening to my mother? Was she going crazy, too, like my dad? I know she was constantly studying biblical books and reading old papers about theology. But how and why was my family going crazy over knowledge? Or was it more? Was I going to go crazy? Was it genetic? No. I had to keep my mind. Can't let this make me lose my mind. She had been strong for me many times.

I can remember these two nightmares I used to have

when I was younger. When I was five, I had one about nothing I can understand. I kept hearing voices calling my name over and over. They were saying something else but I couldn't make it out. Some of the voices were deep; others were light and wispy. The annoying thing was that they continued to talk simultaneously and they would keep getting louder and louder. All I could see in this dream were bright lights, much like headlights but arranged like a chandelier; the bigger lights arranged in the middle and the smaller ones above and below. They kept whispering and yelling until I woke up screaming but yet I could still hear them. I ran to my mother's room and she let me sleep there as she sang me back to sleep.

The other nightmare I recall was when I was seven. I was in a big house with a long hallway with only a few doors. The door at the end of the hallway was open and my mother was sitting on a bed in that room reading, paying no attention to me. Suddenly, the door next to me jiggled and something on the other side was trying to push its way through. I backed up in fear waiting to see what might come through and yet hoping that it wouldn't succeed. I watched the knob of the door turn unsuccessfully and then I heard a key on the other side being inserted. I tried to grab the knob to keep the door from opening, but the door swung open. Before me was the most hideous looking man, a mere skeleton in skin. He wore no clothes and he hunched over and looked me directly in the eyes. I was stunned; I couldn't scream, let alone move. He walked past me and walked down the hall toward my mother. I shook myself, realizing that I had to do something.

"Stop," I yelled. "You can't hurt her!" He stopped and slowly turned around. I froze once more. He had caught me in his icy stare like a medusa, and I felt my body turning to stone from fear. He opened his hand and threw a substance that enveloped me like a cocoon. I fell to the floor unable to move, only my eyes were free to see him walk slowly to the room. Once he entered her room my bonds loosed from me and I flew with such quickness down the hall screaming and crying, at the same time yelling her name but she didn't respond. The door slammed shut before I could enter, and I awoke in a cold sweat.

And here I am ten years later comforting my mother in her waking nightmares. What could she be seeing that would make a grown woman scream? I didn't know. I could not understand. My mother had numerous mysteries in her heart and she would barely tell me anything.

I closed her door. I walked to my room, closed my door, and slid down the length of it, resting my head on my knees. Just for a moment.

"I'll rest my mind for one moment," I told myself. I fell asleep and had no nightmares.

Somehow the nap turned into a long slumber and I awoke to find myself sprawled across the floor. I got up and walked into the kitchen. I looked out the window and noticed the setting sun. Why did I sleep so long? Why did I have to be so tired? I didn't like sleeping that long because it made me feel as if my life was passing by. I sat down at the table and dropped my head. My shoulder was sore. I pulled open my shirt collar and saw that my shoulder was bruised. Must've happened when Mom pushed me against the wall. Dang, when did such a little woman get so strong?

"What time is it?" I jumped at the sound of the low, scratchy voice. I turned around; it's just my mom. She looked tired and pale. Her hair was frizzy, and she came into the kitchen with her pink robe on.

"About eight-thirty. Are you feeling better?"

"When did you get home? Why didn't you wake me?" She went to the cupboard and grabbed a glass, walked slowly to the fridge, and poured herself a tall glass of grape juice. She looked different than she did this afternoon. Her face wasn't as dark but she was still sickly looking. Until recently, I had never seen my mother sick . . . Come to think of it, I hadn't ever been sick either. We had lived a primarily healthy life, so I really was unsure of how to handle this problem. At one moment it seemed physical but now it seemed it was affecting her mentally.

"I did wake you," I said slowly, "and you started screaming." She sat there stunned for a moment. She put her glass down and stared away.

"I was awake?" she asked.

"Yeah, and you kept screaming at me and you even pushed me." She looked at me then put her glass in the sink. She seemed to be thinking intensely. She sat down at the table.

"I'm sorry I don't remember. Is that how the lamp broke? Because of me?"

"You threw it." I continued to look at her. She looked as if she was going to cry. *She was scared that she was losing control.* How did I know that? The more I thought about it the more overwhelmed I became with her feelings. How was it that I could almost understand everything she was feeling? She stood up and went to the bathroom and slammed the door. I ran to follow her and stood at the door trying to listen. She had turned on the water. Was she camouflaging her crying?

"Mom, are you okay?" I knocked after hearing no response. I waited. Finally, the doorknob turned and she looked up at me through the open door.

"Andy, there are some things, baby, that I haven't told you."

"Like what?" I was confused. Was something wrong? Why did she look at me so scared?

"I'll explain everything later. But I have something important to tell you. My mother died."

"Grandma?" My mouth dropped open and I was speechless. I didn't want to believe that Grandma was really gone.

"No, baby, not your Me-Ma. My mother, my biological

mother. I found out recently that she has passed. Her funeral is tomorrow and I am going to go."

Mama had mentioned to me only a couple times that she was adopted and really spoke no more of it. I knew nothing about the woman, and Mama was so uninterested in talking about her that I tried not to pry into the whole adoption issue. I think it had something to do with Mom's attempt in college to find her mother, and when she did the reunion wasn't quite what she expected—at least that's what Grandma told me. When I would talk to Mom about the issue I felt rejected. But sometimes I think it was because she felt rejected herself.

"How did you find out? Why didn't you tell me?" Her biological mother was as much a part of my life as she was hers. I was excited yet offended that she had waited till now to tell me.

"Our family isn't as simple as you would want it to be, Andy. That's a part of me that is gone now. I did everything I knew to give you a normal family." She rubbed my head. "I know it's unfair to you that you didn't know a lot about who she was, but it's better that way."

"But why? She's a part of our family!" I was outraged, at what I wasn't sure. My mother had kept a longtime truth from me and my mother's mother had kept family from me.

"And we will pay her respects. There's more to the story, I will tell you later." She sighed.

"I want to know now! I can handle it." I wasn't a child whom she had to walk around on eggshells. She looked at me with her soft smile and opened the door. She rubbed my face with her hand and stood on her tiptoes to kiss my cheek. "My baby is grown isn't he? So strong and I'm gonna need you to be very strong in the days to come." She patted my chest and walked back to her room. I stood silent, choosing not to release the frustration anymore.

I figured every family had secrets. But my mother was my only family and so it made no sense to hold secrets. I didn't understand the whole purpose of keeping a secret. It just raised my curiosity more. I tried not to let it bother me and I went back into the front room. The house was small and it was nothing but a few steps to go from one room to another. I had found comfort in this house, and my favorite spot was the couch. I think the couch was made for me, as it seemed to mold to my very shape as I crashed into it. Maybe calling Tonya would make me feel better. I pulled out my cell phone and dialed her number. Gee, I wonder if she has my number in her cell phone? The phone rang and rang. Dang—voice mail. Where was she? Didn't she know this was a school night?

It frustrated me that I let her frustrate me so much. With all the problems I was having the last thing I needed was female issues. I have always liked Tonya and I have expressed my feelings toward her, except for actually telling her that I liked her, but no, that would be way too much. I mean, the last thing I want is to get the kiss of death. I could only wish it was a real kiss, but it isn't. Every guy has gotten this kiss at one time or another. It's when you tell a girl how much you really care about her and you look in her eyes and you think you just about got her heart and then she tells you: "I just see you as my friend," or even worse, "You're like a brother to me." I was walking that fine line of the "friend zone" and didn't want to fall in that bottomless pit, but then again I didn't want to be desperate. I don't need her! I'm a man! I can have any girl at school! Forget Tonya and all her trifling ways! If she can't recognize that I'm a sexy stud then, oh well, her loss. I'm moving on with life. I hung up the phone.

chapter 4

I dialed Tonya's number again for the fourth time tonight. Okay, this time I'm going to leave a message. I know. I told myself I wouldn't but then I turned on the radio and heard a love song and well . . . you know how those dang love songs get ya every time. She makes me so dang upset because I like her so much and she doesn't like me. I just wanted to scream. I grabbed the pillow off the couch and screamed into it to muffle the sound.

"Baby, are you all right?" My mother walked into the room. I looked up slowly and put down the pillow, gave a sheepish smile, and nodded yes.

"Who were you on the phone with?" Uh-oh, Mom was in the interrogation mode. She was obviously feeling better. There was no escaping. Once she asked one question she would get to the bottom of the problem. So I might as well tell her, besides, I needed to vent.

"It's this girl, Tonya at school, I really like her but she has a boyfriend, and I want her to notice me but I think she just sees me like a friend."

"Well she has a boyfriend, Andy, what do you want her to do?"

"I dunno, but he is so not right for her and I know I would treat her a whole lot better. I do things for her—let her borrow my notes. She talks to me about all her problems. It's like I have her soul but I don't have her heart."

"Well, baby, just keep doing what you're doing; maybe one day she'll notice and give you a chance. I'm sure she knows how nice you are."

"Well, thanks. 'Cause everybody knows that nice guys never get girls." My mom laughed—I glimpsed her old self—and she scooted me over to share the couch.

"Your father was very nice and I loved him. Sometimes it takes girls a while to mature to understand that the nice guy is the one to be with."

"Yeah, 'cause right now all they want are the bad boys. Then all they do is complain about all the problems they have with those guys. I just wish Tonya would break up with Leonard and be with me. He's cheated on her, like, twice, and she's gone back to him each time. He's called her all types of names and made her so self-conscious that she hides behind all this makeup. I really like her because deep down I know she deserves more and she's always coming to me to talk. If I'm good enough to talk to, then why am I not good enough to be with? It's like she doesn't want to be happy at all. Girls want to date bad boys and keep the good guys in the friend zone."

"The friend zone? What are you talking about, Andy?"

"The friend zone is hell and girls are the devil." I looked up at her and my mother just stared at me silently. She wasn't smiling.

"Do you think your mother is the devil?" she asked quickly.

"No Mom, what I meant was . . ."

"Young man, I don't want to ever hear you say anything like that again. Do you understand?"

"But I . . ."

"*Do* you understand?" She just stared at me, and I realized the conversation was over.

"Yes ma'am." I felt hurt but I realized that somehow my words had hurt her. She went back to her bedroom. I stretched out on the couch and looked up at the ceiling. I just wanted this horrible day to be over.

Mom called to me from her room: "I'm going to call the school in the morning. We gotta go out of town for the funeral, so pack your clothes tonight." I didn't respond to her, I just went to my room. I looked at all my clothes and figured I would pack in the morning. I was tired—mentally. I took a shower and washed off my funk and wrapped up in a towel. I didn't even dry off. I flopped my partially wet self on top of the bed. The ceiling fan felt good, and I closed my eyes and fell asleep.

chapter 5

My alarm clock went off at six as usual and I awoke underneath the covers. I pulled back the covers and put on the nearest pair of jeans and threw the towel aside on the floor. God, please let this day be better than yesterday. I shook my curls loose with my hand to alleviate the matted-down "bed head" appearance. It wouldn't take long for me to pack. I grabbed my duffel bag from the closet and threw in a few outfits and some underwear.

From the hallway I could hear the shower, so Mom was already up and about. The house was cold and quiet and the old floor creaked beneath my footsteps. I thought about how awkward I was going to feel to see my biological grandmother for the first time at her funeral. It's hard to mourn someone you never knew. What kind of woman was she? Did she look like my mother? Where was my grandfather? Did my mother know him? All these questions filled my heart and I became excited about this little trip. That alone made me stop and feel guilty, too. I mean, this *was* a funeral. I felt bad for going to a funeral like it was a family reunion. I'm sure people were not going to be interested in answering any of my questions.

Even though it was a funeral, maybe I could still learn some more about myself.

All my life I had never really fit in. When I was younger, all the kids in school picked on me for my lankiness, but as I grew taller, I became more acceptable. People always asked me where I was from. My friends claimed I neither talked nor looked like a country boy. But Texas was all I knew. I had always been what people call a dreamer. I never really thought anything of my dreams in my young age. There were always bits and pieces of weird images I could never understand. But one day about three months ago I saw something on cable TV about Joseph. He was in the Bible and he was a dreamer. There was something about this biblical character that I could relate to.

For those that don't know the story, Joseph was a favorite of his father, and Joseph kept having these weird dreams. The way it went was that the meaning of his dreams prophesied his upcoming power. Well, his brothers didn't like that so they mistreated him and sold him into slavery—big bummer. To make a long story short, Joseph became a slave in Egypt but slowly worked his way to being one of the most powerful men in Egypt using his God-given gift, dreams. He even got stronger as he got older, being able to not only dream but also interpret other people's dreams.

Well, after seeing this show, I started believing that there was something greater in me that was more influential than my environment. Just like Joseph, my gifts would make room for me in this world; I just had to figure out what my gifts were. Sometimes I could just sit and talk to a person when he or she had a problem and could tell so much about the individual and what was going on without even knowing certain things. Occasionally it would freak people out. I think that I just figure people out pretty fast, that's all.

The one thing I knew least about, however, was the one

thing affecting me the most. That thing was my family. My mom had this problem with not telling me the whole truth. I should just sneak and read her journal. As long as I had been alive she had always kept one. All I had to do was track down one of her old journals to figure out this mystery. But that would defile the trust we had between each other. Plus I'm sure she would find out. My mom had a way of knowing what I was up to all the time. Maybe that's just a gift mothers have.

Finally, the bathroom door opened and from the steamy room my mother walked out wearing her pink robe with her hair wrapped in a towel. She looked way better than she did yesterday, yet her eyes still seemed tired. She smiled and went to her room. It was a scary thing to see her sick. She came back out wearing a pair of jeans and a white tank top. Mom looked so young—she was practically knocking on forty and she could very well pass for my sister. Her complexion was bright and she had short curly hair much like mine and small dimples in each cheek. Her blue eyes appeared to look right into your very soul when you stared at them. My mother was beautiful, totally untouched by time.

This sickness was getting the best of her, however, and I feared it would begin to age her. She took two big bags and put them at the door.

"Have you packed yet?" She didn't glance up.

"Yes ma'am." She continued to situate her bags, and I thought that maybe she was in the mood to explain what happened to her so long ago. "How much do you know about your mother?"

She paused.

"I'll tell you on our way there. It's quite a long story and I don't know if I have enough time to tell you everything. I would have to write a book," she laughed.

"I'd buy it." She looked up at me with a flattered look and shook it off like it wasn't that important. But to me it was. My mother's life apparently was full of secret experiences.

She went to the kitchen and sat down at the table. She appeared to be tired and began to breathe heavily. Words can't describe the fear that filled my heart as I stood in the doorway. I just stood staring. What was wrong with her? Why didn't she get help?"

"Hey, Mom, are you feeling okay? I mean, maybe we shouldn't do this. You're ill and it may get worse. Maybe . . . maybe you should go to the doctor." She glanced quickly at me, avoiding my eyes. She shook her head.

"I don't need a doctor. I can heal on my own. There's nothing a doctor can do for me anyways but tell me what my symptoms are. I know what's wrong and I know what to do about it." True. I had never known my mother to ever frequent a doctor, which was awfully weird. But this sickness was weird, and nothing was making sense.

"Well, if you know then, what's wrong?"

"Andrew, don't concern yourself with this. You know I'm strong, nothing is going to happen to Mama." She rubbed my head and patted my face but something in me didn't believe her. "I know this is going to be weird for you, but this funeral is something I feel I need to do."

I gritted my teeth. I was mad at her because she was holding secrets from me. I could feel tears welling up in my eyes, but I would not allow them to fall. I took a deep breath and smiled instead.

"Have you decided what school you want to go to?" She still didn't look at me. She was hiding herself. I knew she was. "I really want you to look into Morehouse. They've been sending you a lot of paperwork. Did you finish your scholarship application for them?" She was trying to change the subject of an unspoken conversation we were having within our minds.

"No, Mom."

"No, what? You didn't finish your scholarship? Andrew . . . that's an expensive school and . . ."

"No . . . I didn't mail the application for Morehouse in, Mom." I cringed slightly knowing how upset she was going to be about my not putting my all into this college thing, but I just wasn't feeling *college* right now. I didn't even know what I wanted to be in life yet. Mom had been pressing different schools and I understood that she wanted me to better myself, but there was this hunger inside to do something other than school.

"I thought about college but I'm not sure. I haven't applied to any particular one."

"You need to do something, Andrew. You can't just sit around here."

"I know Mom, I didn't say I was going to."

"So what do you have planned?"

"I said I don't know."

"Damn it, Andrew! Think about your future and figure something out! I'm not going to be around forever to baby you!" She slammed her fist on the table and stood up so fast that the table toppled over. I flinched a bit but stood for the most part shocked and frozen. The tear I was trying to hold back dropped without my permission, but I held the others under captivity and bit down on my lip. I think she saw the tear roll down my cheek, but she saw how I tried to hide it. She came to herself and looked down at the table and around at the kitchen aimlessly as if she were confused. She kneeled slowly and picked the table back up.

"Can—can you help me please, baby. Help me pick this

mess up." Her voice was calm but her hands were shaking. She looked down but I saw a tear drop on the floor. Crying was contagious. I walked over to the table and knelt beside her.

"I got it, Mama. Don't worry." I started to clean up the broken pieces of the ceramic saltshaker and place them in my hand. She frantically picked up pieces and she nicked her finger on one. I grabbed her hand.

"Mama, stop! You're hurting yourself." I held her hand and grabbed the towel next to me and dabbed the blood. But it looked unusual. Her blood was dark, almost purple, and it came out slow. It looked old and dead. She pulled her hand back when she saw that this had caught my attention, and she stood up and in a very straightforward voice she told me to get in the car and get ready to go.

"It's a long drive to Dallas, and I don't want to get caught in traffic," she said. The tears were gone. Her moods were like the ocean tide, in and out. She controlled them for now, but I had this feeling that the high tide had not arrived yet. She walked to the front door and grabbed her bags and went outside. The screen door slammed behind her. I looked at the towel and the stained blood on it. I held the towel, grabbed my duffel, and proceeded out the front door.

I looked at my mother. She was all I had in this world. She brought me into this world—she *was* my world. Now that very world was crumbling, slowly. I threw my duffel bag in the trunk and sat down in the passenger seat. Crickets chirped as I closed the door to cut the morning chill. I reclined my seat back some and looked at the towel again. I rubbed the dark blood with my thumb and for a moment my mind jumped—I closed my eyes and instantly started dreaming—deeply.

I was in another place, a club. It was dark and smoky.

"What'll be, kid?" the bartender asked. I was confused. I

looked at my clothes. I had on a black polyester disco shirt, some really tight pants, and my hair was slicked back. I looked like a retro pimp.

"What'll be, kid?" the bartender repeated like a broken record and gave me the same stare. I looked past him at the mirror, which seemed to pull at me. I didn't see myself or the bartender in the reflection. I saw the most beautiful woman on the dance floor behind me. Suddenly, I was on the dance floor, too. People were dancing all around me and this beautiful girl was dancing before me. This dance was unfamiliar. This music was unfamiliar—so retro. Was this an old school party? Everyone was dressed in sixties' clothing. Everything around me was brightly colored. The club had a red essence about it. The beautiful woman stared at me and winked. She was a drop of chocolate with matching dimples. I approached her, and she teasingly backed up some and continued her dancing, shaking her hips fast left and right. Her green dress stopped at her thighs and she had on white go-go boots. Her lipstick was pinkish and matched her eye shadow. She had large hoop earrings that barely hid under her flipped-out hair. She would not allow me to get any closer than the arm's length I already was. I laughed and began to dance, mimicking her moves. Everything was on rhythm. Everyone did the same dance.

The music stopped and she stopped dancing, but everyone else kept dancing, only slower. It was as if she was the only thing in color. I couldn't move. Her stare left me frozen. She walked slowly to me. She rested her head on my chest as if to hear my heart and stared up into my eyes. She was quite pretty and her eyes had that teasing look. She whispered so softly but it seemed to echo all around me.

"See you at the after-party."

"What after-party? Where is it?" I couldn't move and I

watched her back away into the crowd. As soon as I could move the crowd sped up in their dancing. It was almost impossible for me to get through. I could see she was already far in the distance at the front of the club. She walked up the steps to a tall white gentleman who held out his hand. He was wearing a brown leather jacket and only his collar from his white satin shirt peeked through. He had what some call "presence" and he was more than handsome, he was beautiful. I couldn't stop staring at him. His hair was black and long like velvet and silk. His skin seemed to have a luminance to it. I could not see his eyes clearly behind his dim sunshades. He had an eerie perfection to the structure of his face. He took her hand and they walked out the door but not before he stopped and looked over his shoulder and stared me square in the eyes. Yeah, he was looking at me and smiling. His smile made me dizzy and the room appeared to be spinning. What was he saying? I tried to read his lips. He was telling me something.

"Wake up, Andy!" I shook awake. My mother touched my shoulder. "Wake up, you got me worried. You've been asleep for the whole trip."

I squinted a bit. The countryside was passing away and the cityscape was approaching. The sun was high so it must've been almost noon. My mother drove with one hand and wiped my forehead with the other.

"You must've been tired," she said calmly.

I was disoriented. I could not have been asleep that long. I looked at the clock—10:30 a.m. The strange man at the end of the dream had spooked me. The whole dream seemed too real.

Mama rolled down the windows and the fresh air seemed to help ease my mind. Her coughing startled me again. I looked at her. She looked like she was trying to catch her breath between coughs. Her eyes still had those rings and her skin had a sweaty glow about itself. She tried to smile to not worry me.

"Get my cell phone out of the glove compartment please, Andy." I opened up the compartment and handed her the phone. She pushed a button and waited for an answer. "Hello?" she spoke into the phone.

"This is Andrea, is Karen there?" I had never met Karen Hendricks but my mom had spoken of her a few times. Karen was my mother's most trusted friend. They would talk on the phone a lot and I had only seen old pictures of her in my mother's scrapbook.

"Hey, Karen, I'm on the road still—we'll be there in about twenty minutes . . . okay . . . no, not yet . . . okay . . . see you then." I could hear Karen's voice responding but couldn't actually make out what she said to my mother. I rested my head on the back of the seat and let the wind hit my face. I sat my seat back up from being reclined. I thought.

"What did she die of?"

"Excuse me?" My mother looked at me perplexed and quickly looked back at the road.

I looked at her. "What did your mother die of?"

"She had some heart complications."

"Is that what you have, the same thing as her?" Her jaw dropped at my comment, and she pulled the car over to the side of the road. Putting the car in park she turned herself in my direction.

"Andy, I'm not dying."

"Then what's wrong with you?" I looked her in the eyes but she looked away and sighed.

"I'm just a little under the weather." I didn't believe her. This was another lie.

"I wouldn't lie to you, Andy." How did she know what I thought? Just my imagination, my face must be telling my emotions again.

"Then why can't you remember doing some things? I have never seen you sick before and now that you are, you're doing weird things." My voice cracked. Dang, why did I have to be so emotional? I cleared my throat. She looked at me so softly—the look I was so familiar with.

"I could never keep anything from you." She grinned; her eyes seemed to have tears. "Andy, I am sick. That's why I want you to get your life together, because, I don't know—"

"You don't know what? You don't know if you'll live?" I interrupted her. She looked as if she was trying to explain something complex to me but yet still holding back details.

"Andy, I don't think I will die, but I'm changing. My body is changing and it's affecting my mental state also." Her voice was so calm.

"Well can't you go to the doctor, get some medication?"

"No, it's not that simple. I have a genetic issue in my blood."

"Your blood? Does that mean I may have it, too?" Now I was really worried. I mean, maybe this explained why I was always falling asleep so hard.

"No—no, you are okay. I know you are, you have to be. I've made sure of it." She seemed to second-guess herself.

I looked at her suspiciously. I wanted to get out of the car and leave but I was in the middle of nowhere and that was one adventure I wasn't ready for.

"Remember when it used to rain real hard and thunder real loud? You would run crying and screaming into my room and jump in my bed." I smiled at this old memory. "You would think the sky was exploding, and I would tell you that the angels in heaven were just bowling and when you heard the thunder they hit a strike. I would hold you in my arms, and you would get mad at the thunder and tell it to shut up and quit bowling so loud, remember that?" She giggled and poked me in the side with her finger to get a response from me. I laughed.

"I remember," I commented. My mother seemed to always have a situation under control ever since I could remember.

"Whatever happens, good or bad, hold on to the memories that we have made, Andrew. You are growing into a beautiful man of God. Hold on to God. He is there for you. My every hope and dream has been to see you succeed—that's why I get upset when I see that you don't have a plan for your future. If you don't have a plan, then you will do whatever anybody tells you. If you don't dream and work that dream, then you live your life working somebody else's dream."

"Yeah, I have dreams all right, really weird ones. I've prayed for God to bring Daddy back and he's never come back, people tell me that he's gone crazy. I love God, but why can't He keep my parents from going crazy?"

Her eyes widened. Oops, did I say "crazy" to her face? I gotta learn to hold my tongue. She seemed to have this mind-boggling patience with my outbursts, but I would not attempt to test this any further.

"I can't believe you're saying this; I've raised you better and I know you have stronger faith than this. Why are you so doubtful of what God can do? He is all you have when it's all said and done and, baby, your father is not crazy. Some people used to say he was because they didn't understand why he did certain things. Your father and I went through a lot of things that people would not be able to understand. You are more like him than you know. We had to make decisions for your best interests and many people could not understand that. Your father is why you are who you are. I believe that somehow, some way, all the things that have happened so far is the plan of God."

"What are you talking about? Mom, he abandoned us."

"No, you have it all wrong, Andrew, you don't understand."

"What is there to understand? Is he here?"

"Your daddy has always been around and watching you, baby. Trust me, all this is for your own good. I don't want you to be hurt."

"Hurt by what? Is he going to hurt me? Is my daddy an alcoholic or a child molester?"

"No, it's not that."

"Then what is it, Mom? Why do you have all these secrets?"

She paused. I could see she was definitely holding back but wanting to reveal all to me. She looked at me so gently and touched my face.

"Not time." It seemed I could hear her whisper in my mind. Whoa. I felt this peace overwhelm the fire in my heart. Her tears fell once again—one tear, then another. I sat silent, just staring.

I looked away from her and out the window. My mother wiped her tears with her sleeve, started the car, and continued driving. The next twenty minutes felt like hours. What was going on? I wanted answers. I knew whatever I found out would change the way I saw life, forever. But I kept my peace and just sat there in silence.

ndrea! My gawd, it's been too long! Girl, get in this house!" Karen stood on the patio of her beautiful red-brick home. It seemed to be even more humid in Dallas than it was in Heaven. Karen's hair was long and braided and she had a little gap between her front teeth that gave her smile charisma. She was tall, like myself, so I didn't feel weird standing next to her.

"Hey, Karen, how's things been going?" My mother pulled her bags together and took a breath. We walked through the front door and the cool air conditioning of the house felt good to my flushed skin. I stood behind my mother with my duffel bag strapped to my back.

"Oh my . . . and is this your baby?" Baby? I didn't see a baby anywhere. Karen grinned at me, exposing the gap, which I found so fascinating, and extended her hand to me. My mother nudged my side to signal me to introduce myself. It wasn't like I forgot, I mean, dang, I have manners. I shook Karen's hand and smiled back.

"I'm Andrew, I'm seventeen. You have a very nice house," I said, making emphasis on my age.

"Thank you, Andrew. I have a nineteen-year-old daughter, you should meet her. I think she is upstairs. Courtney, come down and meet our guests!" Hmm, maybe this trip will get better after all. I could hear footsteps upstairs, then rumbling downstairs.

Courtney came from around a corner. She was slightly shorter than me but still taller than my mother. She was lanky and thin, wore a very big Afro, and she had on black frame glasses. She wore a dashiki shirt that exposed her belly, and bell-bottom hip-hugging jeans. Her style was different—almost like the people in my dream. She didn't smile. She simply came downstairs and acknowledged our presence.

"Courtney was about two when you last saw her." Karen fixed Courtney's shirt and primped her, which seemed to bother Courtney.

"Courtney, show Andrew where the guest room is while I catch up with Andrea." My mom nudged me again to pick up her bags. Okay, when did I become the official bellhop? I need to calm down, I was irritated still and I'm sure she could sense it. Courtney did little more than look at me before she commenced to walk back down the hall. I grabbed the bags and wobbled quickly to catch up with Courtney. One suitcase in each hand and a large duffel on my back made me feel like I was in boot camp. Courtney continued walking without looking back. Hello? Was this chick going to slow down with these long strides she was making down the hall? I decided to make some conversation; maybe then she would realize that I was lagging at least four feet behind her.

"Hi, I didn't introduce myself. I'm Andrew." She looked back. Good, now I can catch up some.

"I know, my mother has told me about you guys."

"Really, what has she told you?"

"Stuff—your mom and my mom grew up together so she has stories after stories."

"Well, maybe you could tell me some of them sometime." Okay, so maybe I was fishing to get some info and this might be an inside informant.

"Hey, you need some help? You look like you are struggling with those bags." That was a girls' way of saying that I look weak. In no way was I going to ask for help. Besides, if I did ask she wouldn't want to really help me anyway. I found that girls would ask to do things a lot and not really want to do it; for instance, like picking up a check when you go out to eat. No girl really wants to pay for the meal; they just want to see how broke you are or how cheap you are.

"No, I got it." I switched my muscles into second gear and resituated the bags underneath my arms to get a better grip.

"Okay, muscleman." She turned right and hopped up the stairs. I looked at the challenge ahead of me and took a breath. Step by step I hiked up the stairwell.

"You have a pretty big house." (*Translation:* Where the heck are our rooms?) She looked back again and watched me finally get to the second floor. She smiled for the first time. Maybe I impressed her with my mighty strength.

"Your room is at the end of the hall." She turned and walked on to the end of the hall. I must say I enjoyed watching her walk with those tight jeans. Her butt cheeks looked like pistons in an engine moving up and down. She reached the door and opened it and waited for me to catch up with her. I raised my eyes quickly so that she wouldn't notice that I was admiring her assets. Okay, I have to be cool with this girl, no reason falling into the friend zone with her, too.

"Thanks, I appreciate your help." I nodded to her. She nodded back.

"Uh huh, no problem. The bathroom is the third door on the right—now if you'll excuse me, I was on the phone."

Courtney walked off. Man, this was going to be some kind of trip.

My cell phone rang. I threw Mom's bags on one of the two beds in the room and slammed my duffel bag on the floor. Pulling my cell out of my pocket, I pushed the answer button.

"Hey, this's Andrew . . ."

"Drew, boy, where are you?" Mackenzie hollered on the other line. I had totally forgotten that I was supposed to get in touch with him.

"I had to go to a funeral, Mack. I'm sorry, dude, I forgot to call you."

"Yeah, well I was late to school because of you."

"You're always late to school, Mack."

"Oh yeah, well who died?" I flopped down on the other bed and took off my shoes.

"My mother's biological mother."

"Whoa, that's gotta be weird."

"Yeah, kinda, but hey, at least I get to see Dallas."

"Any cute girls there that you've seen yet?"

"Not yet, well there's this one. Courtney, she's the daughter of the lady we're staying with."

"Boy! You better get yo' pimp on!"

"Have I ever told you how ghetto you are?" I laughed at Mack.

"Well call me when you get back. I gotta go to class."

"I will . . . talk to you later."

I hung up the phone and looked around the room. It was fairly small but sufficient. The two quilt-covered beds were separated by a wooden nightstand. A small lamp sat on the nightstand and the only window was next to the bed where I was sitting. The wall adjacent to the window was decorated with a single picture of a flowery field with a gray barn in the corner. What an ugly picture. No wonder they stuck this picture in this small room. It was boring and no one would ever see it in a guest room. The floors were hardwood with only a small circular green-and-white carpet in between the beds. The room resembled a hotel room without as much luxury. I walked to the window and I could see the front yard. There on the street curb sat our blue sedan. It looked real dirty even from here.

Okay, time to be nosy. There was something about being in a new environment that made me want to know my surroundings. You could learn a lot about people from their house or their bedrooms. I wondered where Courtney's room was. I went into the hall. The hall was decorated with the time-frozen pictures of Karen and Courtney, mostly Courtney. Courtney must be Mama's little baby. I liked to look at pictures, especially baby pictures. My first reaction was to laugh when I saw Courtney's snaggle-toothed pictures from grade school. Only a couple of pictures were of Karen and then this one lonely picture, small but nicely framed of some guy. He was young, about twenty-something, but the picture appeared old. Might be her daddy; Courtney looked just like him. The first door on my right was a linen closet. I went to the second door and opened it—a library of some sort. Books were on every wall except the back wall, where there was a large window. A big desk faced me and on it was a computer. Probably Karen's office, I thought. I closed that door. I knew what the third door was, no need to investigate that. The final door was at the end of the hall facing me. This had to be Courtney's room since it was the only door that was decorated with a poster of Bob Marley. I knocked.

"What is it?" Hmm, cordiality wasn't her strong point. I opened the door and peeked in.

"Did I say you could come in?"

"Oops, sorry, I was just seeing what you were doing." Courtney was stretched across her bed on the phone, looking at me. Her eyes were bucked at me. Her room was elaborate, and I considered the idea of sleeping in this room, of course this was a non-negotiable request, I'm sure. To my immediate right were a TV set, a DVD player, a game system, and—what is that?—a satellite hookup. Oh yeah, this was my new hangout. I would suffer the numerous stuffed animals in the far corner staring at me with their cynical smiles to be able to sit for but a moment in this room. In comparison, the guest room was a bologna sandwich and Courtney's room was a Philly cheesesteak.

"Okay, you can leave now, I'm on the phone." She pointed at the phone as if I couldn't see or something. I excused myself from the "queen of England's" quarters. She was cute but I could see now that she had some attitude issues. I backtracked and went downstairs to find my mother and Karen in the kitchen drinking coffee. They didn't hear me come down.

"So did you explain to him how it happened?" Karen asked my mother.

"No, I haven't. I don't think he would be able to handle it right now." My mother pulled her hair back with her hands.

"Andrea, that's not right, he's getting older and you need to tell him everything. Things are getting worse with you and he does not need to be in the dark. What happens if you can't control this?"

"I can control it."

"Did you control it when you first met Donyel?"

"That was different, Karen, Donyel is very powerful."

"Don't you think Andrew needs to be prepared if you

can't handle this, if you don't come out this time or if Donyel comes back?"

"He won't come back."

"How do you know, Andrea?"

"He won't, Karen, there is no way Donyel can get us! Look, let me be honest with you. I'm not sure how much time I have left. I seriously feel like I'm losing my mind. You are my best friend and I trust you."

"I know, there's nothing I wouldn't do for you."

My mother stood and looked out the window. She had a blank stare.

"I need to ask you a favor."

"W hat are you doing?" I jumped and flipped around with a guilty look on my face.

"Is being nosy a bad habit or your profession?" Courtney asked. Dang, she had busted me. She had her hands on her hips and a look on her face as if she needed a good reason not to blow my cover. I grabbed her arm and pulled her back to the stairwell.

"Look, let's keep this between you and me." I implored her to not turn me in.

"What's your deal, kid? Why are you eavesdropping?"

Did she just call me kid? "My mom is really sick and she's keeping a lot of info from me and I want to know what's up, that's all." She looked at me, and I could tell by her eyes that she was considering my plea.

"Please?" I asked her and grabbed her hand. Goose bumps covered my arms. I looked into her eyes and felt that she knew more than she was letting on. *Her mother had asked her to hold some secrets from me and these secrets were . . .* wait, what was I doing? I let go of her hand. I stood shocked. Was I reading this girl's soul? My mother screamed. I had heard that same scream before and my heart jumped as I thought the worst. Courtney looked up and ran past me and I followed her.

We entered the kitchen to find my mother on the floor. This seizure was worse. I could tell. My mother was breathing heavily and sweat was pouring from her face. Her eyes stared blankly as if she was unconscious—or dead. Karen attempted to pull Mom off the floor with difficulty as my mother flopped back down using all her dead weight and resisting Karen as much as she could.

"Mom!" I yelled. I ran to her and tried to grab her hand. I felt this surge of power when we touched.

"Your resistance is futile, you belong to us." I heard that. In my mind, I heard all these voices when I touched her hand. She pushed me back with her foot and slid back on the floor. Karen grabbed my mother's face and slapped her a couple of times.

"Andrea, wake up! It's me, Karen! Girl, don't you do this to me!"

"What's wrong with her?" Courtney asked. Karen looked at me and then looked at Courtney. She said something to her with her eyes. Courtney evidently understood.

My mother calmed down and looked worn out from wrestling. "Don't worry, Andrea, I'll take care of you. Help me carry your mom to her room, Andrew."

"Don't worry, Andrew, my mom knows what she's doing," Courtney reassured me. I was scared. When my mom was like this she tended to get violent. I waited until I was sure she had calmed down. I walked over and grabbed my mother's feet while Karen held her shoulders. Lifting her was fairly easy since my mother was so small—I probably could have done it by myself. My mother passed out after we laid her down in the bed upstairs.

The worst thing in the world is not knowing.

Whoever said that ignorance is bliss? All I wanted to know was the truth. My mom was trying to protect me; that I understood. But evidently Karen felt I was old enough to fend for myself. The question was, from what? Who was Donyel? My dad's name is Anthony; is Donyel some ex-boyfriend or something? What if my mom has HIV or something and this Donyel guy gave it to her? No, that can't be it. She said he was powerful. What the heck does that mean? Is he some kind of drug lord? Is my mother involved with the Mafia? I took a breath. Dang, Mom, what secret did you hold in that mind of yours? I lay on her bed next to her. She slept so peacefully. My only way of finding anything out was Courtney. I knew she knew something. It was just a matter of time. I would wear her down. I rolled over and looked out the window. I was uncomfortable, as if I were lying on a knot. I lifted up my buttocks and pulled out the towel I had before from my pocket.

I held it between my fingers and closed my eyes. I was so tired. Thinking too much made me tired. I dreamed.

"Hey, kid, what'll be?" There he was, the same old bartender. Maybe I should try ordering something this time.

"Hey, kid, what'll be?" he repeated; not in the way that one repeats when they are waiting but the repeat that happens when you rewind videotape and play it over again. This was surely a weird dream, but it had to have some meaning so I tried to pay attention. I looked into the mirror and saw the retro girl again. The mirror became my window. Once again, I stood on the dance floor without even moving one muscle. This dream was like a roller-coaster ride that took me through a journey of different scenes. I knew what was coming. She danced and I watched for a moment.

"See you at the after-party," she whispered in my ear and ran off into the crowd, which began to speed up their tempo to prevent me from following.

"Where's this after-party?" I yelled. I tried pushing myself through the crowd but I couldn't. There, beyond, was the

luminescent white man with the long black hair, embracing
her. His presence made the whole room seem to change col-
ors. I tried to look at what he was doing. He whispered some-
thing into her ear. She slapped him. This was different. There
was some more to this dream that I hadn't seen, but now I
could see that he was grabbing her and pulling her out of the
club, not her leaving with him. I struggled to get through the
crowd, but they turned into oceans of people pulling and
pushing me into the depths. Was this a club or was this hell?
I didn't feel like I was going to wake up. I felt like I was suf-
focating. Suddenly I felt hands pulling me up from the floor
of the club and picking me up and pushing me out.

I awoke. It was nightfall and my mother was still sleeping. I got out of the bed. Man, these dreams were really
beginning to bother me. God, what could these dreams
mean? I looked out the window at the night sky. I watched
the wind blow the trees back and forth. I thought about the
girl in the dream. Was I going crazy?

First, I was hearing thoughts of people and now this
crazy dream. I wondered if these dreams and these feelings
were related to each other. Maybe I was being silly and this
dream meant nothing at all. No, this was a recurring
dream. What if God was trying to tell me something? What
if I was like Joseph, the dreamer?

In the Bible, Daniel himself had dreams and was trou-
bled by them because they were about future things he
didn't understand. But my dreams were about the past—a
past I knew absolutely nothing about. I went downstairs to
find Courtney reading at the kitchen table.

"Hey, whatsup, what cha doin'?" I asked, stretching a
bit to loosen up my muscles.

"Look who decided to wake up, Rip van Winkle. I'm
reading some stuff for my philosophy class."

"You're in school?"

"No, I like reading incredibly large books so people will respect me for my brain and not my stunning good looks," she said sarcastically, but I wasn't sure for a moment. "Yes, I'm in school. I go to the community college to get a few classes out of the way."

"Oh, okay. Well where's your mom?"

"She's on duty—night patrol. There's some food in the oven if you're hungry."

"Thanks." I opened the oven and looked at the moist meatloaf and the vegetables that had been prepared for our arrival. It smelled good and my mouth salivated accordingly.

"Ya mom should be a chef, not a cop," I joked. Courtney grabbed some plates and some forks and helped me remove the dish from the oven.

"I checked on ya earlier but you seemed to be sleeping real hard and I didn't want to disturb you." She cut a piece for me and then for herself, and brought them to the table. "You want something to drink? We have soda, water, and some milk." I cringed at the thought of drinking milk with my meatloaf.

"Soda is cool."

Courtney went to the fridge and popped open two soda cans and laid them on the table. Wow, not even a glass. She was quite hospitable but as real as any guy. I figured most girls liked to drink out of a glass. I got the feeling that Courtney was one of the guys, yeah, that was the type of girl she was. There was only one way to find out. I grabbed the can, took a swig, and let go of the biggest belch my stomach could generate. I watched her reaction.

She looked up at me, frozen. Disgust took over her face. Oops, maybe I goofed up again.

"That was horrible, Andrew." Dang, I guess she is a girly

girl. "I mean, honestly, that burp was about a four on a scale of one to ten." I looked up surprised and listened as she released the longest most repulsive belch in the world. Yeah, her belch made me look like an amateur. I laughed.

"Eewww, now that was nasty!"

She laughed at my comment. Okay, Courtney was cool. She passed the "cool" test. Maybe she would be comfortable enough to fill me in on what her mother had been telling her about my mother. I slid the big book on the table around to my side so I could look at it.

"Philosophy, wow is that a hard class?"

"No, I enjoy it. We talk about different schools of thought and it challenges our own belief system and why we believe certain things to be true."

"Really, sometimes I don't know what to believe." I opened the book and thumbed through a few pages, not really reading but looking at the pictures.

"Well, in class, that's what we do. We break down what we believe, what we've been told is true, and what truth actually is."

"Sounds pretty cool. I may take that class when I get to college 'cause that's all I wanna know—what the truth really is."

"Yeah, I have to be real careful, I seem to be one of the only Christians in class so it can get very hectic if I use the Bible as a reference. There's a lot of things that I find in life that are true or have some truth but are not the truth."

"So you're a Christian too, cool," I said. "So explain what you mean about truth."

"Well just because you find something true doesn't mean it's the truth. Truth is relative according to your point of view. The reason that we have so many people out there with so many belief systems is because everyone is looking to themselves for truth. And when you do that, you will develop a system of truth that works according to your experience. But just because it works for you doesn't mean it works for everyone else."

"Well, why even tell people about Jesus, if you believe like that?" She was intriguing me with her conversation.

"When we received the gospel of Jesus we didn't look into ourselves for the answers or the truth. We went to God knowing we had no real truth but seeking the truth. We believe Jesus is the truth and that He has truth because He is omniscient. But as I was saying, it's like creation, some believe in the big bang theory. The big bang could be true, but, what would make nothing all of a sudden bang into something? The truth would be that when God said 'Let there be Light,' that light exploded in such an awesome power that it created a big bang similar to what scientists speak about. How about the Ice Age? It's true that there are animals and people frozen in the arctic regions and so scientists believe an ice age to be true. But when I read the Bible it says nothing at all about any period in history where the entire world was frozen."

"So what are you saying? There was no Ice Age?" I challenged her. "How do you explain all those frozen animals and Neanderthals? Com' on, Courtney, maybe the Bible skipped over that part."

"But then how could I count the Bible to be the truth?" she asked me. "In fact, I believe the Bible tells us what happened and how it happened that those people and animals got stuck in ice. Open your mind, Andrew, and think. This is stuff church just doesn't talk about 'cause they are too busy telling people how to make money versus telling them the mysteries of God and why we exist. Ice is true but it's not the truth. Water is the truth."

"Sorry, you lost me; back up please." Courtney knew she had my full attention. She stood in the middle of the floor to pace back and forth, which seemed to intensify her points. Evidently she had taken a speech class too.

"There was a massive destruction of the entire earth and animals with the exception of Noah, his family, and two of every kind of animal. The Bible says that it rained for forty days and nights. Where did all that water go? Sure, some of it evaporated. Some of it receded and became the seven seas, but that was a lot of water. Think about it. They say, that if global warming got to its extremes and the arctic regions were to thaw out, the entire planet would flood. God didn't make all that water disappear; he froze it! That's how the animals and people got stuck in ice. So that Noah wouldn't step on ground and witness the unburied bodies of thousands of people and animals. When the water pulled back, it grabbed what the ocean couldn't hold and froze it in ice. That's how you get animals in the arctic region that obviously look like they are from the African regions such as the woolly mammoth and the saber-toothed tiger."

"Wow, that's pretty deep. But I have to disagree with you about the Ice Age. I read somewhere that the Ice Age probably very well happened and Noah's ark is probably the cause versus your explanation replacing it."

"Okay, Andrew, kick some knowledge." She smiled at me and I smiled back at her attentiveness—finally, all that reading was paying off.

"Well, I read somewhere that in order for the water from the flood to evaporate then the water would have to heat up. The underwater volcanoes and all the molten lava could raise the temperature of the water enough so the evaporation could begin. Evaporation creates clouds, so much cloud coverage that the sun would be blocked for some time and the temperature would go down outside, creating an immediate ice age in certain areas. The evaporation and ice is the reason the water went down so fast. Noah then was able to leave the ark. Sea creatures, those that didn't need to be in the ark, probably ate the dead carcasses. As the clouds precipitated away the ice began to thaw away. Many of the mammoths and tigers probably got caught in the ice after the ice began to thaw and they got stuck in avalanches."

"Not bad," she said.

"Your theory is cool, too, but since we're on the subject of Noah," I said, "explain this to me. How did he get two of every animal in a boat? I don't care how big that boat is, there is just no way that you could get two of every animal. What about the dinosaurs and other big creatures?" I wanted to see if I could stump her, but Courtney seemed to invite the challenge.

"You ask a very common question that most people ask," she giggled. "People don't really study the Bible, they skim the Bible and think they know it. Noah took two of every *kind* of animal, not two of every animal. He didn't have to take water-bound animals, so you can take those off your list. But everything else he developed a system to decide which animals were of the same kind—or same family—for example, rather than find two African elephants, two Indian elephants, and two mammoths Noah probably grabbed an African and an Indian elephant and called it a day. Six becomes two. That's a rough example but you get my point. When it comes to dinosaurs and other big things he most likely took the young small ones, not full-grown adults."

"Yeah, I get it. That was pretty sharp on how you understand things. What do you feel about cavemen and the missing link?" She stopped and looked at me. What was wrong? She looked at me blankly. She walked past me and began putting away the meatloaf.

"I talk too much. You don't need me filling your head with my thoughts on the truth."

I jumped out of my chair and followed her. "No seriously, I want to know."

"I don't believe that the bones they are finding sometimes are fully human."

I laughed at her statement, what did she think they were? "What are they then, aliens?" This time I was being sarcastic.

She stopped and looked at me. Dang, were they really aliens? If she started talking about spaceships, I was about to go back upstairs.

"No, they weren't aliens. But Genesis talks about other creatures that used to dwell on the planet. This is why God destroyed the planet's life with the flood because of the Nephilim."

"What the heck is a Nephilim?"

"It's in Genesis, chapter six. Talks about when the angels took wives from human people and their hybrid children were half angel, half human, called the Nephilim. Some say these people were super-strong but others say they came out looking deformed, like mutants. And well . . . if you want to know more, then you need to study yourself. I'm not your professor and you ain't paying me for this info."

"Why study when I have you?" I joked. She rolled her eyes at me and continued cleaning up the kitchen.

"Is your mom going to wake up?"

"I don't know." Our discussion had made me forget about my problems, and now I was back to my worries about my mother. I sat at the table finishing up the bit of food I had on my plate. I raked the plate with my fork. I have to get my mind off these problems.

"So uhh, Courtney, how did your class react to your comments?"

She loaded the dishwasher, every so often looking up to acknowledge me. "Well, the professor was intrigued by my reliance in proving history with the Bible. But the rest of my class seemed to get on my case. I really don't get it."

"Get what?"

"Well, people can talk about Buddha, Wicca, astrology, and Scientology and no one cares, but the minute I talk about the Bible and my Christian beliefs they want to crucify me right there in class. One guy even told me to shut up." She laughed. Evidently, she took scrutiny very well. I didn't know if I would be able to take such challenges against my faith, but then again I was still young. She was a strong-minded college student. I'm sure there would come a time when my faith would be tested as well. Wow, if only I could muster half as much courage to express myself like she did; maybe then I would be dating Tonya. Dang, can't go a day without thinking about that girl.

"Hey, Courtney, I want you to know, despite what your class may have said about your ideas about the truth, I believe you."

"Thanks, Andrew, but don't believe me, believe the truth. The truth's something you have to discover on your own." She smiled and wiped her hand on a towel. Courtney was good at jump-starting the brain. It may take some time before I get back to sleep with all these things on my mind.

"Hey, Andrew, when you finish, make sure you put your dish in the dishwasher and turn it on. You're welcome to watch TV if you want. My mom will be home later from the station."

"Okay, thanks. Good night, Courtney."

"Good night, Andrew." I watched her as she left. I liked

watching her leave and that is the truth. I got up and placed my dish in the dishwasher and turned it on. The room was dark, lit only by a small chandelier. I plopped down on their couch and grabbed the remote. This couch felt much different from the one at home. I turned on the TV. You can never go wrong with *I Love Lucy* reruns.

I slept without dreaming. I heard that people dream every night, but I couldn't remember any of it if that was the case. I remember reading somewhere that everybody dreamed, every night. But I was glad I didn't dream. It was good that my mind actually had the opportunity to relax like the rest of my body. I was still on the couch with my nose in the corner of the cushions. When I awoke, Karen was cooking eggs.

"I saw that you were sleeping kinda hard when I came home so I didn't want to disturb you. I didn't know you were going to sleep the whole night down here," giggled Karen as she went to the fridge to grab some more food to throw in the skillet. She dragged her feet in her old house shoes and they made a sweeping sound when she went from one point to another. All the windows were open, and the sun shined brightly through the whole room. I flipped over and covered my eyes with my arm. I groaned some and attempted to focus before getting up.

"You hungry?" Karen asked, still smiling and making that sweeping sound with her house shoes. Swish, swish, swish; that noise alone could wake me up. I didn't verbally respond but merely nodded my head. Okay, I didn't want her to think I was a bum. I gathered my senses, sat up, and took a deep breath. Whatever she was cooking was filling the room with the most pleasant aroma. I looked around. Karen's front room, living room, and kitchen were almost one room with the exception of where the carpet separated the living room from the kitchen. The kitchen was bordered by two large countertops, one of which contained the sink. The stove was against the far wall.

The couch and the loveseat were all plush and leather. They surrounded the large television as if it were a campfire. Karen set up some plates on the kitchen table. She was moving fast. Had she been a waitress before?

Groaning some more, I decided to go upstairs and get myself cute before I ate. Just as I reached the stairway, Courtney was coming down.

"Wow, did you sleep the whole night down here?" She looked at me with a look of half disgust and half concern. Did I look bad? I must have slobber dried on the side of my face or something, 'cause a girl doesn't look at you crazy for just any reason.

"You look like you got hit by a bus."

Okay, Courtney's comments weren't making the situation any better. I knew I was looking bad. I was in unfamiliar territory, so sleeping in a strange bed was just difficult. I slept hard but the couch had done me no justice. My back was even slightly sore. She continued on to the kitchen and I could hear her and her mom giggling. Were they giggling about me? After finally getting upstairs (have I mentioned how incredibly long I think these stairs are) I saw my mother all dressed and looking far better than she had these past few days.

"Hey, baby, I was wondering what happened to you when I woke up." She attempted to rub my hair down, which I assumed was sticking up in the air.

"Did you sleep all night?" I asked her, looking deeply in her eyes. "I was worried about you."

Her thoughts switched inward and she simply gave me a smile.

"Actually, I woke up early this morning, around four o'clock probably. I've been praying most of the morning."

"Praying about what? Healing? Are you praying that He'll heal you from being sick?"

"Something like that. I'm going to need you to pray more, too. Okay, Andrew?" I nodded. She paused and looked as if she would say something else but continued on downstairs. Tomorrow was the funeral. She hadn't mentioned about going to see the family before the funeral, and I was wondering if that was on the agenda for the day.

I walked to the bathroom. Whoa! I looked in the mirror. I did look bad. My curling hair looked as if it were mad. My face was pressed on the side from where I laid on the couch, and the couch print was embedded there. I rubbed my face to smooth out my skin. My eyes were crusty and my lips appeared dry. I turned on the water faucet and pretty much put my entire head underneath it.

I washed up some more and went to the guest room. I found some shorts and a red muscle shirt and threw that on in place of what I already had on. Okay, now I was ready for the world. It didn't feel like a new day until I put on some different clothes and washed up. I balled up my old clothes and stuffed them under the bed. When I glanced out the window by the bed I could see Courtney getting in her car and backing out of the driveway. She must have seen me because she waved. I waved back. My hair was still damp so it wasn't its normal curly appearance. No good, never mind, just screw it. It seemed that my hair had a mind of its own sometimes. I slipped my feet into some flip-flop sandals and went downstairs. Karen and my mom were eating at the table. The television was tuned to the morning news.

"Look who's back! Well, Andrew, I'm not sure what you like to eat but we have waffles, sausages, and eggs on the stove. If you don't like that, then there's cereal in the cupboard." Karen smiled, showing that charming gap between her front teeth.

"He may eat both the waffles and the cereal! Girl, that boy eats everything."

I laughed at my mother's comment. I did eat a lot. I couldn't understand then why I was so skinny. I must have a high metabolism or something. I grabbed a plate and scooped some waffles and eggs. I sat down with my mom and Karen at the table.

"Where did Courtney drive off to?"

"She had a morning class. She'll be back before lunch," Karen answered me.

"Must be that class she was talking about last night. Courtney is pretty smart. She went on and on last night about her theory on Noah's ark."

"Noah's ark? I'm sure you know that story, Andy," my mother added.

"I do, Mom, but she was getting all deep about it. Talking about Nephilim and stuff."

My mother looked up at me and looked at Karen.

"Nephilim? What did she say about the Nephilim?"

She had stopped eating and even Karen stopped for a second. This attention struck me as odd for a second but then I continued.

"Well, I had never heard of them before and she simply told me what they were. They are like the children of the angels, right?"

"That's my Courtney. I used to tell her bedtime stories

about angels, guess that sparked her interest," Karen said, looking over at Andrea.

"That's all she told you about them?" It seemed my mother was in interrogation mode again. She looked as if she were trying to read me in my eyes.

"Yeah, do you know what Nephilim are?"

"Yeah, she's right about the angels. I-I am just surprised that you were so interested in a subject like that. You don't even read your Bible that much when you are at home." She continued eating.

I smirked at her comment. What did she mean by she was surprised I'd be interested? It wasn't the Bible I was afraid of; it was the issue of going crazy from reading the Bible. Ignorance had been my bliss in childhood but now I was dying from the lack of knowledge. My mother was holding back from me. My interest in the Bible had concerned her, oddly enough, and probably had something to do with whatever her secret was.

My mother looked back down at her plate. Karen was looking odd also. I had this crazy feeling that everybody knew what was going on except for me. The tension was intensified by the silence. I had to say something, but I didn't want to reveal my suspicions yet.

I broke the silence by changing the subject. "When is the funeral?" I asked. I could feel the tension passing like clouds on a windy day.

"Tomorrow afternoon. Did you call your boss at your job to tell them you were going to be gone?"

It slipped my mind totally. So much was going on and my normal day-to-day life was being put totally on hold. I would be sure to call my boss later because I really took pride in my job. My mother wanted me to be responsible all the time and this was my way to show her that I was a young adult. It seemed she always wanted more, however.

She constantly insisted that I go to college out of Texas and start a new life. That was really weird, especially because she had been so overprotective of me most of my life. She'd freak out anytime she heard about somebody robbing a store on the news. Being in grocery wasn't the best job in the world but it was my job. I remember one time when I had just started and I was so nervous.

I had just learned the computer system that they had installed and there were thousands of codes for the produce, but somehow I had crammed all that information into my brain. I had one of those ribbons on that read "new employee," and for the most part everyone was fairly patient with me except for him, that one guy who had to give me trouble, Leonard Freeman. I guess I would have been cool if Tonya hadn't been at his side at the time. Leonard wasn't even my customer yet, but his taunting made me self-conscious of how slow I was.

"Damn, Turner!" he yelled two customers back in the line, "can you speed up? I've got thangs to do!" Leonard was the big football jock type. I could not figure for the life of me what Tonya saw in Leonard. I don't make it a habit to judge the appearance of other men, but . . . Leonard was ugly. His teeth looked more like fangs, all crooked and spaced out. His lips were always cracked and black as if he smoked weed every day. He kept his hair cut low and he had rolls on the back of his neck that gave him that bulldog appearance. What was the purpose of that extra skin on the back of his neck? One of his crooked teeth was gold and he flashed it often when he smiled. He had hoop earrings in his ears and his eyes were dark and smoky, most likely from the weed again. Leonard Freeman: obvious proof that Darwin's theory may hold some truth. I wish I hadn't let him get to me. I wish I hadn't let Tonya's cuddling under his arms irritate me. I wish . . . I

hadn't dropped those eggs. Leonard enjoyed that spectacle. He busted out laughing at my goof-up.

"Clean up at register four!" he yelled. "You're such an a**-drip Turner!" I hated when he made up cuss words to describe me. I just wanted to punch him right there . . . I just didn't because . . . well . . . I was at work. Not only did he want to embarrass me in front of Tonya but he wanted the whole store to know also. This is why I don't like Leonard Freeman. Well there are other reasons too . . . but this story is about me, not him.

I looked up, and Karen was washing up some dishes. I looked out the window and realized my mother had left the table also and was sitting on the porch swing enjoying the weather. I went out to join her.

She didn't look up when I stepped out on the porch; she just stared out—to what I don't know. She had that gaze as if she saw beyond time in the clouds and she could interpret what the birds were saying.

"Nice day," I said, getting her attention. She looked at me and smiled and patted the space next to her. I sat down and she put her arm around me.

"I'm not being fair to you, am I?" she asked, still looking into the sky.

"What do you mean, Mom?"

"Taking you to this funeral. You don't know what has happened with me and that side of the family."

I laid my head on her shoulder. "I understand that it's probably difficult for you. It's just that I don't like it when you keep these secrets from me."

"Andy, I'm trying to protect you."

"From what? Mom, I'm about to graduate, I'm gonna be a man and be on my own. How can I know where I'm going if I don't know who I am?"

"You are . . . Andrew Turner, my beautiful son." She rubbed my hair. "I used to be like you—always on the pursuit of truth. I remember when I went to college and my life turned upside down. There was so much I didn't know. It turned out the more I found out, the more that life ceased to be as normal as I thought. I found out by accident that I was adopted. You can't realize how that made me feel because here I was, an adult, and my whole life that I had grown to know was a lie. I was so mad at Mama. I later met your daddy on campus. He taught the campus Bible study and I guess God brought us together. He was also majoring in theology and some of the things he knew amazed me."

She giggled and looked at me. "You have his smile. Karen was always trying to get us to be alone together; she was such an instigator. I remember when I first saw him at the campus Bible study. I was looking for answers and I really never intended to fall in love. I really didn't even like him; I was into this other guy who wasn't really good for me at all. But I couldn't help but notice how beautiful your daddy was, not just in body but in spirit. He was tall and thin. He had chocolate skin that was so smooth and hair that was faded. He wore a red and blue sweater with some black denim jeans. I could tell he worked out; his shoulders were broad and he had this cute tight butt with his bow-legged self!" She grinned and fanned herself. Okay, my mother was zoning out and scaring me now. She looked at me and blushed.

"Sorry, but baby, your daddy was cute. And of course, I felt bad 'cause I was in Bible study scoping him out like such but I couldn't help myself."

"So why aren't ya'll together anymore? Why did he leave us?"

She stopped grinning. She looked back at the sky.

"Andy, he didn't leave. We agreed to separate. I still love him. We are husband and wife and haven't divorced; it's just that if we were together . . ."

"Ya'll are still married?" I sat up. "If you two are still married, then why isn't he here?" This news was another shock. I wasn't sure how much more of this I could take.

"He's always been here—if not physically then in other ways. He knows that you are okay and he loves you very much."

"Then why hasn't he ever tried to visit me or invited me to come visit him?"

"It's not that simple, Andy." Here we were back where we left off from the conversation in the car. We had kept an emotional distance because of the argument and the road had looped right back around to the same question.

"Where is my daddy?"

She sighed. There was so much she didn't want to reveal and so much she wanted to tell me at the same time.

"Your daddy will come back when it's time."

"Well, when is it time—time for what? What are you talking about?" Once again I was letting my frustration get the best of me. I had sat up trying to tune into her and she was emotionally blocking me out again.

"Andy, I realize that for many years I have tried to protect you from everything under the sun. But I can't do that forever. Whatever happens I want you to remember that your mother loves God and I love you; I want you to remember all that I've taught you. That's why I need you to get stronger in Christ because whatever's out there you have to learn to fight it."

"I'm strong in the Lord! Tell me what you're talking about! Fight what?"

"You will learn, in time. No truth can be held from you because you are a child of truth."

Okay, now my mom was really freaking me out. Not only that, but she was scaring me. She was talking as if she wasn't going to be around. She got up from the porch swing and went back into the house. I stood and looked up. God, what are you doing to my life? Everything that I had ever known was changing.

Courtney arrived home around noon. I was still hanging around the front porch sitting on the steps. It ended up being a day that I wished for rain. The humidity was almost unbearable, but every now and then a wind would soothe my burning skin. She got out of the car with her satchel strapped around her shoulders. She walked up the sidewalk with her little faded denim shorts on and a green tank top that revealed her midriff slightly. A bandana covered the front part of her Afro. Had I been that exhausted this morning to not have noticed how incredibly lovely she was today? She smiled when she saw me and invited herself to sit on the spot next to me.

"Why you looking so down, kiddo?" she said, placing her bag at her feet and readjusting her bandana.

"What are you talking about?"

"I'm talking about you. You sitting outside in this heat looking like you just missed the ice cream man." A smile cracked despite my effort to hold it in.

"Seeee, there ya go! Show Courtney them pretty-boy teeth."

Okay, now she had me blushing. I turned my head so she couldn't see how she'd got to me. I was twisting several blades of grass in my hands, which were becoming slightly greenish from the nervous repetition. I wiped my hands and looked up at the sky.

"Courtney, so many things are happening so fast. I mean, first my mother tells me she found her biological mother after the woman dies. My mother is definitely sick, and I feel deep inside she knows what the problem is. Today, she tells me that she is still married to my daddy and she won't tell me the reason why they are not together."

Courtney put her head down. I felt she knew something and I wanted to get some information from her. She tried to keep from making eye contact with me.

"Courtney, what do you know?"

"What are you talking about, Andrew?"

"Courtney, don't play with me, girl. If you know something that pertains to my life don't you think I should know?"

Courtney sighed and stood up with her back to me. I grabbed her arm and stood up, turning her around.

"Excuse me? I don't know what you are talking about, Andrew." She pulled her arm from my grip.

"Please, Courtney. I need to know what you know," I said softly. I was determined.

She shifted her weight from one leg to the other and crossed her arms. Her eyes burned into my own. It was like a showdown at sunset in one of those Old West movies. Finally, she gave up. Her eyes softened and she bit her lip. She grabbed my hand and pulled me to her car.

"Get in." She opened the door to her car. I did as I was told. I sat in the car and watched her walk around to the driver's side.

"Where are we going?"

"Away from here, I don't want my mother knowing

what I'm going to tell you." Finally, some truth was going to be revealed. She backed the car out and began driving. I could tell she was thinking. We drove for about ten minutes in silence. What was the big secret? I looked at her and wished I knew what she was thinking—what thoughts consumed her being. She glanced at me.

"Andrew, my mother has told me a lot about you and your mom."

"I figured so; I mean, they grew up together."

"Andrew, there's more to this story than what you've been told. I understand how you feel to some extent. I didn't know a lot about my dad. He died before I was born. My mom didn't tell me for a long time until she thought I could handle it."

"What are you saying? Are you insinuating that I'm not mature enough to know about my own family?"

"No, not that at all. What I'm saying is that people keep secrets for a reason. Some things are better left unsaid." Courtney glanced my way.

Maybe she was right. Only God knew what I was getting into. Was I about to open my mother's Pandora's box? But I had to know.

"I have to know, Courtney. I know you understand, not knowing your daddy. It's like a missing puzzle piece. Although you see the majority of the picture and basically know what it is, the picture stays incomplete and that bothers you until you find that piece."

"What if you find that space is not for one piece but actually many pieces?"

"Excuse me?"

"Well, Andrew, I only know so much about your family but there are things my mother still doesn't tell me. I know there isn't one answer to your problem."

"What do you know, Courtney?"

Courtney pulled the car into the parking lot of a nearby school. She stopped the engine and rested her forehead on the steering wheel.

"My mom was a friend with your mom and dad. They all met in college here in Dallas. Something happened during college that affected your mother, and my mom says that if it wasn't for your dad she wouldn't have made it. That's about all I know, but my mom did tell me to watch your mom 'cause she was really sick and that she . . ." Courtney paused and tried to hold back.

"She what?"

"She may be dying, Andrew. She wants you to hang around here because my mother is like a sister to her."

"And she doesn't want me to be alone when she is gone."

"Exactly." I sat there confused and shocked. I knew my mother was ill but I wasn't sure to what extent. This was a reality check to think she may not be around. What would I do if my mother died? Evidently she had thought this through already and she didn't want me to be scared. That's why she came here and wanted me to be close to Karen and Courtney. But if she knew my dad was alive, why not let me meet him so I could live with him?

"What about my dad?"

Courtney shrugged. "Your dad is alive, I know that. But I don't know his whereabouts. I figure he's in this city somewhere. My mother has pictures of them in this old box. I can't understand why you haven't met him yet."

"That's what I'm wondering and I'm going to find out if you want to help me. When we get back can we check it out?"

Courtney agreed to my request and patted my hand.

"I'll help you any way I can but I'm sure that your mother will let you know the whole story soon enough." I hoped that Courtney was right.

We got back home and Mama was cooking some things for dinner. Karen was asleep. I felt weird seeing her there all happy, pretending things were okay when they really weren't.

"Hey, Mom, how are ya feeling?"

"I'm fine, baby, just fine. How are you?" She smiled and cut some potatoes and washed them in the sink. I walked behind her and kissed her cheek.

"I'm fine." Courtney watched me and motioned me to follow her. I walked off, and my mother looked confused for a moment but continued to wash the potatoes.

"Don't act differently, then she'll suspect I told you something," Courtney whispered to me around the corner. She had me against the wall and she pointed her skinny finger at me.

"What do you want me to do? You just told me that my mother was dying," I whispered, attempting not to yell.

"I told you that it may be something that you might not want to know."

I walked past her. I was opening a can of worms. I gritted my teeth. The worst thing about someone having a secret is finding out and then having to pretend you don't know. This game was getting hectic and new rules were being added every minute. I walked up the stairs to my room and looked out the window. The funeral was tomorrow, and I was sure to find out more when I met my mother's family.

The rain poured down. Perfect weather for a funeral, I thought. My mother had not spoken a word to me as she was driving and my mind was beginning to wander. The windshield wipers of the car squeaked back and forth and the windows were beginning to fog up. I glanced over at her and she was biting her lip. She must be nervous. But why? Why was she even going? If this woman who gave birth to her could not even care less about her existence why were we even bothering to go to her funeral? My mother looked at me. She smiled but her eyes were sad. Her sadness was enough to answer my question. Evidently, my mother had parts of herself still missing. She was an incomplete puzzle. Her own husband, my dad, was a significant piece of that puzzle.

"Andy, baby, you're thinking too much."

"Huh?" I looked up, surprised. Was my face betraying me? Was I all frowned up? I tried to smile. She knew this whole thing bothered me. Karen was on duty again at the police station and Courtney was asleep at home. I adjusted my tie. I hated ties. What was the purpose of a tie? Everything else you wore had a purpose. The belt held up your pants, the handkerchief was a necessity for those with

allergies, and the cuff links were more than decoration—
they . . . well . . . linked the cuffs. But the infamous tie.
What was its purpose? It was merely a strip of extra material meant solely to choke the crap out of you. It wasn't a
useful commodity. It was just an accessory, a necessary evil.

I could see this old white church through the rain, the
Greater Glory Church, and my mother pulled into the parking lot and parked the car. She sat there silently for a while.
She wore the traditional black dress and around her neck
some white pearls. She took a breath and patted my leg as
if to say, "Ready or not here we come."

I grabbed the umbrella and got out of the car and ran
to the other side of the car to cover Mom from the pouring
rain. She bowed underneath the umbrella and I wrapped
my arm around her, bringing her more protection underneath it. We skipped up to the church door and could hear
an organ playing. We entered the church foyer. The carpet
was green and flat. It looked wet from previous guests trying to escape the rain. To my left was a big picture of an old
man in clergy apparel—must be the pastor. Underneath the
picture was his name—Reverend Thomas Francis. The
organ was more distinct in the foyer and the sanctuary
doors were in front of us. I closed the umbrella and shook
it dry. My mother took my hand and opened the right door
of the entrance and we slipped into the back row.

The church was maybe twenty rows deep and all the
rows were filled. We were late, people had already begun
viewing the body. I'm glad because I hated to view a dead
body, it simply gave me the creeps. Had my mother intended
on being late? Was she attempting to keep a low profile? I
must admit her hat was quite big and much of it hid her face.

At the front of the church an old woman caught my
attention because she had begun screaming and throwing

herself on the open casket. Ushers grabbed both her arms and pulled her to the first row, fanning her in the process. Her limp body flopped onto the row as if she had died instead of my grandmother. I wanted to laugh but I held my composure; I did not want to show disrespect—but I had to admit it was kinda funny. The tears of others reminded me of the weather. I could not see the body, but it dawned on me that that was my grandmother up there in that casket. It dawned on me that she was dead and I had never met her. It dawned on me that my grandmother never loved me. That was enough to almost make me cry. I excused myself and went to the foyer.

I sipped some water from the fountain and looked out the glass door at the rain. The rain was lighter than it had been on the drive here and . . . what was that? Someone across the street was looking at me. He was wearing a long coat and the shadow from an umbrella hid his face. Was he thinking about coming in? I stared hard and concentrated to make out his face. Was he aware I was looking at him? My heart raced and my very soul jumped, and every hair on my body stood up as a chill ran down my spine. He was across the street but it was as if I was right in front of him, staring into his eyes. I wasn't touching him but I could feel him in me because I was part of him. His face came into focus and I flashed back to what my mother said to me earlier:

"I couldn't help but notice how beautiful your daddy was . . . He was tall and thin. He had chocolate skin that was so smooth and hair that was faded." I realized that everything she was describing was this man. I could see his eyes as if they were right in front of me and in his eyes I saw myself and even deeper into his eyes I saw myself again but different, even stronger.

I was about to open the door and run to meet him but

I heard another scream. My mother! Just then the man across the street walked off and jumped into his car. I ran back into the sanctuary. My mother was on the floor between the pews holding her head, screaming, and the ushers were grabbing her shoulders. Her screams were not of sorrow but were screams of pain. I ran to the ushers.

"Let her go, she's sick, she's not crying, she's sick," I yelled at them and pulled them back. The pastor walked up the aisle. I grabbed my mother and tried to pull her from the floor in between the pews but once again her strength was greater than my own. She was breathing hard and I could feel through her dress that she was perspiring heavily.

"Get that demon from out of this church!" yelled the pastor. I looked up at him.

"She doesn't have a demon, my mother is just sick, Reverend," I told him. He was the same man in the foyer's picture. He looked at me with eyes open wide.

"You are a spawn of this demon also! Get out!"

"What are you talking about?" I could hear the other people in church praying and casting us out. What was wrong with these people? Was this a church or was it a cult? No one seemed to be paying any mind that my mother was having convulsions. They were acting like mindless slaves to what their pastor said.

"Please, Pastor, call a doctor."

"No hospital can help this demon woman, this child of the devil. Leave my church, Satan!" My mother cringed at his words. I looked down at her and I held back my tears. She was getting weaker and I was confused, hurt, and rejected. But they weren't my feelings, they were my mother's. I was feeling her pain. I picked her up with all my might and walked past the crowd; they moved back when I stood up as they realized how tall I was. I could still hear them casting me out in the name of Jesus. I felt a tear drop from my eye. The very Jesus I loved and worshipped was the same Jesus they were using to insult me.

I left out of respect for those who deserved no respect. I carried my mother out into the rain. We were both getting wet, and I struggled to open the passenger-side door and hold her safely at the same time. I placed my mom inside and knelt beside her as the rain rolled down my face. Her eyes darted back and forth at nothing.

"Mama, what's wrong with you?"

She gasped. And her eyes stopped moving. My heart stopped because it appeared she had died, but she slowly directed her eyes toward me.

"I'm sorry. I'm . . . so sorry, Andy," she whispered weakly. I was about to get up but she grabbed my arm and she looked me directly in my eyes.

"See and understand . . ." She whispered and more chills ran down my spine. The wind blew and that instant my reality changed into my dream that I had been having before.

My mother wasn't holding my arm anymore, the strange dark-haired man from the club was holding my arm—no, he was holding the beautiful girl's arm and I was safely outside, my mother's image but an apparition around me. They could not see us. The young girl screamed and struggled to escape from his grip. This seemed all too real. It was as if I were really there.

"Stop, let me go!" she screamed. He didn't even struggle to hold her but seemed to pick her up with the greatest ease. His laugh was dark.

"Struggle some more, Maggie. It will do you no good. Why don't you leave with me and stay with me forever."

"No! Don't do this."

He pulled her close to his face and rubbed his lips across her neck. "You are so beautiful. I want to have you as my own."

She screamed and pushed her hand at his face, but he didn't budge; he smiled bigger and began to levitate in the air. He spun around with her in his arms, and his hair flowed freely as if he were underwater. His skin illuminated brightly like the sun, and his clothing ceased to bind him as his entire being held her against his nude body. He was both beautiful and hideous at the same time. He floated in the air yet had no wings. Solar flares expelled from behind him and proceeded around him, and they seemed to have something to do with his flight. He ripped at her dress and exposed her breasts. His long nails ripped at her flesh on her back as his tongue licked over her chest. Her blood poured down upon the pavement, and the girl who was so happy in my dream before cried in this violation and seemed too weak to fight the rape from this creature. I jumped from the apparition of my mother that surrounded me and advanced to help her.

I could feel my mother trying to pull me back but my will was too strong. The girl looked at me through weak watery eyes and her frail, shaky hand reached out for me. I couldn't reach her and the luminescent man continued to have his way with her. He was so much larger than she in his actual state, and I thought he would kill her as he sexually consumed her without any regard to the torture she was experiencing. By my feet a puddle of blood formed, and I backed up because it appeared to be moving. The blood was alive. It no longer was a puddle, it was a deep red abyss and something was attempting to emerge from it. It bubbled and churned, and a bloody hand broke the surface. I didn't want to touch the grasping hand . . . Finally, another hand came out of the blood and then a head and a face. Oh, my God! I was looking into the bloody face of my mother.

The man dropped the girl and she plummeted into a Dumpster. He had thrown her away like an old newspaper. He *picked up my mother from the blood pool and cradled her. He spoke in some unknown tongue and simultaneously I could hear the translation.*

"You are mine!" he said. I was shocked and frozen like in my nightmares when I was young. I couldn't move so I did all I could do. I screamed. I screamed so loud that everything in the alley shook. The man stopped and looked at me for the first time. It was as if I had broken some barrier and now I had been revealed to him.

"Andrew . . ." he whispered and began floating toward me. I fell back and stumbled backward on the floor. In frantic fear I got to my feet and ran back to the corner. I could still see the cloud of protection that I had left and I could hear my mother's voice within it. I jumped into the cloud feeling its power around me.

The man stopped just before it, laughing and slamming his fist over an invisible barrier. I crouched down within the cloud. His eyes were afire and he stopped trying to find me in the smoke screen.

"You can't hide forever, Andrew. The winds will blow and your cloud will be gone." With that he laughed and disappeared.

In a flash I was back outside the church and my mother so weak before me in the passenger seat. I was drenched with sweat and jumped back, releasing her grip from my arm.

"I'm sorry, Andy."

I stood there quietly and closed the car door. What had I just seen? My mother had provoked my dream into my mind while I was awake. Was she really a demon? A tear rolled down my cheek. I had to get her home before I could make sense of this . . . this . . . mess. I looked back at the church. I needed so many answers and I had nowhere to go.

I jumped into the car. My heart was beating a thousand

times a minute. I couldn't get the face of that evil man out of my head. He knew my name. He knew my mother. He wanted both of us, this rapist. I drove down the highway at high speed. I couldn't go back to Karen's house. I decided to drive back to Heaven, where I felt safe. Evidently, this demon man had not found us in Heaven and it was only logical to go back there. Ever since we had left, things had become more intense. Yes, get back home, that's the answer. Once I was home I could figure things out. I could get Mama some help and get things back to normal. Normal—what the heck was normal? Who was my Mama? She wasn't normal. All these secrets; I had to calm down. Breathe.

I was still driving when my mother came to. The rain continued to pour down, and I stared at the road with only one aim—to get home.

"What are you doing?"

"I'm driving us home . . . now."

"Andy, no, wait . . ."

"Wait, wait for what? Do you realize what just happened back there? You had another convulsion in the church. The preacher called you a demon! You grabbed my arm and shot an entire dream into my mind. The same guy who's been haunting my dream seemed more real than I would like him to be. Not to mention, I think I'm going crazy like everybody else in my family!" She sat up and tears filled her eyes.

"Andy, I'm sorry, I should have told you."

"Yeah, yeah, you should have told me a lot of things. Does Daddy come to mind?"

"You aren't crazy, you're gifted just like me."

"So you are a demon."

"Yes and no."

Okay I was being sarcastic, but her answer threw me for a loop. I looked at her, shocked.

"What! You gotta be kidding me; you have to be kidding!"

"Listen, Andy, it' s real complicated. I want you to listen very carefully."

I clicked the windshield wipers another notch to speed them up. The rain was hard and my visibility was unclear, among other things.

"I'm about through listening. Every time I listen you tell me one more thing to shatter my whole world. So that preacher was right when he called you a demon, how did he know you were a demon? Am I a demon, too?" My voice quivered like I was going to cry.

"No, no, no, you don't understand."

"What, what is it that I don't understand, Mother? How the heck did this happen? Is that why I can see things that people are thinking? Is that why?" I hollered at her and she didn't rebuke me. I slammed my fist on the steering wheel and tears ran through my nostrils.

"You are not a demon. Your father is a human man. You are redeemed to God by his blood. But my father raped my mother many years ago and he was . . ."

"Your father was a demon?"

"No, an angel."

Can I take any more of this? I rubbed my forehead and my eyes were stinging.

"Do you really expect me to believe this?"

"It's true. Donyel, that's his name, he's a fallen angel. Many years ago he lusted after this young preacher's wife, so he took her and gave her a child."

"Donyel? Is that the dark-haired man in my dream?" My mother nodded. "But that would make you a Nephilim like Courtney was telling me about."

"Right," she said softly as if she were ashamed.

"Not a demon. So why did he call you a demon?"

"Because my soul may be damned; I'm losing my mind slowly and his blood is making me go crazy. People were not meant to have these types of powers or to have the blood of angels. God won't accept my spirit into heaven because I'm the product of an abomination. Now, I can't control any of my powers anymore, and the demons—I can hear them calling my name. They say they want to destroy me and they want to destroy you."

"Me? What did I do to them?"

"Like I told you. You have the blood of men because your father is a man and a Christian man at that. You were born under a covering of protection that God himself created. I knew that would happen because God works under certain principles. I've studied this since I was young and I figured that if I couldn't save myself I could make sure that you were saved. You are his seed and that means that you are eligible to be redeemed from hell like any other man is but you also have the power of angels; that's why you are a threat to not only the demons but Donyel himself."

"This is crazy. This isn't fair—you can't be dying!" I laughed but there was no joke.

"Life isn't about what's fair. It's about principles and laws. When those laws are broken then there's chaos. That's why I need you to be prayerful, because God is your only hope to get through this. I don't know how long I have or where I will go after all this but you have to survive."

"So you have no choice but to be hell-bound because of some principle?" It sounded so preposterous to me.

"In some ancient Hebrew books they say the Nephilim were destroyed during the flood. Because they were an abomination to God their spirits had no heaven to return to, so they were cursed to walk the earth without bodies."

"Ghosts?"

"No, their spirits became known as unclean spirits and to what we now know as demonic spirits. There's no account of demons before the flood but afterward there are many."

"So . . . you are telling me that demons are the disembodied spirits of the Nephilim and that's what you are going to become?" Why couldn't she just have been crazy? That I could handle. But somehow this made too much sense. She was telling me things that were in my dreams. All those feelings that I was having inside now were making sense. But maybe this was all some dream. I should have listened to Courtney—this truth was overwhelming.

"Yes, whatever happens I want you to know that what I am going to become is not who I really am. Look at me . . ." I attempted to drive and look at her, glancing every so often. "You are not to believe anything I say or contact me after I'm gone. My spirit will transform and my soul will be lost. Do you understand me?"

"So you will be able to talk to . . ."

"Do you understand?" She grabbed her stomach in pain and folded over.

"Mom, are you okay?" She was scaring me. I could feel the car swerve some while I was trying to comfort her. As I touched her head the hairs on my arm stood up. A whisper in my mind like a passing wind simply said:

"Antonio."

My mother screamed again. I removed my hand and started adding things up. It seemed that every time I got a chill I could see into people's minds. Every time I used this gift, my mother went into a convulsion. I was the reason. The whole reason why she was getting sick, the whole reason why she was advancing in her transformation was because I was getting stronger. I was the catalyst for her sickness. I was killing my mother.

"No, it's not your fault; don't blame yourself, Andy." She was reading my thoughts. She had my gift to read the soul and probably many other gifts that I didn't have. I slammed my fist on the steering wheel. A bridge loomed a few feet ahead.

"You have to go back," she whispered, "go back to Karen's. I have to tell you about my pregnancy. You have a . . ." Suddenly, the car skidded and hydroplaned. I panicked and attempted to regain control but the car began to spin. We had just merged on a bridge and I was determined to keep control.

"Mom! Hold on!"

"Andy!" She grabbed my shirt and I heard it tear. I couldn't even see the street. The car was spinning and I put my head down. The car hit something hard and I heard the sound of metal slamming on metal. Next thing I knew we were sideways and I had a horrible feeling. No skid sound, no resistance, just the sound of the wind. We were falling. It happened so fast and before I knew it, all I could see was water. I was jerked forward on the impact and only my seatbelt kept me from hitting the windshield. The car was now sinking into the river below the bridge and the water exploded into the car, blinding my eyesight and filling my mouth. I unbuckled my seatbelt and gasped for a quick breath. The sound of the rushing water was replaced by the muffled sound of being underwater. I couldn't see anything. I felt for my mother's hand but she wasn't moving. My lungs felt as if they were going to explode. I kicked at the door and tried to open it, but to no avail. Bubbles rolled up my face. I wanted to scream feeling the cold water numb my skin, but I knew I couldn't release my breath. I rolled down the window and attempted to squeeze through the space. The deeper the car sunk the darker it became. I flapped my arms with everything I could to fight the pull from the car. The icy waters were taking their toll on me and my legs were feeling numb. The current was pulling me backward. I was blacking out. I blacked out. I think I was dead. But if I was, the story would be over.

chapter 11

Hey kid, what'll be?" I must be knocked out.

"Hey kid, what'll be?" Why am I having this dream and why does this guy keep repeating himself? I've seen everything there was to see, or have I? I looked in the mirror and my reflection was getting direct eye contact with me as if it were someone else. I saw my reflection banging on the mirror trying to tell me something but I couldn't hear. This was different. I tried to focus on what my reflection was trying to tell me, and then I saw him. Just as evil as before. Behind my image in the mirror there was Donyel. His eyes were black like his hair. He zoomed up behind my image so quick that it startled me to look behind myself. Nothing—just people dancing. There I was without even moving on the dance floor. And the beautiful girl . . . what did Donyel call her—oh yeah, Maggie.

"Maggie, you have to get out of here." The girl continued to dance and look at me and smile.

"Andrew, what's done is done, just change what you can; you must fall suit to the most divine plan." Nice. Sounds like this woman should be a songwriter. The club lights went out and there was silence.

Dark silence.

"Is he going to be okay?"

"Well, he's been through a lot of trauma but it appears as if he's going to be fine."

"Good, is it okay if I stay here a while?"

"You're welcome to stay as long as you like. About his mother, it's usually customary for the doctor to give such news." Another voice whispered.

"I think it would be best for the news to come from me." I could hear everyone talking but I couldn't get myself to move or even open my eyes. But at least my mind was awake now. I was aware of someone's presence in the room around me. I wanted to move so badly but couldn't. There was a sharp pain on my head. I felt a hand rub my forearm and grip my hand. Had to concentrate. I felt the chill and I took a gasp of air. The wind of thought like the breeze in a tunnel filled my mind. I could hear the echo of a voice in my mind.

"He's been through so much." Karen's image flashed through my mind with the sound of her voice, *"How am I going to tell him that his mother is dead?"* Oh, my God. I couldn't cry, but in the prison of my mind I was screaming and I couldn't do anything. It was like overhearing a conversation and being locked in a closet. The voice I was hearing was Karen's. Her image had flashed with the sound of her voice. I couldn't do a thing. My mother had died in the accident. She was gone. It was my fault. The car accident was my fault, her convulsions were my fault; I wanted to kick or scream, but I couldn't. It should have been me. I should have died. If I had died instead of her she would have been at peace. She would've been able to live a full life. I could only feel Karen's hand on my head.

"Poor Andrew, you already know don't you?" She rubbed my forehead. I could feel a single tear roll down my face and into my ear. I felt another tear hit my hand. Was

Karen crying too? Who would be there for me now? I'm sure Karen would. But could she understand me? I'm . . . I'm not normal.

I've been born into some freaky family line and the only person who could help me through it was my mother and now . . . she's dead. My own father is nowhere to be found, my grandfather is some crazy fallen angel, and . . . oh, God, what is my relationship with God? I've been a Christian all my life. How could my mother be sure that I was not damned to hell like her? How could she be sure that I wouldn't go crazy too? And what about these demons? How was I going to protect myself? There was one person I needed to help me through this and she was gone. I didn't want to do this by myself. I didn't want to be alone. I did not want to be alone.

"I don't want to be alone . . . ": I startled myself. My own voice had broken through the mental darkness.

"Andrew? Baby, can you hear me?"

"Amazing," the doctor said, astonished. "This is a strong young man. He seems to be healing at a remarkable rate, too."

"Thank you, doctor, for all your help," Karen said. I could feel both her hands cupping my right hand. I still couldn't open my eyes but I attempted to move my head.

"Take it easy, baby. Shhh just rest, Andrew, just rest." She began to hum this tune that I couldn't recognize but it was so sweet. I wished I knew the words to the song. I felt her sit on the bed and her arm wrap over my shoulders. She held me close and I could hear her heartbeat. I was still crying inside but I became lost in Karen's song and I went from the conscious darkness into the unconscious darkness, the darkness that slumber brings. Her voice faded away as did the sense of everything around me, except for the sense of Karen holding me. I'm not sure for how long, but I slept for a while.

I awoke some time after, but Karen was not there anymore. I struggled to open my eyes to see that Courtney was sitting next to me. My eyes were hurting from the light in the room. I tried to talk but my voice seemed to have other plans. I grunted, and Courtney jumped from the chair. She had been asleep also, and I tried to reach for her but a few tubes had me bound.

"C-Courtney . . ." Good, the voice was still working.

She looked at me and smiled. "Hey, pretty boy. Glad to see you're awake."

I cracked a smile. I was still squinting my eyes because it seemed my eyelids wanted to close more than they wanted to stay open.

"Where's your mom?" I asked.

"At work, she's been here praying with you all night."

"My mother's dead, isn't she?"

Courtney's eyes glazed over and her lips tightened. "I'm sorry, Andrew." I didn't want to show my emotion but sooner or later I was going to have to let go. I turned my head to look out the window on my left. The silence was uncomfortable. Courtney wanted to help me but she had absolutely no idea the right words to say.

"You can stay with us, Andrew."

"No, I gotta get back to Heaven. I got all my stuff there and my mom's stuff. I gotta find something to do with all that . . ." I paused to think.

"What's the matter?" Courtney rubbed my hair.

"Nothing," I lied. God forgive me. I was thinking about the numerous diaries my mother had stashed away; surely there was something that could help me in there. She had to have written about what happened to her. In those diaries were probably information about my dad too. I had to get those journals. I looked back at Courtney. Now I knew more than she did. Her mom probably knew of my angelic heritage, but this knowledge was probably too much for Courtney; crap, it was too much for me. I still couldn't believe this but I didn't have much choice. Everything happened so fast, and now I was being taught how to swim by being thrown in the deep end of the pool— sink or swim.

"Courtney, could you excuse me? I have to go to the bathroom." I think she blushed. She nodded and left the room. I bought myself some personal time—not to use the bathroom, however. When I knew she had left, I safely released my tears. I still couldn't comprehend my mother's being gone, not forever. I still couldn't comprehend her leaving me by myself. I grabbed my pillow and hugged it and almost choked on my own tears. I tried not to make a sound, muffling my own mouth in the process. I tried to stop, but the tears wouldn't obey my command. I had opened a floodgate and now the waterfall was pouring. I was trying to remember everything she told me and nothing was coming to mind. The fear of failure crept up on me. She had so many expectations for me, and now I was scared that I would not be able to complete the task set before me. Demons—what if the demons tried—no, can't think about them right now. I had to get myself together. I attempted to sit up. A stiffening pain held me down on the bed. I would wait a little bit longer before I tried that again.

Courtney knocked on the door.

"You can come in." I wiped all emotional evidence from my face. She returned and looked at me so blankly, so solemn.

"Please don't stare at me like that. I'm starting to think that the accident disfigured me or something."

"In actuality the doctors are really amazed that you came out of it with hardly any scratches at all. The ones you came with are almost healed and you've only been here twenty-four hours."

"Good cells in my body I guess."

"I guess." Courtney stood at the foot of my bed. I was going to tell her about me being a—whatever I was, but first *I* had to figure it out. I mean, I wasn't an angel and I wasn't a Nephilim. I was half Nephilim, but she would flip if I told her that. I had a difficult time as a teenager trying to figure out who I was already, now I had this to worry about. I had to speak to Karen. Karen probably knew things that could help me since my mom confided in her so much.

"They say you might be able to leave as soon as they run some more tests to make sure everything is okay. We'll take care of you at the house, that is—if you want to go there because . . ."

"Because what?"

"Well they found your car way on the outskirts of the city limits. Were you going to leave without telling us?"

That was exactly what I was doing but I had to figure a way to tell her without offending her. My running had nothing to do with Courtney or Karen.

I could hear the hurt in her voice. I spoke slowly. "Well, not exactly. I mean yes . . . but, well, I was scared."

"Scared of what?"

"We had gone to the funeral and my mom had another convulsion there."

"Inside the church? During the funeral? What did the people do? Why didn't you call my mom or bring her to the house?" Her eyes got bigger until I could see the sun reflect off her irises; she had such beautiful eyes. Focus, Andrew, focus.

"Well, I panicked. Plus, the pastor told us to get out."

"Oh, my gosh, the pastor told you to leave? He didn't help?"

"No." Now that I was thinking about it, I wanted to talk some more to that pastor. I didn't have time to be sitting in this hospital. If something was out there trying to get me, whether it be some demon or Donyel himself, I wanted to be ready.

"My mom will be back later to see you. I'll tell her you're awake and we'll probably be able to take you back to the house tonight."

"Okay." Courtney grabbed her satchel and threw it around her shoulder and waved good-bye. As tough as she tried to appear, I was beginning to see her softer side. I had to be honest with her and I would be. God forbid something bad happens to her because of me. I had to stop whatever madness was coming. How much of my personality was genetic?

Did my genes choose if I were to be evil or good? But this is more than good and evil, because my mom was good and yet she was still consumed by the evil. How could it be possible that something could be good and yet still evil? Evidently evil had no discrimination between good and bad. I thought for a second about the Sunday school lessons I had learned as a child. The beginning of time—Adam and Eve had sinned against God by eating the fruit of the knowledge of good and evil. It didn't say the knowledge of bad and evil or the knowledge of good and bad. Good and evil came together as a package, and when Eve saw the fruit she said it was good. So there has to be something to this being "good."

Satan comes as an angel of light, God forbid I meet him. Donyel, himself, didn't have horns or anything in my dreams; he was glorious and beautiful in himself. The evil side seemed to come from the fact that the glory emanating from him didn't come from God, who created him.

I wonder if good and evil can be the same thing. If evil was "bad," then people wouldn't enjoy doing it so much and I think it's the attempt of obtaining "good" without God that goodness becomes evil. I think too much. I knew that being good could still make me like Donyel and pull me into hell like my mother. She was good, but she was searching for righteousness.

Righteousness is goodness obtained from God alone and recognized by God. If I could obtain heaven and God's love just from being good, then I could work my way to heaven. However, from what I knew from church, I understood that there is nothing I could do to work my way into heaven because Jesus already paid the price when he died on the cross. So I had to have faith—faith in God, faith in Jesus, faith in this destiny set out before me to conquer this evil that plagues my family. Donyel was like my family's generational curse. I would break that curse for my mother, for Maggie, and make Donyel pay.

～ chapter 12

It felt weird being back in the guest room of Karen's house and my mother not being there with me. I had not faced the reality that my mother was really gone—I didn't want to think about it. The other bed in the guest room looked so empty, and at night there was an eerie silence in the room. When the loneliness became too unbearable I would grab the pillow Mama had laid her head on. It still held the scent of her perfume. Karen had notified my school and my job of the tragedy. For the next couple of days I didn't feel like leaving my room. It was like someone had ripped out a piece of my chest and there was this empty hole. I was losing hope and slowly going into depression.

Some nights I would awaken thinking I heard her say my name. One night, I jumped up and looked around the room.

"Mom?" Maybe I had been asleep all this time. Maybe her dying was simply a nightmare. Maybe this whole thing was a nightmare and we were still in Heaven, Texas. But after looking at the bland, quiet, poorly decorated room, I knew that all that had happened was real. It was all too real and I was still alone. Nothing in the room to keep me company but my silent shadow given off by the moon.

Karen would ask me to come downstairs to eat but

wouldn't force me to do any more than I would have to. After a while, the pain of hunger would be more unbearable than the pain in my heart and I'd venture downstairs. I knew she wanted to help me and I did want to be stronger, but my mother's death had weighed down on me like a load of heavy bricks. I had so much inside and I didn't want to cry. I walked around the house silent, hair uncombed, face with no expression. What more could I do? I was in shock. Courtney came to the table where I was eating and sat down.

"Glad to see you're up and about," she said.

I looked up from the bowl of cereal I was eating. I hadn't spoken to another in so long that I wasn't sure if I could still talk. My nose burned the way it always did when I felt as if I was gonna cry, so I decided not to say anything.

"Please don't shut me out, Andrew." I tried to look up but I felt my vision blurring from the tears in my eyes. Only a small voice came from my mouth.

"Please, excuse me." I left the table and went back to my room. It amazed me how the angelic blood had healed my body so quickly. I had no physical pain but inside my heart was so torn. It's amazing that my heart, which pumped the powerful blood, was unable to heal itself spiritually. I stood at the door of my room and looked around. I didn't want to go to bed and I didn't want to go to sleep.

Something caught my attention. I looked down on the floor and saw something peeking from under the bed. I leaned down to pick up the towel that had my mother's dried blood on it. I'd forgotten all about it. I touched the blood and the hair on my arm stood up.

"*Andrew* . . ." My mother's face flashed before me. It startled me and I dropped the towel. I stood staring down at the old towel on the floor. Had I seen into my mother's life by touching the towel? What could I see now that she was dead? What did I want to see? I wanted to see her again, to tell her I loved her. Would I be wrong to do that? Was I holding on to something that I didn't need to hold on to? I decided to try. I picked up the forbidden fruit and took a bite. I touched the blood on the towel and closed my eyes. I had to know where she was.

I felt my face get warm. A breeze that wasn't in the room gave me chills over my body. A warmth covered me. The room around me ceased to exist and I was standing back at home, in my own house. *Everything was the same except for the dreamy haze that told me that it was only a vision.*

"Mom?" I walked around the house. I could hear breathing, but from where?

"Mom, is that you? Where are you?" I could feel my heartbeat increase. I heard a whisper in my mind telling me that I shouldn't be here. I continued walking through the house. I stopped at the door of her room. I felt the door and it was hot. I grabbed the knob, and it was hot, burning my hand. I jerked it back quickly and rubbed it against my leg to alleviate the pain. Remember, it's just a vision; just control the vision. I stared some time at the doorknob, which appeared to turn red before my eyes, attempting to keep me out. I concentrated wholly on the knob with everything inside of me. An aura of frost surrounded the knob, and soon the ice made the knob bearable to touch. I grabbed the knob and it shattered in my hand, leaving the door free to open. A draft pulled the door open and a smell unlike I have ever experienced filled my nostrils. My stomach turned from the old, rancid smell. What was that? The room had no light and seemed to pull me inside. I held my balance and tried to focus on what was around me. The darkness was moving, and all I could hear were whispers around me. All the whispers were unfamiliar.

"Andrew . . ." One whisper called me, and I felt a breeze

sweep around my legs. I lifted my foot, thinking something was touching, and I looked around but nothing was there. I will not be scared. I am in total control—I think.

"Mom, it's me, Andrew." The whispers increased. They were so inaudible it frustrated me and I wished I knew what or who it was. I wasn't sure if the room was filled with darkness or smoke because I could see myself plain as day, but the rest of the room was filled with a fluidlike darkness. It appeared like smoke but I smelled no smoke, just that old smell. It was enough to make me want to throw up, but I covered my mouth with my shirt to prevent my stomach from turning. I stood in the middle of the room and I couldn't see to the other side. I had made small baby steps because I was nervous to not run into anything, but it seemed the room was empty. Maybe I could fill it with things from my imagination. The darkness slithered around my hands like a snake and I shook my hands to keep it from sticking to me.

A gray cloud whirled from the darkness and formed a face; a white pale face with no eyes. It was Andrea, my mother, and the clouds had molded into her face. Had I created this image? Everything was white and pale: her hair, her lips, everything. She looked cold like stone.

"Mom? What should I do?" The mouth motioned as if it were talking but no sound came out. Only these dark shadows that leaked from her lips like words. These shadows, in the same snakelike fashion, slithered and attached themselves around my legs and around my arms.

"What? No!" They were pulling me against my will farther into the darkness. I struggled and tried to resist but couldn't. My mother's face became harshly evil, and I could see the bony, skull structure underneath her skin. Her teeth sharpened and her mouth enlarged as if she were ready to swallow me. I gotta wake up! But I couldn't snap out of it.

"Nooo! Mom, it's me! Andrew!!!" The shadows wrapped

around my neck and I tried to pull them away, but they wrapped around my arms, too, and I felt the air ceasing to enter my lungs. The veins in my forehead started to swell, and I couldn't scream even if I wanted to.

I felt myself choking and the darkness slowly about to consume me. I had nothing else left and no one else left. The whispers around me were telling me to give up.

"Andrew!" *Courtney's voice pierced through the darkness and I could feel her hands tugging at my leg.*

I awoke.

I fell to the floor and dropped the towel.

"Oh my . . . Andrew . . . you were floating in the air!" Courtney stood over me.

I felt weak and I opened my eyes. I was free from the darkness. I looked up and realized that Courtney had seen me . . . flying?

"What are you talking about?"

"When I came in the room you were floating, how did you do that? What's going on, Andrew?"

"Calm down."

"No, what's going on? I told you what you wanted to know, now you talk to me!"

I got off the floor and sat on the edge of the bed. I felt weak. Whatever I had done, whatever was in that vision was strong and had tried to kill me. How did I manage to fly?

"Umm, Courtney, there are some things that my mother told me before we got in the accident and I don't even know what to think of it, so how can I explain it to you?"

"Are you into some kinda witchcraft?"

"No, Courtney. I'm not a witch. I am . . ." I couldn't get the words out of my mouth. She would not believe me even if I told her. Who was I kidding?

"You're a . . . you're a what? Andrew, tell me."

"I'm a . . ."

"He's part Nephilim"—wait . . . who said that? I looked in the doorway and Karen walked in behind Courtney. Courtney backed into the corner of the room.

"A Nephilim? That's impossible, tha-that's only biblical theory."

"Well, actually, Andrew is half Nephilim. And evidently the Bible is more real than you give it credit, Courtney." Karen spoke more seriously than I had ever known her to.

I looked back at Courtney, and she was still in shock. She still stood in disbelief in what she had seen and what she was hearing.

"How much do you know about me?" I asked Karen. "What's wrong with me?" I was still weak and I couldn't control the tears flowing down my face.

"Courtney, sit down." Karen pointed to the next bed and Courtney obeyed. Karen stood before both of us like a teacher and we were the diligent little pupils. She paced back and forth.

"Andrew, honey, there's nothing wrong with you. I realize that you are confused and I wish I had more time to prepare for this but it all happened so fast. Your mother asked me to take care of you if anything happened to her. She thought she would be able to tell you completely of who you were before she died."

"She did . . . when we were in the car she told me that she was half angel and that the angel blood inside of her made her an unclean spirit, but my father's blood gave me a chance to be redeemed by God."

"Yes, this is true, Andrew. But you have to make that choice. You have strong powers inside of you but you are more human than you are angel. If you let those powers overwhelm you and pull you into evil they will."

"What do you mean?"

"You must not use your gifts to do your own will. You must understand God's will and obey Him."

"How do I know God's will in my life?" I shouted. "It's not like He is just speaking audibly to me. I mean, I have all these gifts and I would trade all that in to be able to hear from God." I was so serious. Knowing the will of God was something confusing for me. Everyone wanted to do God's will but somehow we got sidetracked into our personal agendas. I wanted to do right but I didn't want to be a person who did my personal agenda and said it was God's will.

"Andrew, have you prayed?" Karen asked me.

I wanted to be honest. My prayer needed work. But that didn't mean I didn't love God.

"Sometimes. Karen, I'm a Christian. I just really don't know where I stand in this spiritual thing. Am I human or am I something else?"

"Did your mother tell you about Donyel?" I nodded to Karen's question. His name was starting to give me a headache.

"Donyel is your grandfather and your mother had to fight him years ago before you were born. Together, with Christ, we bound him up and the evil inside her for a time, but I'm afraid that he will be coming after you now. Once he knows you are of age he will attempt to find you."

"But my mom said he was locked away."

"But he is eternal. We can't be sure how long he will stay bound. Her fight was won; one day you must fight."

"She won? How did she win? She's dead now. Not only that, she's some kind of demon."

"Andrew, she won because her hope was for you to survive. She did her part and now it's your turn to do yours."

"I don't understand."

"Andrew, the spirit of man is the very essence of God. It's the fire, the breath, and the power of God inside of him to be alive. The soul is the essence of that person to be an individual and not a robot, and the body is made from earth and is the only thing that allows our spirit to exist in this realm. Donyel was a fallen angel and gave your mother a part of his spirit, which was an earthbound spirit, and she took an earthbound body, so when her soul attached to both, well, she had no choice but to be earthbound. God could accept neither her body, which is a fallen state, nor her spirit, which is in fallen state."

"So I'm different because my father has given me a part of his spirit that is not fallen?"

"Men have fallen spirits from Adam, but Jesus came to earth to die for the fallen state of men, not angels. So your mother died under a broken covenant of the angels and God but you are born under the covenant between God and men." I grew even more frustrated.

"There's gotta be a loophole. There's gotta be some way to save her!"

"I don't know, Andrew. But you can't worry about that now. You are not to try to link with her. It is against biblical principles to be a medium and contact the dead. You are a very strong empath from what she told me, and if you don't watch yourself the darkness will take you over; there are many things about your gifts that you don't understand and if Donyel can't destroy you he will try to use you."

"Wait—wait, what's an empath?"

"It's something your mother could do and it increased when she was pregnant with you. She could simply know or feel what people were going through as if it were her very own experience. Is that what you do also?"

"Yeah, sometimes I just can see what people are going

through if I touch them and know things without them telling me."

"Stop! Stop! This is all too crazy!" Courtney interrupted. We had forgotten she was there in the room, and she wasn't sure how to take this.

Karen looked at her daughter and tried to be as patient as she could.

"Courtney, we need you to keep yourself together. Andrew has a gift and he's gonna need you to help him in the long run. No one is to know this secret. Also, Courtney, you must be just as strong in Christ spiritually as Andrew is going to have to be. Donyel can't do much to you, that's Andrew's fight, but he has demons that he may send after you and you must be ready."

"Demons? How do I fight those? I'm not a vampire slayer! Do I get a wooden stake or some kind of silver bullets?"

"If you fight them with bullets you won't win. Christians fight the demons differently. The Bible tells us that our weapons of warfare are not carnal but mighty to the pulling down of strongholds. We fight not a fight of flesh and blood but of spirits and principalities. The principalities are the angels. Andrew, you have the power to do that."

Now I was getting overwhelmed. I hadn't cracked open my Bible in some time and Karen was spitting out scriptures like nothing. If I needed to be a strong Christian to do this, I was in serious trouble; especially since I was supposedly so strong.

"I don't know if I can do this Karen. This is too much for me to do, I'm just a kid."

Karen sat next to me and gently touched my shoulder. "Most of the people in the Bible were just kids when God called them to do something extraordinary. Don't put faith in your mother, or your own powers, but put faith in God because when it comes down to it, you're going to need Him to finish it." She sighed and rubbed my hair like my mother used to do and gave me that motherly look. It comforted me some for a minute. I felt like I could do it—just for a minute. Karen grabbed two Bibles and gave one to me and then to Courtney.

"I'll talk to you later about the funeral arrangements. It was your mother's decision that she be cremated. The ceremony will be in Heaven, Texas, so we will be heading back there." I was glad to hear that, and in the light of all the tragedy that had taken place, deep inside, I was happy to finally be heading to familiar territory. Karen left the room and left Courtney and me to our own thoughts.

I could tell that Courtney was still uncomfortable with what all had happened—didn't take my gift to figure that out. She looked at me through the corner of her eyes but her head was looking down at the Bible in her lap.

"Look, Courtney, I'm the same guy you met before."

"I know, it's just so much going on. I mean my mother knew all this about you and your mother and I didn't. All this stuff has been going on and I don't know how to feel about it and no one has asked me what I want to do about it."

"How do you think *I* feel? This is happening to *me*. Everything you heard about is about *my* family, *my* mother, *my* grandfather. This evil is not some outside influence, this is my actual family, Courtney."

"I'm sorry, Andrew. I'm not helping you any and I should."

"You are. It's good to have someone to talk to about this stuff. You are a real friend." She smiled. It was true—everything that I told her. I had felt outcast before but now these past few days had really made me feel totally unattached to this world. I had no example to pattern myself after, and nobody who could seriously understand what I was going through. Courtney taking my hand and encouraging me that she would share the burden that I was about to go through gave me a sigh of relief. It helps to think that you have a friend who will pray for you or help you fight a battle. It helps to know that you're not in a battle alone and to have a friend who will stick with you till the end—not to mention to have a friend as fine as Courtney. Oh, sorry, male hormones at work again.

"Get some rest boy and, uhh, chill out on the floating around the room, okay?"

I laughed. "I don't know if I could do it again even if I tried. That one happened by accident." She took her Bible and left the room. I laid down and cracked open my Bible. Where the heck do you start reading a Bible? There are sooo many scriptures. I guess I'll start with Genesis.

I turned the Bible to Genesis and started reading. "In the beginning God created the heavens and the earth . . ." I continued reading and slowly read myself into a long slumber. I awoke with a sudden jerk and a whole hour had passed by.

"Dang, this Bible study thing is gonna be harder than I thought."

That night, I decided that before I left Dallas I needed to take it upon myself to visit old Pastor Francis one more time. My mother was dead and he owed me some type of explanation. How was I supposed to accept the rejection that he threw at me? He was half the reason for the accident that killed my mother.

I wanted to know more about Maggie. She was still my grandmother no matter how he felt about my mother or me. I wanted to get out of the house without Karen knowing I was leaving. I opened the door to my room. Why couldn't I have the gift to make myself invisible? Hmm, maybe I do. I concentrated real hard, looked at myself in the mirror—nope, still there. Dang. That's okay, surely I was sneaky enough to get out the house. I walked out the guest room and proceeded down the hall. It seemed the sneakier I became the more the floor made noise. Courtney peeked out her bedroom door, her eyes looked like she was already asleep.

"What are you doing?" she questioned.

I thought of something quick. "I'm going down to the kitchen. Do you want anything?"

"Uh, no." She closed the door and I proceeded to go downstairs. I didn't know if Karen would go along with the story. The hallway had a horrible draft and I had to remove my sandals because they made too much noise when I walked. I felt my toes curl on the cold floor. Goose bumps covered my skin. I walked alongside the wall and I felt the most horrible sensation. My nose began to tingle and my lungs began to fill with air. I felt as if my nose were going to explode. Can't sneeze—she might hear me.

With all my willpower I attempted to hold the sneeze in. I held my breath and tried to control my breathing. I pinched my nose and tried to be still for a second to avoid the eruption of my sinuses. Finally, I could not stop the inevitable any longer. A small tiny snort shot from my nose. I peeked around the corner and saw Karen on the couch watching television. Good. She hadn't heard me. I just had to get past the kitchen to the front door of the house.

Where the first sneeze came from there were others trying to follow. I had to be quick. I made one step. Karen resituated herself and I jumped back. My heart was racing. I had to be creative or I was going to get caught. Maybe I could just tell her that I was going out. Yeah—I'm a man. I would do that and she would . . . tell me to go back to my room. It was quite obvious she wouldn't let me go out to merely investigate. Maybe there was another way.

I walked back upstairs to my room. Even if I did get out I would have to sneak back in. I didn't want to get caught sneaking back in, then I would really be in trouble. I closed my door. My mind was getting frustrated. I needed an idea. I looked out the window. Hmm, how far a drop was it to get down? I opened the window and looked down. Whoa—it was a healthy drop down if I wanted two broken legs. The wind blew through the open window. The ledge underneath the window was narrow, but it followed along the side of the house and up to the roof. If I was careful I could walk along the side of the house with no problem. I threw my sandals out the window. No need to have any extra things in my hand if I didn't have to. I tested the ledge with one foot to make sure it wouldn't break with my weight (not like I weighed all that much anyway).

I grabbed the two sides of the windowsill and pulled myself slowly onto the edge. The breeze blew and I could feel my shirt flutter up some. It was really dark outside— no, take that back—my eyes were closed. Okay, Andrew, get some balls and open your eyes. I took a breath and scooted sideways toward the roof. I didn't want to make any major movements because I was sure that a thud on the roof would make Karen suspicious also. I scooted another step. Suddenly it dawned on me that I was outside on the edge of the house in danger of falling—was I crazy? Yes, there was no doubt that I had lost my mind. The breeze blew and I closed my eyes, gripping the wall with my fingers. There was nothing to hold on to.

I moved my foot and it slipped on some moisture left over from the past rain. My heart jumped and I held my previous spot. I turned my head and looked to my right. It had to be only three feet to the roof where I would be out of danger of falling. Those three feet looked like a mile. It was okay, I would just take my time. The wind blew and I closed my eyes tight. Okay, on second thought, I just had to move quickly and get to the other side. I attempted to scurry across the ledge, but this time my hand slipped and the attempt to grab the side of the house again caused my feet to lose balance; I had that feeling again . . . of falling. Next thing I knew I was surrounded by a pile of bushes. I had fallen safely. I lay still, trying to see if anything in my body was giving me the signal that it may be broken. I sat up slowly with a few leaves in my mouth. I spit them out and raised my arms and wiggled my toes. No pain. I pulled myself out of the bushes and to my feet—good—no broken ankle. I grabbed my sandals and put them on.

"Andrew, what are you doing outside? I thought you were going to the kitchen." Courtney was looking outside her window. Evidently she had heard the crash. Dang, I hope Karen didn't hear anything.

"I'll be back; I need to investigate something. Don't tell your mom I'm gone. I'll be right back."

"Investigate? Who are you, Sherlock Homeboy now? Where are you going?" I didn't wait to answer her question. I had already run off down the street. It was still early evening and I thought I could get to the church and back in no time. Of course all that seemed logical until I realized how hard it is to go so far a distance on foot. The bus seemed a logical answer. I rummaged in my pocket for some change. I hopped on a nearby bus and asked the driver how close he could get me to the Greater Glory Church. He seemed to know what I was talking about but told me he could only get me within a block of the church.

A block didn't discourage me and I took my seat. I watched the other people on the bus. These bus people looked, for lack of a better word, interesting. I wouldn't say that they were ugly, because all of God's creatures are beautiful, but I would say they were definitely . . . creatures. The guy to my immediate left had a stench about himself that set my nose on fire. His odor resembled that of onions inside an old gym sock. He seemed unaware of his own smell as he rested his arms up on the top part of the seat. Another person across the aisle, an old woman with a greasy curl, commenced to smack on some chicken that she attacked like a tyrannosaur. I was slightly unsure if the grease I smelled was from her hair or the chicken. I felt uneasy on the bus. I tried to look out the window, yet it seemed like someone was watching me.

I closed my eyes and laid my head against the window. I didn't want to sleep for fear that someone would try to mug me, even though I didn't have any more money in my pockets. Besides, I didn't want to miss my stop.

"Andrew . . ." I heard a whisper in my ear. I looked up and all around. The smelly man was looking in another direction and the hungry woman with the curl was still devouring that poor chicken.

"Andrew . . ." Okay, I heard that whisper loud and clear that time and I saw no one's mouth moving. The whispers continued and laughing followed each one. I was getting more uncomfortable because I couldn't pinpoint where it was coming from. The whispers were like a breeze—here and then gone.

"Andrew, you belong to us . . ."

"I belong to no one!" I jumped up. Silence. The woman with the curl stopped chewing and stared at me for my outburst. I smiled and looked around, realizing I had proven myself to be slightly crazier than the rest of the people on the bus. I didn't think anyone would try to touch me now. The bus driver let me off like he said, a block away. I could see the church from where I was standing.

People were talking in the church parking lot. I assumed that a service had just ended and this would be the perfect opportunity to confront the pastor. I ran up the block as fast as I could and ran across the street to the church. I entered the foyer and stopped before the sanctuary doors. I could almost still hear my mother screaming on the other side of those doors from the day of the funeral. I could still feel the hurt and rejection of how this church had cast me out like I was Lucifer himself. I was angry; so why had my eyes started to water? I didn't want to cry. I shook my head and took a breath and walked into the sanctuary. The pastor was still talking to another church member by the front altar.

"Pastah' you sho'll did bless my soul." The church member exhorted the old white-haired reverend. He was way older than the picture hanging in the foyer. He was a short, pudgy old man. His skin was dark and wrinkled and his cheeks were even darker. He wore glasses on the tip of his nose and his hair was receding from his wrinkled forehead. He still had on his gray-and-black clergy robe with two gold crosses on the front. It resembled a choir robe. I walked down the middle aisle and stood by the second row, staring at him.

He looked at me and dismissed the member with a wave of his hand; the member walked away like a servant in a royal court.

"I thought I told you never to come back h—"

"I know what you said, but I'm not leaving until you give me some answers. Maggie was my grandmother, and she's dead. Her daughter, my mother, is dead now. There are some secrets they had and I think you know something and I want to know what it is."

"Your mother was the devil."

"Stop saying that!" I shouted. "You don't know my mother. Why are you saying these things?"

Pastor Francis's whole face frowned up and glared at me like he was a devil himself.

"You need to leave my church, and you need to leave now." He turned and began to walk off. I needed answers and I wasn't going to leave until I got them. So I decided to take this matter into my own hands.

I followed him. "I'm not leaving until I get my answers, Pastor."

Pastor Francis turned around and pointed his old hand at me. "Young man, do I have to call the poli—"

I didn't wait for him to finish. I grabbed the forearm that he pointed at me, and with my other hand I gripped his hand tightly. With everything I could I held on to him and I focused inside of him. The hairs on the back of my neck raised up and I got that chill feeling. The pastor ceased to speak and I looked into his eyes and in a flash I saw everything and then nothing.

I filtered through his thoughts until I saw Maggie. She was young and she looked way more innocent than I had seen her in my dreams. This must be his perception of her. I was looking into Thomas Francis's mind. *Maggie hugged me.*

"Yes, Thomas, I will marry you!" I backed out of her hug and she looked at me. "What's wrong, Tommy?"

"Tommy?" I said. I looked around me and I was no longer inside the church. I was outside at a church picnic of some sort. It was a bright day. Everything had that dreamy hazy look. I had not only looked into this man's soul, I had jumped into his soul—but could I get out? Maggie looked at her ring. She smiled and her eyes glittered like the diamond she had on her finger. My mouth moved and made words without me trying to speak—these were Thomas's words, his memories.

"I'm about to get my minister's license," Thomas said.

"My husband is gonna be the big preacher."

"And you're my first lady." She kissed me, or Thomas. I couldn't tell and I was getting confused. I pulled away remembering that this was my grandmother. She smiled at me with a confused stare.

"Tommy, you're acting really weird today."

"Sorry, Maggie, I'm . . . not feeling well," I said. I closed my eyes and when I opened them I could see nothing again; I heard voices.

"*You never have time anymore!*" was one voice that I could make out. It came loud and clear. The voices echoed like I was in a tunnel. Time itself was moving forward like a strong wind.

"*What are you doing? You can't have this stuff in my house being my wife!*" I saw fading images of the young Tommy Francis throwing candles and tearing pages from books. "*This is how I find answers, Tommy! You're throwing away my family heritage! You don't understand, please stop! You don't love me . . .*"

"*You are my wife and I won't have you opening the door for devilry in my house!*" The images faded away and I felt time passing again. Then, a scream; was it his or hers? I heard Thomas's voice whisper, "*Oh, God, it's all my fault. It's all my fault. We are being punished.*"

"*I'm sorry,*" she said, "*it was the devil, Thomas. It was the devil who did this.*" There were no images to comfort me in the darkness this time. Just the eerie sounds of whispers that I couldn't make out. Under these whispers I could hear crying, and I felt tears hit my hand in the darkness; then I heard a baby crying in the distance. The crying faded away to my left and a dim light began to illuminate the room.

I was standing inside the church. The pastor was standing across from me with a blank look on his face and I was still holding his hand. He looked at me.

"D-Donyel . . ." he said and then passed out on the floor.

I stood over him and panicked. Oh crap, did I kill him? He was old and I had pushed myself into his mind because he had built a wall to keep me out. But I had to force myself inside of him. I had to get what I wanted. In the process had I killed him? I checked his pulse. It was weak. I slapped his face to wake him up.

"Come on, Pastor Francis, wake up." My heart was

thumping and I could almost swear I could hear it. His eyes jumped and his eyes slowly opened.

"Get out of my church, demon." I tried to help him up but he snatched his hand away and stumbled back to the floor. He was defiant, yet scared of me. I ran out the church and onto the street. I didn't stop running until I reached the bus stop down the block where I had arrived. I held my head down.

"*You belong to us . . .*" the whispers told me again. No one was around so I spoke back.

"No. I do not." A shadowy figure moved within my own shadow.

"*You are so much like him, beautiful, and so self-indulgent.*" It startled me to see my shadow move of its own free will but I did not show my fear.

"Leave me alone."

"*You are the first male from him, you are Donyel's first-fruit. You are like him—so powerful and so much potential. You are more a part of him than you are of men. Be one with him, not your mortal life.*" I couldn't tell whether the rusty voice belonged to a man or a woman.

"I am not like Donyel." I ran faster but it didn't seem to get me any farther from the voice.

"*You raped this man's mind and took what you desired. Donyel, your grandfather, is more in you than you know and he will find you.*"

"I resist you, demon, in Jesus' name, I resist you." The whispers immediately stopped. I stopped running. I was so out of breath and near tears. I was scared—more so of what the demon had said than of the demon itself. And I wondered, was I running from it . . . or my fears? My shadow was normal again and the night was still. Was the demon right? Had my selfish use of my gift drawn me closer to Donyel than I had hoped? I had repeated a pattern of evil from Donyel by seeking to do things my own way. Maybe the pastor was right. I was a spawn of the devil. Donyel was evil and a horrible being—and he was my grandfather. Even though my mom claimed that I'm redeemed by the mortal blood of my dad, didn't the fact remain that I still had claim to the same dark genetic tendencies of Donyel just like I laid claim to some of his powers? But maybe I choose to be who I want to be.

I had to watch out, this whole escapade had even opened me up to hear the demon taunt me. I had never heard anything like that before. My mother must have heard thousands of voices like the one I heard, and it drove her crazy.

Headlights beamed in my eyes. I squinted. Must be the bus. I put my hands in my pocket. Crap. I had given all my money to get here. What was I going to do? A horn honked. It wasn't the honk of a bus. I squinted to see past the headlights and it was a car—Courtney's car.

"I drove all over looking for you. I figured this might be one of the places you would come," she said through the window. I jumped in the car.

"Yeah, just take me back home."

"What happened, Andrew? Why did you come here? Did you try to talk to the pastor again?"

"I'll tell you on the way . . . back home." I closed the car door and reclined my seat back and closed my eyes. She sighed. We went back to the house.

chapter 14

Courtney leaned against her bedroom door with her arms crossed.

"I can't believe you did that to that old pastor."

"I didn't mean to. I was trying to find out what happened." I sat on her bed with my head down and hands on my forehead. How was I supposed to know that Pastor Francis would pass out?

"Well, it seems to me that you are getting stronger every day and you don't know how to control this gift you have." I looked up at Courtney. She didn't even blink. I could see her disappointment but I knew she was trying to help.

"I can control what I'm doing."

"Oh really? Well, could you control it when I saw you in your room floating?"

"Well, I didn't know I was doing that. Besides, that's different."

"Exactly, Andrew, there's no telling how many other gifts you have. I saw you floating, you can enter other people's minds and memories." She seemed slightly perturbed. "What if you had killed that man? What would you have done then? What would you have told the police?" I hadn't thought about that. Courtney was acting like my mother.

"You didn't tell your mom, did you?"

"No. She doesn't know." She came over to my side and sat on the bed next to me and looked up at the ceiling.

"Andrew, I can't believe this is happening. This seems so unreal. I want to just wake up and pretend this was some dream."

"I'm sorry. All this is my fault."

She looked at me and paused for a moment. "No, it's not your fault. You're a great guy. It's just taking me some time to put all this together. Whatever the reason, God has a purpose for your life and you're going to do whatever that is."

"What do you think that purpose is?"

"Well, I dunno. Andrew, you have a special gift to see into people and know things. Once you learn to control it, there's no telling how much you can help people."

"Yeah, if I don't kill them first." I was still trying to figure out what had gone wrong when I touched Pastor Francis. Why had he passed out on me? Maybe he was too old.

"Don't beat yourself up, Andrew. This is going to take time. I'm going to do some more studying about Nephilim to see what I can find out. You do like my mom said and study your Bible."

She was right. After confronting that demon at the bus stop I needed to be more prepared. If one came, surely there would be more.

"I have so many questions. I don't even know where in the Bible to start reading."

"Hmm, your best bet may be to start with Genesis." Courtney smiled at me and grabbed her student Bible from her shelf.

"I have other biblical references and I have even done online searches, so I should have more about your history pretty soon. But that doesn't get you off the hook with studying. Here, my student Bible may break it down a little better. Welcome to Remedial Theology Class 101 with your most beautiful instructor, Professor Courtney."

I laughed. Does that mean I was going to get a grade? I think I could actually enjoy having Courtney tutor me in this spirituality stuff. If all my teachers in school looked as good as Courtney, maybe I would actually pay attention.

"Pay attention and quit daydreaming."

"Sorry, um, what are we going to study?"

"I want you to read Genesis. Don't skim, actually read it."

"But . . ."

"But what?"

"It's so long with all those people's names that I can't even pronounce."

"Andrew, suck it up. It's your history. Once you realize that maybe you'll look at it differently."

"Okay, professor, I have a question." I raised my hand like a good little student.

"Yes, you, the funny-looking student in the front row." I looked around. Maybe there was another student in here I hadn't seen. She laughed at my response.

"Well, since we are discussing Genesis, I do have a question. It's about Cain and Abel."

"Yes, what about them?"

"Well, after Cain killed Abel, he was exiled to another town called Nod, where he got married. Where did he find a wife?" I felt that this was a valid question; it had bothered me so much. I figured that it would be a good test for "the professor."

"Well, grasshoppa . . ."—Did she just call me grasshoppa?—". . . you must ask yourself this question. How old was Cain when he killed Abel?"

"I don't know."

"Exactly. The Cain and Abel episode could have happened many years after they were fully grown. Remember, people back then were living for over 900 years. Just imagine how many full-grown children you could have in 100 years."

"Hmm, probably a lot."

"Then within that same 100 years think about how many children those children could have."

"So what you're saying is that by the time Cain had committed the murder of his brother Abel, Adam and Eve had already had several more kids and those kids had some more kids and so on and so forth."

"Yep, they were popping babies left and right to the point that there were probably tons of people by that time. But the Bible focuses primarily on the lineage that led to the Israelites and ultimately Jesus. Which is why it starts with Seth and goes on, but Adam and Eve had many children."

"Wow, that makes a whole lot of sense. You are so smart."

"That's why I'm the professor." Okay, Courtney was cool. But Cain and Abel didn't explain my issues and I wanted to know more about what I was going through. I flipped to Genesis, chapter six. I skimmed, oops—I was supposed to be reading—oh, well, she wouldn't know. I read it to myself:

4 The Nephilim were on the earth in those days—and also afterward—when the sons of God went to the daughters of men and had children by them. They were the heroes of old, men of renown.

Was that the only scripture there was? Dang.

"What are you looking at now?" Courtney stopped reading her reference books for a second to see what I was doing.

"Reading about the Nephilim in the scripture you had told me about, trying to figure out why all this is happening now." She looked down at her books and did some writing. She looked back at me with concern.

"What if," she said, ". . . what if, all this has something to do with the end of the world?"

"The end of the world? Are you saying that I'm going to end up being the reason for the destruction of the entire world?" Okay this was surely messing up my self-esteem.

"No, Andrew. I think that everything that has happened until now has something to do with the Apocalypse; including the reason your angelic grandfather was able to run around crazy." There was something about the way she spoke that made her even more beautiful. It seemed that even though she was talking about the end of the world her face lit up. I must admit, my heart thumped a little faster. This was both scary and intriguing. I had to know more. My young mind was a little sponge. She continued.

"Look at this scripture, Andrew." She flipped her reference Bible to Matthew 24:37:

As it was in the days of Noah, so it will be at the coming of the Son of Man.

I read over the scripture in Courtney's Bible. Wait one second. I flipped back to the scripture I read in my Bible and laid it in Courtney's lap.

"Look at this. This scripture in verse four says 'in those days *and* afterwards,' and then your scripture pretty much says that the days of Noah will be repeated."

"This means that even though the Nephilim were destroyed in the flood, there could be another rise of Nephilim. This could be a sign of the coming of Christ back to Earth."

We were both quiet before I had the courage to say what we were both thinking. "I'm not the only one. Could there be other people out there like me?"

"Or like your mother. Looks like Donyel is trying to spread his seed like the fallen angels in those days," she answered. "From what I've studied, the Nephilim seed was evil and the people from that lineage had no desire to love God or His children. These were the children of the devil, just like the Israelites were the children of God. Other giants like Goliath were said to be a part of that lineage."

"That's why when I saw my mother in a vision, she looked so evil. She was fighting so hard to repress her evil side when she was alive." This thought made me distraught and I felt my faith begin to break. How could I be sure I had not inherited this evil seed? "I have the powers of angels, I'm tall for my age, like a basketball player, how do I know that . . ."

". . . that you're not evil too?" Courtney interrupted. "I think you're overreacting. You're tall but you're not a giant. Andrew, your mother fought as hard as she could. She knew her destiny and she knew yours. Women can't pass a seed. Even though you inherited her powers—you're not like her. There's a reason Donyel hasn't taken you. There's something you probably have to do."

"Like surrender," I said slowly. My mother's warnings came to my mind. "I'm not exempt from evil, Courtney. Even if I was all human I wouldn't be exempt and now I have this angelic side to me that's just as—if not more—sinful to God. What if I find myself like my mother, unable to fight the darkness, and then what?"

Why the fallen angels wanted a powerful bloodline of damned humans was beyond me.

"But what makes you human, what makes you a man, is your ability to make choices. The human will to serve God is your biggest weapon against your fears. Mama is always telling me 'Courtney, these are the last days. You gotta be ready.'" She shook her head and giggled. "It never seemed so real until now. Andrew, I really, truly, believe that God has some big purpose for you. But you have to seriously, with all your heart, trust not your powers or your intellect, but Him alone."

Courtney looked scared by her own comment and I'm sure she was trying to see where she herself fit in the big picture. Suddenly all the biblical prophesies we had ever heard were manifesting to a very real truth.

"The world as we know it is ending and the beginning of a new one is approaching." She shook to snap herself out of daydreaming. "But that's not what we have to worry about. The thing is that if the last days will be like the days of Noah, then there's going to be a lot of Nephilim babies popping up, and that's not good. I'm sure Donyel wants you to be a part of his plan."

"What plan? To spread evil through the human race like HIV?" I shouted. I no longer felt gifted. I felt like an Ebola monkey that some scientist had let loose. "What could the bloodline of a fallen angel do?" Courtney's sympathetic eyes bonded with mine. She sat closer to me and grabbed my hand.

"Do you want to be evil?"

"No," I said.

"Then you don't have to be. The Bible says that the devil comes to kill, steal, and destroy. Unless you have an uncontrollable urge to do those things, I don't believe you're evil. The Bible also tells us that you will know a tree by the fruit it bears. Some trees need fertilizer to bear fruit. Fertilizer is sometimes made of some icky stuff that people would never eat. Even if the tree used the fertilizer to produce the fruit, the fruit remains a product of that tree. God can use crap to make fruit. You are good fruit from a good tree, Andrew." She was so sincere. I wanted to cry but I didn't. She reassured me with common sense.

"Well if I'm not evil, maybe there are others with gifts who aren't a part of Donyel's seed but the seed of men."

"I don't know. If you did find one, how could you be sure? You're more human than angel." Courtney put her hand to her head. "I can't figure out why your mom lasted so long before she lost her mind. I think God allowed your mother to be the way she was because He does have a plan. Don't you find it strange that she ended up being a girl? I'm sure that Donyel didn't plan on that since he would need a male to carry on his seed."

"Maybe Donyel has a son somewhere. Imagine how powerful the child of two Nephilim would be," I guessed. "What if Donyel wanted my mother to have a child with his son? Maybe my mother was trying to prevent that from happening."

"If he had a son then that would make sense for him to want your mother to continue his bloodline. But instead she found your dad, a Christian. Maybe, just maybe, the daughters carry the power, and the angel sons carry the evil nature of Donyel. If that's true, it would make plenty of sense to understand why you love God and why you aren't evil. Think about it—it's like when women change their last name when they get married. So now, I can see how Donyel wants those powers back into his bloodline. But this is just my hypothesis."

"It sounds good, but my mother still kept some of Donyel's evil or she wouldn't have gone crazy. The only logical and spiritual answer is that my dad's bloodline overpowers my mother's to a certain degree. But it will take more than that to keep Donyel out of my life. I ain't even trying to be on Donyel's side." I thought for a second about my father. Did he ever look for me? I couldn't help but wonder where he was at this moment.

"Just be careful, I'm sure Donyel is tricky," Courtney said, flipping through some more books. I felt a headache coming on.

"You act like I'm looking for him."

"No, my guess is, though, since your mother is gone he is looking for you."

"I hope not. She supposedly bound him but she never told me where. I wish I knew so I could make sure."

Courtney was beginning to scare me and I didn't want to think that the scary dark-haired angel with the white face in my dream would just pop up for an old family reunion. My family life was screwed up. I had a missing father, a mother who was Nephilim and is possibly a demonic spirit in hell, and a crazy angel grandfather who wanted to end the world. I hope my dad's side of the family was slightly more together.

"What's wrong?" Courtney looked over and closed her books. I must have frowned up because all this thinking was bringing me down. For the past few days I had nothing but one bad report after another. I was in dire need of a vacation.

"Nothing. Hey, Courtney, I'm really tired. I'm going to bed now. Tell me if you find any more info, okay?"

"Okay, no problem. Goodnight, sleep well." I let myself out the room and closed the door behind me. As I walked down the long hall I reviewed the past few days in my mind. Everything was happening so fast—I had to figure a way to keep myself from going crazy. Whatever worked for Mom has to work for me, too. I walked into my room and closed the door. I went to the window and decided to talk to God.

"God, it's me, Andrew." I hadn't prayed in so long I thought that maybe He didn't recognize my voice. "I'm having some hard times here. So much is coming at me at once and I know you are there for me but I'm just so scared. I don't know what's going to happen or what I'm supposed to do. I need some help, please. Whatever you want me to do, God, please help me. I can't do this by myself." I sighed. The clouds moved fast across the sky. The moon was so bright I could see the shadow of a cat move across the street. I wondered if God had heard me.

I walked over to the bed where my mother had slept and laid down on it. I buried my face in her pillow. I felt so alone. It wasn't long until I was in a deep sleep. I felt like I was floating and a peace overcame me. I had so many dreams in the past few days I was readily waiting to see what this one would bring. I saw my mother's face and then my own. It continued to morph into what seemed like a thousand faces. I felt winds blowing around me.

"Why do my actions concern you, Shariel?" I saw Donyel in a grassy meadow standing over a cliff. With him was another (an angel I think), darker in complexion with long black hair in one braid. They were dressed in old nineteenth-century clothes. Shariel, I think his name was, held Donyel by the shoulder.

"Donyel, it is my concern because you are my brother. Why do you grow jealous of these men? We have a job to do and I must see fit that we finish our assignment together." Donyel pulled away and teased the edge of the cliff. As he peeked over, he laughed that Shariel was upset that he played with his emotions.

"You're so naïve, brother. Look down, below us. These mortal men drink and be merry. They take women and experience such joys that we are forbidden! They enslave other men to do their bidding so that they can be like the Almighty Himself!" Donyel's eyes burned with rage for the Lord. "They sin and they should be punished! But He . . ." Donyel held a

laugh in his closed lips, "He loves them so. And for what reason? They pay Him no mind! He pays us no mind! We are His true sons! He should exalt us above them for our faithfulness! We are made of fire and they are made of clay! But He makes us their babysitters. For what? So they can have time? More time, to become more like Him."

Shariel turned his back on Donyel. He didn't want to entertain these thoughts.

"Donyel, you speak folly. I know what you propose, and such things are forbidden. We have lost legions of brethren who lost their fire of the Almighty to experience the pleasures of sinful man. It is ordained that we help man get from this state, not encourage it. Please, refrain from this."

Donyel hovered over to Shariel and whispered behind him, "My thoughts are my own and not the product of what the Watchers have committed. I am not concerned with the ranks of Lucifer. I shall challenge him as well for dominion."

"The Lord rebuke you, Donyel. He who is not for God is of Satan. He is the firstfruit of the Fallen Ones."

"So be it," *Donyel said, and Shariel bowed his head. I could feel the pain that Shariel was experiencing as he let go of Donyel. Donyel didn't seem to care. He laughed and floated back to the edge. Shariel didn't budge.*

"The very ones I watch will be mine. I will experience things you will never know, Shariel. I will make their slaves mine. I will be their master and I will be their god. I will make them in my image until . . . they all worship me. There's a new revolution upon us, Shariel."

"That, there is." *Shariel lifted his head up and disappeared. Donyel's eyes burned at his brother's departure. His cocky smile disappeared, and like a rebellious child he jumped from the ledge to the plantation below. I saw through his eyes as the ground quickly approached. I saw Donyel surrounded by fire as if he were a shooting star. And I saw the eyes and the horrified faces of the black slaves below as Donyel descended like a devil.*

I awoke in a cold sweat.

∼ chapter 15

We arrived back in Heaven, Texas, the next evening. Courtney stayed behind so that she wouldn't miss her classes, but told me she would come up later. Besides, Karen thought it was better that way since there was little room in the house. Out of concern for me, she didn't feel comfortable having anybody sleep in my mom's room, but I told her it would be okay. At least I was trying to tell myself that. Karen took total charge of all the memorial preparations, and my mother's body had already been cremated. The urn that held her remains was being brought in by the funeral services that Karen had selected. Karen even called Grandma, the grandma I actually knew. I couldn't call her myself. When Karen called her I could hear Grandma screaming over the phone.

The house felt so lonely, so cold without my mother there. Whatever she had become in the spirit world was evil. I had lost her forever. That thought alone put a pain in my heart. She was evil and totally damned, but yet I still loved her. That love wouldn't stop, but her love for me was dark and would pull me into the darkness with her if I gave her the chance. She wasn't the same person I had known. Maybe she had become the person I had known in order to save me. I couldn't figure it all out. She had told me not to seek her out because she knew I had the power to do it. She knew that she would fall to the dark side.

"Yes, ma'am, I have Andrew with me here at the house—he's fine," Karen commented on the phone to Grandma and looked in at me from the hallway. She was walking around with the portable. I sat on the edge of my bed. My "Me-Ma," the name I gave my grandma many years ago, was very elderly. I never knew my grandfather. He died before I was born. Me-Ma was my only next of kin I knew and there would be no way she would be able to take care of me, so I was glad Karen was around for now. Karen looked at me and motioned to the phone to see if I wanted to talk to my grandma. I shook my head because I knew if I talked to Me-Ma I would not be able to hold my composure. I needed more time.

"Mama Gail, Andrew is still tired from the trip but I will make sure that he calls you back, okay?" She looked at me in her peripheral vision, hung up the phone, and stood at my doorway. I was looking down but I knew she was there, just standing and staring at me.

"You okay?"

I looked up. I didn't want to cry, but I was so exhausted from holding it in.

"Yeah, I'm cool."

"We can stay at your grandma's house if that would be more comfortable." Karen came inside my room and picked up a couple of shirts that were on the floor. She loosely folded them and laid them next to me, then sat down on the bed.

"It's cool. I mean, this is my house."

She gave me that silent smile as she often did, revealing that charming, demure gap between her teeth.

"I talked to your school. Since the school year is almost

up you can finish the rest of your classes at home and still graduate."

"No seriously, I'm fine."

"Andrew, you lost your grandmother and then your mother and you were almost killed. I think you need to take your time. Baby, you're stressed, and I think it would be better if you were at home." I knew there was no arguing with Karen. Behind her kind smile was an enforcer of laws.

"It just seems like yesterday we were here together," I said, looking around.

"I know, Andrew."

"Have you ever lost someone so close to you and it hurt so much that you didn't know whether to cry or scream or just sit silent?"

"Yeah, matter of fact I do." Karen held her hands out and leaned forward. "I had just had Courtney, and her father and I were planning on getting married. His name was Dewayne. Dewayne was an all-around nice guy. We had been high school sweethearts and went to the same college and everything. He had become real good friends with your dad and that's how Anthony met your mom. Dewayne was so funny. He had a way of always looking on the brighter side of things. I remember how he would distract me so much when I tried to study, jumping on my bed and singing at the top of his lungs. He said it kept the stress away. When he found out I was pregnant, he was so calm about it. I was sure he would freak but he didn't. He just said we'd get through it together. He held me so close. I don't ever remember seeing him cry until that moment."

Karen bit her lip and her voice cracked a bit. I felt her pain—without even using my gifts. I had to realize that Karen had also lost my mother, her closest friend, and she was dealing with all this as well.

"How did he die?"

"Donyel. He came after us all. Of course, we all didn't survive."

"Courtney's dad was killed by my grandfather?" The guilt hit me in the pit of my stomach. Karen stood up, attempting to shake off the memories that had haunted her for so long.

"I don't know how much your mother told you about how dangerous he is, but you don't want to have to deal with him. It took all of us to get him last time and . . ."

"So you think he's going to come after me?"

"You must always be ready." Karen turned back in my direction.

"Courtney thinks Donyel wants me to be a part of his family. Do you think he would really hurt me?" Karen looked surprised at our discovery.

"He tried to do the same with your mother, and she might have fallen totally if it hadn't been for the help of your dad. He is a very brave man. Donyel doesn't really care about people. If he can't use you anymore, he will destroy you. He is an angel, a fallen angel, and he has no love for people at all."

"You said that my dad helped my mother beat Donyel last time. Do you know where my dad is?"

"I don't know. I haven't seen him since the Donyel episode." She looked at me, knowing how all these missing pieces must be affecting me. She took my hand in one of hers and rubbed my curly hair with the other.

"When he gets word I'm sure he'll find you." Her words sounded good and were timed just right, but I wasn't sure how true they were. I hadn't seen my dad in all these years; what was his reason for not being around? Why would he decide to come around now? From what my mom told me their marriage was hunky-dory. I had a thought. I stood up and walked past Karen into the hall and into my mother's room. I stood there looking for a second. I could still smell her perfume in the room and it seemed as if she should still be lying in bed. Karen followed behind me and stood at the doorway. I think she felt the same, as a quiet reverence came over her. I went to the closet and retrieved a box, and inside of it were two journals. I knew there were more old journals all over the house and all I had to do was read them to get a better idea of my mother's struggles. I looked at the dates on the two I had in my hand and they were both last year's and this year's. I looked at Karen, who had not come any farther than the doorway. She was still looking around the room and I caught her eyes.

"What are those?" she asked.

"My mother's journals, but I'm sure she has some more somewhere else that she wrote when she was a kid." I flipped through the pages, not really reading anything. They were long and written with such finesse. I was impressed at her handwriting.

"Yeah, Andrea was always writing." Karen folded her arms together as if she were cold. "Come, Andrew, let's go to the living room."

I put the journals on the bed. I could come back and read them later, but I was really interested in hearing more about my mom.

The doorbell rang. I looked at Karen to let her know I would answer it and she walked into the kitchen. I cracked open the door and there, chilling on the porch, was my boy Mack. Here was one face I needed to see.

"S'up, Drew, how ya been, man?" With a solemn look he walked in the door and patted me on the shoulder. I took a breath and rubbed the temple of my forehead.

"Mack, man, what are you doing here?"

"The teachers at school told everybody what happened and said you wouldn't be coming back." Dang, it's amazing how news in a small town travels fast, faster than e-mail. Well, at least I didn't have to go over the details of why I've been gone so long.

"Everybody at school is getting together to give you cards and everybody is coming to the funeral."

"Thanks, Mack, I appreciate that. I mean, really I do."

"You my boy, damn, you had me worried about cha. But look at you. You ain't even got a scratch on you after a car accident." He was right. I did have some explaining to do. People would surely wonder how I survived without a scratch on me.

"What can I say? I'm a quick healer. Besides, I almost drowned, you don't need to be scratched up to drown."

"You right," Mackenzie said, as he sat on the arm of the couch. Karen had started cooking; it smelled like pork chops. Was there nothing this woman could not do?

"So, how you holding up?"

"What? About my mom?"

"Yeah."

"I don't know. I really don't know, Mack. I really don't wanna think about it."

He nodded his head. "That's cool. You know I'm here if you need me."

"I know, man." He gave me a dap-hug combination and pounded my back with his other fist twice. I reciprocated.

"Guess what?" I hated *guess what* games . . . did people really expect you to guess?

"What?"

"Ya girl broke up with Leonard."

"Oh, fa' real!" God had finally smiled down on me. But I wasn't in school so what good would it do me now?

"Yeah, they got in a big argument. Maybe you should call her."

"Man, I dunno." I walked around the couch and sat down. "They always break up; they just gonna get back together again."

"Yeah, but if you interfere, that wouldn't happen. I tell you what, I'll see if she's coming to the funeral."

"Mack, please. That is my mother's funeral." He really doesn't think sometimes. "I am not even thinking about that girl. Come on, man, use your head."

"I'm sorry, man. I just thought maybe she could help . . ."

"I . . . don't . . . need Tonya right now. Okay? My life has been flipped upside down."

"I know, man."

"No, you don't know!" I shouted with such force that it seemed to shake the air. I had held in my emotions way too long. I had blown up on Mack. But all the Donyel issues, the powers, the reading people's souls, my mother's demonic conversion—was too much of a heavy load. Karen stopped cooking and turned around. Mack just stood there and his face turned red. I wanted to cry because I was so upset and because I had lost it in front of him. I didn't say anything to him after that; I turned around and didn't even look in his direction because I had tears in my eyes. My male ego was too much; I didn't want to cry in front of my boy.

Karen silently whispered to Mack and gently led him to the door. Chills ran up my spine and my gift took control. *I could feel all Mack's hurt and anguish, which was dumped on what I already had inside. He felt that way not because I had yelled at him, but because I had turned my back on him.* I thought of my dream the previous night. God knows I wasn't trying to hurt him. Crap, I didn't want to share his pain, but my failure to control my emotions resulted in me reading Mack's soul. I clenched my fist, trying hard to make it stop. I closed my eyes and gritted my teeth but the heaviness of his heart was too much for me. It was as if I could feel two hearts beating in my chest.

"What are you waiting for? Get out!" I had to say something. I was about to explode and I could feel everything in me. He stormed out the door. The tension in my chest released and I began to breathe deeply. Karen closed the door and just stood there.

"What was that, Andrew?" A tear dropped. I was careful to not let her see it nor let another one fall. I took a breath.

"Nothing. I'm okay now."

"You have to get control or you won't be okay for long." Her words were strong. She had nothing more to say and went back to the kitchen. My own temper scared me. I did what my mother had done. My gift had controlled me and I had become overwhelmed. First, I was raping someone's mind and now I was losing control. My eyes were wet and my nose began to run. I sniffed. No, I didn't want to cry. I had to be strong. I had no one else but me, really. I am Andrew Turner and I can deal with this.

I got up from the couch, went to the hallway, and stood under the access door to the attic. I reached up and pulled on a rope above my head. The access door opened, revealing a ladder. I unfolded the ladder and climbed up. A musty smell permeated the attic as I waved my hand around in the darkness, looking for the small string at the top of the attic ceiling that would give me more light. My fingers finally grazed across the string and I gently tugged on it. The dim light helped me a little bit and now I could begin searching for what I wanted—my mother's journals.

I rummaged through bits of paper and photos in many

different boxes but found nothing. I could hear the sounds of Karen still cooking below in the kitchen. She hadn't noticed that I had gone up in the attic because I had done it so quickly and quietly. With the noise from the cooking she couldn't hear my footsteps above her. I found another box sealed with duct tape. I grabbed it and stuck it in my lap.

"Yeah, this has got to be it." Using my chewed-up fingernails, I ripped off the duct tape. I searched the box. I needed answers. I needed to know more. Information was becoming my drug. The ripped cardboard flaps revealed nothing more than old photo albums.

"Come on, where did she put it?" I whispered to myself. The light was not nearly bright enough to reveal what lay in the corners of the attic. I couldn't stand up completely, and the hunching over was beginning to hurt my neck. The farther I walked into the corners of the room, the more I had to hunch over. I felt a sheet with my hands and tugged at it. It wouldn't give so I pulled harder. Something very heavy was wrapped in it and when I tugged harder, the object slid across the floor.

"Andrew, what are you doing up there?" Karen must have heard the noise. I stood still, thinking maybe she would ignore what she heard. I didn't respond. I was too interested in what this thing was. I pulled away the sheet and grabbed the object. It was heavy and metallic. I had to slide it across the floor because it was too heavy. Once in the light I saw it was a metal chest. My eyes widened. I just knew that my mother had stashed her most precious belongings in here, but when I tried to open it a padlock stood in my way.

"No key, how am I gonna open this?" I thought about kicking it but then that would make way too much noise.

"Andrew!" I had to go back down there or she would be

snooping up here too. I threw the blanket over the chest and started back downstairs.

"Huh, did you call me?"

"What are you doing up there?" I walked down the ladder, folded it back up, and closed the attic door. I looked at Karen.

"Nothing, I just needed some time to think."

She stared at me before she spoke. "Okay, well be careful. I thought you fell up there. Dinner is almost ready."

Did I feel okay about keeping things from Karen? No. But I didn't feel like totally trusting her yet either. So much was swimming around in my head.

I put on a fake smile. I had to. It was the only thing I could do. There were too many people to count. I thanked people for coming—people who had never at one time even really cared for my mother, people she had never even shared her life with. I did it for her.

I had combed and slicked my curly hair to the side. My suit was black, my shirt was black, and even my silk tie was black. My mother would have appreciated my wearing a tie. I was daydreaming most of the time. I could barely remember how I even got to the funeral service.

Courtney wore a pantsuit and her hair was nicely braided back with little beads. Karen wore a dark dress and veiled hat. We all sat in the front pew of the church. Me-Ma was sitting next to me, patting my leg. She softly hummed "Precious Lord" and swayed back and forth; I hated that song. It was so depressing. At the front of the church was the golden urn that held my mother's ashes and a beautiful picture of her. She was so photogenic. The camera loved her . . . I loved her.

I held back. Courtney looked at me. I tried not to make eye contact with her. I wasn't even paying attention to what the preacher was saying. No one understood, and I couldn't explain to anyone because no one would believe me. I was numb, or at least wanted to be.

I didn't want to feel a thing—but that was not the case. When I was out of control, I became so emotional and my gift became even stronger. I could sense not only my sadness but also everybody else's in the room. I made my face like stone. I don't know why I did that. I don't know why I felt the need to control my emotions; I was a magnet for everyone else's. I closed my eyes to block them out, but it wasn't working. *Sorrow from one man hit me because he had known my mother since she was a child. Guilt slapped me when another woman who gossiped every moment she could about my mother now felt bad. Depression set in my heart when a young church member announced that she admired my mother like her own. Then something different warmed my heart; somebody was sympathizing alongside me. Someone had lost a loved one, too.* I glanced over and Courtney was still watching me.

I sat there—my skin was all prickly and electrified. I kept sensing more and more—too many pictures and people connecting in my mind. Of course, they didn't know it. But I knew it, and I knew them. I had to get out, had to get some air. I left the sanctuary and sat on the steps outside the church. I held my head down and tried to collect *my* thoughts. I tried to differentiate which emotions were actually mine to begin with. I refused to mourn over other people's emotions.

"Andrew, hey, are you all right?" Courtney had followed me outside and she stood on the step above me.

"Courtney, there's just too much energy inside and I can't focus." I felt dizzy and put my head in my lap.

"Are you sure it's the other people?"

"What are you talking about?"

"Andrew . . . you're still holding on. You haven't really cried since your mother died."

"What do you want me to do? You want me to scream and fall out on the coffin? Oops, my mom didn't have a coffin so I guess that's out."

"You know what I mean. I know everything is going so fast and you probably feel you have to stay focused because of Donyel, but that doesn't mean—"

"You're right," I interrupted, "I do have to stay focused. Because the moment I let down my guard something is going to happen. You forget that I almost killed Pastor Francis. My mother was going crazy every time I used my gift. I don't want to be all crying and feeling sorry for myself when my grandfather is out there sending demons after me."

"Sounds like you're already feeling sorry for yourself. You can't help who you are. What are you going to do, Andrew? Are you going to let yourself just swell up like a big balloon until you explode?"

"Who has the gift, you or me? I'm trying to deal with this the best way I know how but I don't know if I can. I know what my family has done doesn't have anything to do with what I will do, but I still carry that inside of me. I look at you and I think that if it weren't for Donyel you would have your . . ." The guilt of her daddy's death overcame me and I bit my lip. "Look, I don't even want to talk about this anymore."

"No, what were you going to say?"

"I said I don't want to talk anymore!"

Courtney bucked her eyes at me. I knew she was getting frustrated. I turned back around and looked out at the street.

"Am I interrupting something?" I looked up and there was Tonya. She had just arrived. I felt sort of relieved to see

her. Even though I had gotten so mad at Mack for mentioning her I was glad to see her. Her hair was pulled back into
a ponytail and she was wearing a black blouse with a brown
skirt and black boots. Man, she was looking good. I felt a
static connection with her and that made me feel good.

"Uh, no, Tonya, Courtney was just about to leave."

Courtney looked at me. I turned away. I could hear her
walking back up the steps and the door of the church closing.

"Did Mack tell you to come?"

"Mackenzie? No, I haven't seen him at all. I came
because the teachers told us what happened. You're my
friend and I was worried about you." She sat down on the
step next to me. I looked at her and smiled.

"Where's Leonard?" I pretended not to know they had
broken up. This was my chance to talk about her and not
think about me.

"Well, actually, I don't know where Leonard is."

"What? Did something happen?" I asked, trying to hide
my sarcasm.

"Well, me and Leonard broke up. Actually, I broke up
with *him* this time. I found some evidence that he may have
been cheating on me and, well, we had this argument and,
well . . ."

"You guys broke up?"

"Exactly, so who was that girl you were talking to?"
Okay, at this point whatever I said would either make me or
break me.

"That's Courtney, my mom's best friend's daughter. They
came here from Dallas. Her mom is going to watch over me
to make sure I'm okay and crap like that."

Tonya looked at me with that teasing look. It took
everything in me not to try to read her thoughts, but I liked
not knowing. For a moment I felt like the normal Andrew I

knew before I was so bored of normal Andrew, but now I appreciated the life I had. Having Tonya there was a break from this nightmare that had begun in my life. Somebody coughed and I looked up.

Mackenzie was standing by the steps. He was expressionless. His hair was all slicked back.

"I thought I would come to pay my respects to your mother." I didn't say anything. I felt guilty that I was talking to Tonya in front of him.

"Hello, Tonya, good to see you again." He walked up the steps and into the church. Tonya looked back at me—I could tell she felt uneasy.

"Wow, he looked upset. I guess your mother's death is pretty much taking its toll on everybody."

"I guess so . . ." I didn't feel like bothering her with the details of the argument between Mack and me, especially since she had been the subject.

"So how have you been?" she asked.

"Cool, I just get tired of everyone trying to tell me to cry."

"Good for you, who says you have to cry? Is death an end or just a transition?"

"Well, I know it's not an end."

"Exactly, people who cry don't have an understanding of the unknown. A lot of people in my family have died, my dad, my grandma. Of course, this was before I was old enough to remember, but my mom taught me things about death. They are a part of the greater universe," Tonya said in her charming southern belle twang. I loved listening to her talk about things other than makeup; it made me like her even more.

"Wow, I didn't realize you were so aware of things. So, what if you found out something that you didn't know before? Would you be scared?"

"No, there's a lot in this world I don't know about, I'm

sure." She was so open-minded and that seemed to help me.

"Do you believe in angels?" I asked her. I had to know if she'd be willing to accept who I was.

"Yes, Andrew, I believe in angels." She grinned at me and gave me a playful pinch. "And I believe that there's an angel watching over you in this hard time."

I thought about what she said and I was hoping she was wrong. These angels were starting to sound like spies or stalkers.

"Hey, I got an idea; let's get out of here," Tonya suggested to me. Her eyes lit up and her power of persuasion was difficult to break.

"But this is Mom's funeral."

"These people don't understand. You must celebrate the dead, not mourn them. Let me take you to a place where we can celebrate." In some weird way this seemed to make sense. Tonya seemed to see the light that she had ignited inside of me and didn't wait for me to answer. Before I knew it, she had grabbed my hand. We ran off into the field behind the church and into the woods. What crazy idea did Tonya have? Whatever it was, she had snatched me into the realm of her world and I was going deeper.

I forgot about the world behind me as Tonya and I walked along the trail in the woods. Tall trees and brush bordered the trail as the sun peeked through the branches. I felt like I could breathe out here and the air seemed fresher. I looked at Tonya and even she seemed different, like she had been let free herself. Her small hand gently took mine and we walked along the narrow trail.

"Your mom was a beautiful woman, Andrew."

"Yeah, she was so . . . oh, God!" I felt like I was falling in despair. I rushed my mind to gain control. "I don't know what I'm going to do!"

Tonya looked at me. "It wasn't my intention to get you upset."

I looked at her. "I'm cool, I'm really glad you are here today." I shook off the feeling and she smiled. Her hand gently tugged me down the path until we saw Lake Papa Pete. It wasn't really a lake at all—more like a small pond. They called it Lake Papa Pete because years ago, Papa Pete, some old guy who was one of the first founders of Heaven, Texas, used to go fishing there all the time. But that wasn't the significant part at all. Papa Pete was about eighty years old and they (I'm still not sure who "they" are) say that Papa Pete would strip butt naked, jump in the lake, and come back out with a fish in his mouth. He would do that whether it was August or the harsh cold of February. Some say that he had learned that from an old Indian but others say that he was just crazy. Anyhow, Papa Pete disappeared and was never seen again. It was believed that one winter he drowned and froze in a block of ice.

That was all I knew about Papa Pete. They used to tell us his ghost would get us if we went skinny-dipping in the lake, but I think that was just made up to scare us from trying. Now here I was so many years later with Tonya, both of us sitting by the shallow part of the lake wading our toes. The sun danced across the ripples like diamonds. I looked into her eyes and they reflected the same image as the lake. She was so beautiful.

"Do you believe in heaven?"

"Of course, silly, we're in it."

"No, I mean real heaven." I looked at her with all sincerity. I was looking for more things to relate to her with.

"If you're asking me do I believe in the afterlife, then yes."

"Tonya, what do you think happens to us, I mean, after we die?"

"If you're wondering where your mother is, I believe she is all around us. She is one with this universe. That's my belief."

"So you don't technically believe in a heaven and a hell?"

"Why should I? Hell is a state of mind. If I find peace within myself, then when I die I will have peace. Come on, you can't actually believe in an actual place called heaven, can you?"

"Well, yeah."

"Andrew, please, just think about how big it would have to be after hundreds and thousands of years of so many people dying."

"So, when people become 'one,' what are we doing— melting into the universe?"

"Well, it's a scientific fact that energy is neither created nor destroyed; it just comes back in another form."

"Sounds like you're talking about reincarnation, Tonya; I thought we went to the same church."

"And after being at the same church, seeing how people are, how these supposed 'Christians' act, you still seriously believe in all that mumbo jumbo?" She smiled at me to lessen the impact of that verbal blow to my heart.

I sat up a little straighter. "My faith isn't in the people, Tonya. It's in God. God is all I have left. My mom told me to stay close to God."

"Then stay close. Where is He? You need to find Him if you're gonna be close. God is everywhere, Andrew. There is not a way you can't be close to Him. And you are created in His image, so you are godlike yourself, more so than any creation. Find God within yourself." Despite my sorrow and questions about Nephilim, something Tonya was feeding my mind sounded both correct and factual, and yet wrong.

"So this is the way you live your life and you're happy?"

Tonya turned away and stepped out of the water. She knelt over and slipped her boots back on.

"Sometimes I don't know what to believe, Andrew, but I don't accept what I've been given. It's all perspective." That was one thing I could relate to. Whether or not we saw eye-to-eye didn't matter so long as we had the same goals. I retrieved my shoes and sat next to her and put my arm around her shoulders. The time had relaxed my grip and Tonya's head fell nicely on my chest. Her hair smelled so good.

"Thanks for being my friend, cuzzin." It was the same nickname but now it sounded different.

"Thanks for being mine." The warmth of her against me seemed to make things so much better. The fireflies started to become visible.

I got back as the sun was going down, because I walked Tonya to her house before I made my way back to the reception. I knew that Karen would be awfully upset that I had disappeared during the funeral service, but I figured the worst she could do was yell at me. Yelling never killed anyone. The church was connected to another building, the dinner hall, where most receptions and activities were held. I could tell it was nearly over since only a few cars remained in the parking lot. I walked up to the door and went inside. Courtney was sitting at the table with Mackenzie. She looked at me as the door opened and walked over to me.

"Where did you go?"

"I went for a walk. I see you've met Mack."

"Yeah, he's pretty cool. You okay?" Courtney asked.

"Why does everyone keep asking me that like I'm fragile or something or I'm about to explode?"

Mackenzie walked up. "Look, Drew, I'm sorry man—about what I said before. I was being real insensitive to what you've been going through."

Man, I didn't want to get emotional with apologies; everything at this point made me want to cry. The only emotion I could express safely was anger.

"It's cool, man, I know I've been shutting people out. Still cool?"

"Still cool." He gave me a hard hug. Courtney grabbed my arm and pulled me to the side.

"Look, I know you're hurting and stuff but this is your mother's funeral. You just can't . . ."

"I can do whatever I want to, Courtney." I stared at her without an inkling of breaking. She twisted her lips, not like she was gonna kiss but like she was aggravated.

"My mom is in the kitchen. She told me when you come in that she needed to talk to you."

Oh, God! Here we go. I wondered how long I could avoid this. Courtney waited and directed her eyes to the kitchen. I guess I should go now. Courtney was like a hound that had been sent out for me.

I walked in reluctantly. All my senses were rising again and I felt like something was literally pulling me into the kitchen. Karen was talking to a gentleman, probably someone paying his respects. She hadn't noticed my entrance through the door.

"I'm going to have to leave real soon, I have no idea where he's gone off to and we need to get them both at the right time," the gentleman said. His back was to me and all I could see was Karen's expression.

"I know but I really want him to meet you . . ." Karen looked up and saw me at the door. The gentleman turned to see what had caught her attention. They both stood like a couple of mannequins, eyes frozen on me.

"Uh, why are ya'll staring at me?" The man walked up to me. He had a goofy grin on his face—I could tell that he was excited to see me and yet saddened by the death of my mother. He took my hand and shook it. Maybe I had met him before and couldn't remember.

"How are you doing. Andrew? You've grown so much."
Must be another one of Mama Gail's cousins.

"Fine, thank you. I'm sorry I haven't been here I-I just
had to get some air." I walked past the man, putting myself
between him and Karen. Karen seemed unconcerned with
my ditching the funeral.

"Andrew." Her eyes were full and trying to communi-
cate to me. There was an irritating air of silence that was
tempting me to start reading some souls if this continued.

"Andrew, this man is your father."

Stop, and back up. Could somebody please make sure I
heard what I thought I heard? Did she say "father"? At this
point, everything and anything that could have happened to
me had now happened—so I thought. I think I must have
been frozen for quite some time. I don't know how long but
probably a long time.

I tried to turn around but I couldn't. He waited for a
second and I guess he felt my uneasiness so he tried to
break the silence.

"I know I have some explaining to do, Andrew."

". . . Yes, a lot," I whispered, not sure if he actually
heard me.

"I'm sorry about your mother." I turned to face him. He
was just like my mother had described him. I could see how
we looked somewhat alike—he was a handsome black man.
He was thin for someone his age; his hair was cut short and
his skin was dark. All his features were strong from his
brow to his jawline. I could tell his age only from some pre-
mature gray that spotted his head here and there.

"You're sorry, huh?"

"Look, I know you're upset that I haven't been around,
but there's a reason for all of that."

I walked past him and out of the room. I didn't want to

deal with this at the moment. My mind was spinning out of control.

"Andrew, please let me explain." He came after me.

"Look, nothing personal, sir, but I just can't deal with this right now." I started to walk out but he grabbed my arm. I had that feeling again. My skin electrified and I saw his soul. I saw . . . my grandmother's funeral, I saw him outside the church watching me. I pulled away from his grip.

"That was you—at the funeral! You were following us?"

"I had heard that your grandmother had died so I figured your mother would be there."

"Did you see the accident?"

"Andrew . . ."

"Did you see the accident?" He stood there. His eyes were frozen but they appeared to be thawing, and so were mine.

"I did. I was the one who pulled you out of the water and called the hospital."

"Why didn't you get her?" I stood in his face and I was slightly taller than him.

"It was too late, the car was already too deep."

"If you hadn't been trying to get me you could've got her!"

"Andrew, you don't understand . . ."

"No, you don't understand, you should've let me die! I don't know what's going on and she was all I had and you just let her die!" I turned away from him and kept walking. Mack and Courtney walked after me while Karen grabbed my dad's arm, stopping him from continuing.

"Wait, Anthony, he's gone through too much already. Just wait before you tell him any more." I stormed out the door and outside. The tears rolled down my face, blinding my path. My head was hurting and I growled under my breath as I turned around, slamming my fist into the door.

"I shouldn't have come; what am I thinking?" I could hear my father's thoughts in my head as clear as if I were still inside. Faces flashed in my mind that I couldn't block out. I covered my eyes.

"Andreeew . . . hahah Andreeew . . ." I heard those whispering voices again. I covered my ears. Tears blinded me, and I hunched over on the ground.

"Andrew . . ." *I heard Donyel whisper. I saw him buried somewhere. I could feel him . . . I could smell him. In this vision, the ground was on fire and the only thing emerging from the stony ground was his face, pale as a corpse. I walked through the fire and stared down at his face.*

"Andrew!" *Donyel's eyes popped open.*

Mack grabbed my shoulder and I screamed.

"Hey, bro . . . it's me, Mack. You wanna get outta here?" I couldn't speak, every time I tried tears filled my mouth. I felt Courtney's head hit my shoulder on the other side. I jerked slightly.

I felt Courtney's love inside and she was hurting to know that I was hurting and I wouldn't open up. She was scared for me. I shook my head, trying to gain control again.

"Come on," she said, "Mack and I will take you back to the house." They led me to her car and I got in the passenger side while Mack jumped in the back. I loosened my tie, which seemed to choke the air from my lungs and made the blood rush to my face. Courtney drove, holding my hand. Tears were making me lose my sanity.

"What happened back there, bro?"

"My dad . . ." That's all I could get out of my mouth. Courtney glanced at me in surprise. I didn't think she even knew that he was coming and why now?

We arrived at my house, and I didn't bother to wait for either Courtney or Mackenzie to get out of the car. I simply stormed through the door and retreated to my spot on the couch. Head bowed—not in prayer but in thought, my eyes stared into nothingness—trying to digest all that was happening to me. Mackenzie came in first and then Courtney slowly stepped in, closing the door behind her.

"Andrew, come on, talk." I didn't respond to her. She was quite aggressive as she knelt in front of me and grabbed my face.

"Look, you were the one talking about you didn't want to lose control because of Donyel. So don't lose it just because your dad is here. Now before—you wanted me to talk and open up to you. Now I'm asking for that favor back—talk to me." She didn't blink or take a breath once in that whole sentence. But she was right. I was being selfish and I needed to get this out.

"Who is Donyel?" Mack stood in the kitchen and both Courtney and I looked back at him. Should I tell him? Besides, he was my best friend and it might be good for him to know.

"Donyel is my mother's father."

"Wow, you are meeting somebody new every day, huh?" Mack had a way of making light of any situation.

"Well, I've only heard of him; I haven't actually met him. And from what I hear I don't think he is the kinda guy I would actually want to meet." Courtney looked at me, warning me with her eyes not to give away too much information.

"I don't get it, what's wrong with him? Is he a real ass?—excuse my French," he said to Courtney.

"Uhh, look, Mackenzie," she interrupted, tugging his arm, "I think it's best that we leave Andrew alone—let him rest. All these questions aren't good and I'm sure he'll fill you in on the details later. Let me take you home."

Mackenzie looked at me and I nodded in agreement with Courtney. Courtney stood up and looked at me.

"I still want you to talk to me, Andrew," she whispered.

"I will." She followed Mackenzie out the door.

"Talk to ya later, bro."

"A'ight, Mack." I got up from the couch to close and lock the door. Then it dawned on me that I was alone in the house. I leaned my head against the door; the silence seemed so loud. I wanted something to interrupt the quiet solitude.

I needed an escape from this reality. I needed some noise. I didn't want to think anymore. Television wasn't working and neither could bumping to the beats on K104 FM. Sleep was a good escape. Nothing that had happened in the past seemed real but it was. This was no sci-fi movie of the week, no comic book, or some fairy tale story; no—it was my life. Things were happening to me that I could not explain. I walked through the house to my bedroom and sat on the floor underneath my window. I watched the stars in the night sky. I pulled my blanket off of my bed beside me. The bed was close enough to the window that I was almost hidden between the wall and the bed. I tucked myself lower and closed my eyes.

I'm not sure when exactly I fell asleep. I'm not sure when my mind went from actual thoughts to dream images, but they just happened. The first few thoughts or dreams blurred away. But then, like focusing a lens, another dream filled my mind. *Tonya—she was dressed in a beautiful white dress. It seemed to be blowing in the wind and her hair flowed with it. She looked like an angel. She was floating over Lake Papa Pete in the forest. I ran through the forest with my chest and feet bare. Sweat is covering my face. All I can hear is the beating of my heart—or is it hers?*

"Andrew." I hear her calling out to me. Her hands stretched out, beckoning me to join her. I stand at the edge of the water. Tonya smiles and motions me to come. She giggles and she sounds like a little girl. I have never seen her so lovely as she is now. Only the winds seem to keep her elevated above the water. I swim out to her. I swim to her feet in the cold water.

Her toes barely touch the water, but I am immersed in it. I try to grab her but she elevates higher, giggling. Is this a game? She does this three times and kneels down. The winds are at her command and they maneuver her body so that her face is but inches from my own.

I want to kiss her so bad. I swim to get closer—closer, but to no avail. Then I feel the winds push her back higher into the sky as she giggles. Does it tickle? Where is she going? I feel a hand on my foot, pulling at me. I panic. The clammy cold hand pulls at me but I manage to keep my head above water, but the second tug pulls me completely in.

I want to scream but nothing but bubbles come out. Must hold my breath! Then I see her, my mother, looking hideous. Her face is even more sunken in. Her hair is thin and waves underneath the water like snakes on her head. Her jaw doesn't appear to be attached as it opens wider than any mouth I've seen. Is she trying to consume me? The darkness in her mouth is darker than the depths below her.

Pushing against her, I feel the pressure to my lungs. Her grip is tight. I want to scream but can't—can't move, can't breathe, then—Boom! The thunder cracked outside and woke me up. I took a breath like I was resurrected from the dead. I looked outside my window. Clouds were forming. I scratched my head.

"Calm down, Andrew, just a dream," I told myself. Tiny raindrops tapped on the window. I pulled myself off the floor and slid off my black silk tie. I unbuttoned my shirt and threw on my old T-shirt that had been laying on the floor by my door. I could hear whispering coming from the kitchen. Did Courtney come back? Naw, I locked the door—didn't I?

I went into the kitchen, where Karen and my dad sat at the table. I didn't feel like talking with him right now. They sat there drinking tea. My presence once again interrupted their conversation.

"Grab a chair Andrew. We all need to talk." Karen stood up and pulled over a chair. I walked into the light of the room and noticed Courtney on the couch silently watching television in the front room. I stood by the table. I didn't feel like talking to him.

"There are some things that need to be explained, Andrew." I did not want to talk. I had the impression that they had prepared all their thoughts and my thoughts were still unorganized. But there was no escape so I gave in and sat down. My dad gave out a sigh and gathered his thoughts to say his piece.

"Son, I've always been watching you even though you haven't known it."

"So you're a stalker."

Dad looked to Karen, then spoke to me. "No, it was best that our family wasn't together for your safety."

"You mean *your* safety. Did you leave Mom and me because we were different? Maybe possibly you were scared that she might go demon on you all of a sudden."

"Your mom and I both knew what would happen to her but we had to take account of the safety of both you and Antonio. That's the reason we separated. Because together Donyel had a better chance of locating you, it was your mother's idea that by separating you two the intensity of your powers would not be enough for him to track."

"Wait, hold up. Who is Antonio?"

"Antonio is your twin brother." My response was solely on my face and yet another bomb was dropped, destroying the last bit of truth that I knew to be my own.

"Does he look . . ."

"Yes, he's your identical brother," my father admitted. "Antonio, however, has a different gift than you. Your mother told me that you were developing a more empathetic gift. Antonio has a more aggressive gift. His strength is remarkable for a young man. He doesn't look like he has muscles but he's incredibly strong. He's even tested my authority a few times and gotten slightly rebellious. He tends to do his own thing."

"So where is he? Why didn't he come?"

"After Andrea's death, I knew that the covering of protection that your mother had created would stop—that Donyel and his demons would try to find you and your brother. After I told Antonio he didn't take the news so well and he left the house."

"So you don't even know where he is?" I was angry that my father did not have the relationship with my brother that I had with my mother. It was my dad's own fault for not being honest with him (something I could relate to).

"Look, Antonio is real bullheaded when he wants to be. He thought that his mother had abandoned him, and when he found out that she was dead and that he had a brother, he stormed out. I haven't seen him since."

"I don't blame him. For the longest time I thought you were crazy and had run off somewhere."

"Crazy?" He chuckled to himself and I saw where I got my smile from. "Where did you get that?"

"Different townspeople. So did you get a chance to tell him about our angelic heritage?"

My dad looked at Karen once more as she sipped some more tea. The vibe in the room wasn't good.

"So you're telling me that . . . Antonio, my brother, has no idea who he is. And you don't know where he is. What if the demons come after him, or worse, Donyel?!" I jumped up from the chair. Courtney came to my side.

"Calm down, kiddo." She patted my chest. Karen kept her composure and looked at my dad, who seemed convicted by my words.

"As far as I know Donyel is still bound," he said calmly.

"Well my visions keep telling me other things." Dad looked at me and I almost saw fear in his eyes as he thought about Donyel escaping.

"Let's stay focused," he said. "Antonio is not spiritually in tune and his gifts are more physical, so he won't know what's coming, but you can. Your empathetic gift lets you see into the soul of people. Your twin brother is a part of you and I think maybe that if you tune in, maybe you can find him."

"Karen, I just realized that I have this gift, and I don't know how to use it all that well yet."

"You have to try, son. Your brother isn't a Christian and that makes him more vulnerable to Donyel's deceptions. I'm worried about Donyel using his telepathic powers to get into your mind." It felt weird to hear my dad's voice call me "son." "Antonio is confused. Donyel wants both of you. If you can help me find him, maybe we can be a family once again. Now that you boys are old enough to know what's going on you'll be safer together than if you were separated."

"You said he is real strong physically, right? I mean, if he's that strong, won't he be all right?"

"We are not fighting flesh and blood, Andrew. We are fighting the spirit realm; technically you are stronger in that area since your gifts are soul related and you have a spiritual connection with God. Depend on God and He will teach you how to use your gift."

I needed God and that was no lie. I wasn't sure where God was taking my life. I was sitting at some crossroad and I knew whatever road I took, there would be no turning back. I couldn't imagine myself being stronger than my brother, especially if he were like Hercules. They stood there waiting for my answer.

Okay, I wished for a new life and God had heard me. I had lost my mother but I had found my dad and gained a brother. Not to mention new friends in Courtney and Karen. I recalled that when my mother was dying the thought of my brother had crossed her mind. She was concerned about Antonio's well-being. Maybe she saw something in her mind. My mother not only loved me but she loved my brother, whom she had to give up to protect us both. I had to find him for her.

"When do we start?" I asked. Everyone gave a simultaneous sigh of relief. Courtney looked at me and gripped my shoulder with a manly pat. Harder than I thought she could actually do.

"Hey, kiddo, I'll help you." My dad stood in front of me with a proud look. We were almost eye-to-eye.

"We leave Heaven in the morning."

W hy are you leaving so soon?" Tonya pouted—she was definitely upset. I paced outside the car as Courtney and Dad packed up the trunk. This was the part where I had to make a sacrifice. No good thing comes out of life without a sacrifice. Tonya stood there waiting for my answer, which she deserved. But yet I hadn't even begun to explain why and how serious my situation was.

"I just have to get back to Dallas."

"Are you gonna come back? I mean, you're not leaving forever are you?"

"Naw, I'll be back."

She shifted her weight to her other hip and looked off past me, flipping her hair in the process. She was upset. I guess we had connected and now I was leaving her high and dry.

"Andrew, we're friends, right?"

"Yeah." What else would I say, no? I felt like she was pressing me like a grape, trying to get the very juice out of me.

"It just seems like you're not opening up to me." Wow, that sounded all too familiar.

I looked at Courtney, who acted like she wasn't paying attention to us but I could tell she was eavesdropping. Courtney slammed some bags in the car. If I didn't know any better I would have thought she was jealous of Tonya's being around me. I went to help Courtney with the bags.

"It's not that, Tonya, it's just that I got some family business to take care of." I wasn't sure but I think Tonya rolled her eyes. Courtney grew impatient.

"Well, if ya gonna hang around you can make yourself useful and help us load the car." Courtney gave her fake smile to Tonya.

"Um, that's okay. Andrew, call me when you get back."

"Okay, Tonya." I smirked at Courtney for her comment. She waited until Tonya was safely away and smirked back at me.

"What is the problem, Andrew?"

"I'm trying to figure out what that comment was about."

"She was just getting on my nerves with all that whining." She bumped my shoulder when she walked past. Hmm, this was obviously jealousy showing its ugly green head. Dad came through the door; Karen followed close behind.

"Who was that young lady that was at the car?"

"That was Tonya, she's just a friend." His look was skeptical and I didn't think he believed me. Of course my body action was speaking louder than words, but I didn't want to lie. I mean, she wasn't my girlfriend.

"I don't like her," Courtney said, throwing in her two cents. "I think she's trying to know too much."

"What cha gonna do, Courtney? Kill her if she finds out too much?" I asked, and she looked at me with a light in her eyes. Maybe I shouldn't have given her that idea.

Dad rested his hands on the hood of the car and talked to me across it.

"Maybe you should listen to Courtney. Tonya may not understand what you are going through and who you are. It may be best to keep your distance."

"And you understand what I'm going through?" I snapped back. I felt my anger rising slowly but I tried to control it. "The only person who understood me was my mom and she's dead. Just because you are back doesn't mean you can start being all Mr. Daddy now. I know how to run my life. I'm almost eighteen years old. When it concerns Donyel then you're involved, but when it concerns my friends then that doesn't involve you." I tried to control my tone. He just stood there and then got in the car.

"Andrew . . ." Karen looked disappointed in me but I was tired of everyone dictating what I was supposed to be doing. I jumped in the backseat with Courtney.

The next hour in the car was the most uncomfortable. I knew I was out of line and I shouldn't have said what I said. My dad drove the car in silence, Karen looked out the window, and Courtney pretended to read a book. Why did I have to be such a butthead? He was the only parent I had left and even though he hadn't been there for the majority of my life, he was here now. Not to mention, it seems he was a good father to Antonio. Antonio had him, I had Mom. Why was I so mad? I was mad for the same reason that Antonio was and in that way we were already connected. We had both been deceived. We both had had our worlds shattered. Wherever he was, I would help him not feel alone in the world. There was no doubt he would listen to me. I laughed to myself. I wondered what it would be like to see him—to see my reflection but inside it, a different soul. It was an eerie thought. Once again I felt that excitement rise up inside. I knew that when I did find Antonio, he would have another puzzle piece to this crazy new existence we shared.

I glanced at Courtney as she looked out the window; she seemed intensely bothered. She looked out the window to avoid looking at me. I knew she wanted to talk and I had not let her. Inside the car there was so much tension that I knew she wouldn't say anything. I stared at her—I wanted her to look at me.

Why is it that people can sense that someone is staring at them, even if they are not looking at them? It's the weirdest sensation, as if someone were tickling you inside your head. Like a magnet your eyes are pulled away from wherever you are looking to meet the person's eyes that are summoning you. That is exactly what she did.

Her eyes were slowly pulled in my direction and there was the connection. I slid my open palm across the seat. She stared at my hand, then looked back at me—she knew what I was offering and what I could do. I wanted to know what was on her mind without her talking out loud. After a deep breath she took my hand. Courtney wanted me to enter her soul, and I wanted to enter it. I felt her grip me slightly tighter but this time her strength was matched. I was mindful not to absorb her very life, but take what she would give me. I became heavy and for a moment, discouraged—not because this was what I was feeling but because she had shared her burden with me. That weight was now inside me and in the darkness of my mind, or her mind, that weight was manifesting.

I was beginning to see what was frustrating her so much. Like a cloud it blocked the light of her soul. But the light still permeated through. Along with the light I could hear her voice.

"Andrew, is that you?" she said inside her mind. I couldn't see her but I could hear the echo of her voice. I could sense how scared she was. She could sense only me.

"Don't be scared, I'm here," I whispered back inside her mind.

"I am trying to understand you, Andrew, I am."

"What's wrong with you? You seem upset at me." I could see the cloud move around some more. "Oh my guwd, can you see what I see?"

"What do you see?"

"Nothing, but please tell me what's on your mind 'cause I can really tell something is bothering you."

"Andrew, I know I haven't known you for long but it seemed that we were becoming good friends and now, well . . ." The clouds were thinning and I saw some light break through.

"Yeah, don't stop."

"It seems that you are pulling away now, that you are blocking me out. I'm just trying to be your friend, Andrew, and I want to help you."

"Are you scared of me?"

"No. At first it shocked me, but no matter how powerful you are I still see that same sweet guy and I know you are too smart to let that change. I know that you are good and that what you are capable of is something special."

"Once again, who is the Empath, you or me? Courtney, I'm so scared. So many things in my life have changed in just a matter of weeks. I never knew how one event could change your life forever."

"Isn't that how all our lives are? You don't have to be part angel for your world to turn upside down. God never wants us to become comfortable in the stage of life that we are in. We have to be like water, always fluid, always ready to move, change form, flow over adversity." I saw more light, almost blinding me as the clouds dispersed.

"Your wisdom is illuminating."

"What?"

"Never mind. Look, I know I've been a real jerk. Dealing with my mother's dea—"

"I can feel your pain, Andrew, and it's so heavy."

"My mother's death. I still can't believe she's dead." Hiding thoughts is all too difficult. No matter what a person does on the outside, they cannot hide if you look in their soul.

Courtney was now connected with my soul and I'm sure she could feel every little bit of what was inside of me. I could see her eyes in the light behind the clouds looking for me. Her eyes more beautiful in her mind than her physical eyes could ever be. I wanted to reveal myself but I pulled back. Her beauty, her eyes, her soul scared me.

"Andrew? Andrew, where are you?" Her voice faded away as I pulled myself out.

I let go of her hand and turned away to the window. Courtney gasped for a breath and opened her eyes. The feeling I was left with was icy. She tugged at my shirt. I glanced over. I could still see her soul through her eyes—so beautiful.

"Stop, please," I whispered to her and removed her hand from my shirt. She looked at me, seemingly hurt. But there wasn't an argument on her part and she turned back to her window. Were the clouds that I had seen hers or mine? All I had to do was open up to her. That's all she wanted, and when it counted the most, I stopped. The car slowed down to stop at a gas station. I needed to get my mind elsewhere, and a good bag of onion and sour cream chips would satisfy my mind for the time being. I jumped out of the car when I had the chance. Karen went inside to the restroom. My dad stayed at the pump to refill the car with gas. Courtney was following me into the gas station convenience store. It was more like a truck stop than a gas station. It had all types of things to buy—movies, T-shirts, shot glasses, postcards—all types of things that a truck driver might buy.

Courtney cut me off on aisle three, where the toilet

paper and motor oil were. I looked at her standing in my way. Evidently she didn't intend on moving.

"What happened back there in the car?" I didn't want to look in her eyes because I could still see that beautiful glow somewhat and I could still feel the warmth that was inside of her. She continued, "Andrew, please, it felt as if we were connecting."

"We did connect. But I didn't want to go further."

"Why not, what are you afraid of, Andrew?" I looked away and started browsing down the aisle at some motor oil. She stood closely behind me as if there were magnets attached to our hips. "What are you afraid of, Andrew?"

"Nothing."

"Is it your mother's death? Are you afraid of being alone?"

"I said nothing!" She was provoking me and I didn't want to be a part of this little game any longer.

She stood still. Her voice became much more quiet and airy. "Andrew, I felt you back there in the car. I felt your pain, all your thoughts, your fears—just as you felt mine. I don't know what your problem is or why you are being so short and rude to me, but all I want you to know is that I am your friend." I wanted to look at her but I couldn't. She paused, waiting for a response but I couldn't say anything.

"When you're ready and you're looking for someone, I'll be there for you." With all that said Courtney walked past me. Something inside me wanted to care but to care meant to feel and to feel meant to deal with any other feelings inside of me. It was better to not feel anything at all, to be void of all emotions. Inside, I had built a dam to keep the watery tides of my mind inside. My eyes burned so much from the tears that wanted release but I still managed to hold them back. Why did I come in the store? Oh that's right, snacks.

I searched for my desired road trip cuisine. Karen entered the store and was looking for a drink. I was only an aisle away and I could overhear Courtney and Karen whispering. Yeah, I know it is wrong to eavesdrop but I couldn't help myself.

"What is wrong with you, Courtney?" Karen asked as she looked through a large selection of carbonated drinks. Courtney had her arms crossed and I could see a look of discontentment on her face. She tried to cover it up with a small grin to her mother.

"I'm fine. Just needed some air so I decided to get out of the car."

"Well if you get sick I can always buy some motion sickness pills." In a motherly way she put her hands on Courtney's forehead. Courtney moved her head out of embarrassment.

"I'm fine, Mother." I could still feel the frustration inside of her. I could feel the clouds that I had seen. Courtney walked out of the store. I left my hiding place and opened the clear frosted fridge door next to Karen to get a drink. Karen selected a drink and stood there in what looked like motherly thought.

"Andrew, do you know what's wrong with Courtney?" A mother's intuition had to be almost as powerful as my gift.

"We had some words and I think she is upset with me." Her eyes opened wide as this knowledge illuminated her thinking.

"What type of words?"

"Oh nothing really harsh. It's just that I haven't been that nice to her."

"I see. Well, you guys try to get along. Whatever we have ahead we don't need you guys divided. This battle we're fighting is very much spiritual and we don't want to allow a door for the unseen forces to enter our minds. Remember, they will try to divide and conquer."

Karen was right, and I needed to get my act straight. I didn't know everything and I didn't want to fight this battle alone. I wouldn't be able to even if I wanted. I had to stop pushing people away and finally let somebody in.

We finally arrived in Dallas. Dad grabbed some of Karen's luggage. Courtney stood on the porch and Karen went inside to help Dad. It was night and the air felt humid and damp. I wiped my forehead, upset that I was sweating at night. All that spring rain was evaporating. I didn't enjoy the humidity of this area and this wasn't even extreme. To me, it made no sense to sweat at night. There was no sun but the air just made you feel like you needed to take a shower.

Dad came out the front door, passing Courtney. "Courtney, tell your mom that Andrew and I are going to my place; we'll be back later tonight."

"Okay." Courtney did as my dad told her and went inside. I stood outside the car, silent. It was already weird to have him in my life, but we hadn't really spoken to each other the entire trip down here and now I knew that we would have to speak eventually. He unlocked the door and I got in the front seat.

"Where are we going?" I asked. I don't think I really asked for the sake of knowing, rather, for the sake of starting a conversation. Karen was right, what she had said to me at the convenience store. So here I was making an effort. He started the car and looked at me through the corner of his eye.

"You're so much like your mother."

"Is that good or bad?"

He backed up the car and drove down the road. My dad was a handsome man and very mild mannered. I could sense he was very gentle and there was nothing he would do to hurt me, which made me feel even worse for the words I had said to him. He continued though as if what had happened didn't faze him.

"We're going to my place. I'm hoping that maybe if you see some of Antonio's things you may be able to get a feel for him."

"I don't know how to use this gift. Ya'll act like I know what I'm doing." This was really frustrating for me. My gift basically controlled me. I knew I had a lot inside of me but the issue was that I wasn't sure how to use it or when it was right to use it. The average teenager doesn't have issues like this.

"Andrew, your gift is spiritual. You have to pray and ask God how you are to use it. Being that you are part Nephilim means that you may see things spiritually that most humans don't."

"I already have."

"Like what?"

I felt stupid telling him about my demonic encounters. But maybe he could help me. He helped my mom before I was born and I'm sure she had more issues than me. I was his son and I had to realize that. Mom told me that his bloodline was the reason I was human. Nevertheless, I was still tortured by this "gift." Somewhere Antonio was feeling the same way.

"Well, I was waiting for the bus last time I was here and I think I saw a demon or some kinda shadowy thing." His eyebrow went up and it was obvious the wheels in his head were turning. I continued, "I'm very aware that Donyel is after me. I've had dreams about him; his white face staring at me and his long black hair wrapping around his shoulders like some kind of liquid."

"Yeah, he looks something like that. It seems your dreams are very descriptive. But I wouldn't worry about Donyel. Your mother and I took care of him a long time ago."

He seemed to be very confident of that fact, but that didn't ease my mind any. I knew that there was more to dreams than just random thought. My brain was filled with them. I knew that within the hazy scenery and ridiculous mixtures of imagery was a message.

"What did you do to Donyel?" I asked my dad but he just shook his head.

"Let's focus. We have to find Antonio."

I sighed. Evidently he didn't like talking about Donyel. "So how long has Antonio been gone?"

"It's been over a week."

"Have you asked the school if they've seen him?"

"He graduated early, last semester."

Wow. I couldn't believe that my brother was that smart. Maybe I could've graduated early, too. It wasn't like I wasn't smart but I guess having girls around like Tonya was a distraction. Most definitely if Tonya wasn't in the picture I could have graduated early because there were times she didn't give me my homework back. Tonya was no good for me; why did I put up with her? Oh yeah, she was drop-dead gorgeous; blast these hormones of mine!

I spied an old picture of my mom on his keychain. She was younger and looked like she didn't have a care in the world.

"What was it like when you met Mom?" I saw him take

a breath and it seemed as if it was a struggle for him to formulate the words. Maybe he didn't want to go down memory lane. After a second or four he pushed words from his mouth.

"Your mom," he said. Not exactly what I expected but it seemed to be progress. I thought that maybe I should cancel the question and Control-Alt-Delete on the whole conversation, but finally he started processing a complete answer.

"Your mom was the most beautiful girl I had seen in college. She came to a Bible study where I was giving the lesson that day. She wasn't exactly the most Christian girl back then but I kept trying. That's when Donyel came into the picture. It's a long story but in a nutshell he fought to get her back and I fought to keep her safe. She fought to keep you and Antonio safe. Donyel never intended on her becoming a Christian. It broke a lot of hold he had on her. But the rules of the Nephilim are slightly different from the rules of mankind. It seems that Donyel and possibly some other higher angels are running around trying to build their Nephilim empire—people with their blood, people made in their image with a desire to serve them. If he can keep their blood pure then the children retain more of their power."

My father had confirmed my fears. I swallowed before I spoke. "Why are they trying to build this empire?"

"For the Armageddon, the end of the age and the final war against God," he said plainly. He was without fear and I thought about his courage. He continued, "At the end of the age, Lucifer, his angels, and his people who rebelled against God will attempt to war against God and His people. We believe this interbreeding has gone on for centuries. Jesus even made references to people being the children of the devil and that their father was the father of lies and they would be liars. Of course not everyone with the angelic blood has supernatural power. The blood has been diluted over the years. It still carries its evil power, however; that's how you get people who are serial killers and the insane. Those who have absolutely no love for God or mankind, who want nothing but to destroy this blood. Haven't you ever wondered why people would kill or slaughter people in the name of God and wonder why God would allow them to do that? I mean, He never tells you that. The blood of their angelic heritage becomes dominant inside them and they hear their god, the gods of this world, the angelic beings trapped down here that would want to be like Yahweh themselves. That blood allows them to be deceived by the voices of those angels so they can't hear God. These people are almost oblivious to His existence."

"So who can be saved if you have this angelic blood swimming through mankind's gene pool like a virus?"

"Well, Andrew, when Lucifer and his angels did this they were merely copying a format that God Himself used. You see, the Israelites are the people of God and the only people that were supposed to be redeemed to God for saving because they are His people. The first Nephilim infection was to taint the Israelite people so that there could be no pure-blooded lineage for Jesus. Because if Jesus was Nephilim and He died on the cross, then all the angels would be redeemed and not the men. So Jesus had to have the pure blood of men in order to redeem men. Of course, the angels failed in their first attempt to make the people all Nephilim and the flood wiped out most of them, but not all of them. Others survived and they were named the Anakim and other names. They were super strong or knew great magic that they learned from the angels and were often a part of other nations and warred against the Israelites to keep them out of the promised land and to destroy them."

"Like the Philistines and Goliath, yeah I read some stuff about that—well, maybe not read but I talked to Courtney about it." He smiled at me, maybe impressed that I had taken to something that was similar to his interests.

"Exactly, Goliath had the blood and as you could see he had no love for God in his heart at all. There are just some people like that. The Israelites were supposed to be the only people who could hear from God who were supposed to receive all the promises of God, including Jesus. But the children of Israel became divided over the years because of exile. The twelve original tribes became only two. The tribes of Benjamin and Judah are the only known Israelites or Israelis that retain the laws and customs. We call them Jews, short for Judah, the tribe that the majority are descendants from. The other ten tribes, referred to in the Bible as the tribe of Ephraim, or the lost tribes, were scattered throughout mankind through exile and slavery, and sooner or later they forgot that they were Israelite in heritage. But just because they forgot doesn't mean that they were not. Matter of fact, the intermixing of the Israeli blood from the lost ten tribes with the Gentile, or people not of Israelite descent, is why the Bible says that many Gentiles will be saved and why they can even hear from God and have a desire to be with God. The sanctified blood and covenant made with the Israelites will now pertain to any person with that blood flowing in them."

"And that can be anybody, because in today's world everybody is mixed with something. I mean, just think about how many Jews exist all over the world."

"Exactly, Andrew, you get it. But the Jews only make up about two tribes. So in the world are people who are descendants of the missing ten tribes. No matter what color you are anybody can be a true descendant of the original Israeli people and able to hear from God and be redeemed to Him through the covenant of Jesus."

I felt my eyes were opening wider and wider; it made so much sense but it was awfully deep. It was a lot to take in at once. I wished that Courtney had been here to hear this.

"That makes me look at the Bible in a whole new light," I confessed. "It's more like a book or the heritage of my people and how they fought to stay close to God rather than just some stories of some people with some good morals."

"That's why you have to study. You have to know the promises He made to the Israelites. You have to develop your God-given Christian gifts and powers before you learn to use the powers He allowed you to obtain from the angelic rebels."

"How did you and Mom discover all this?"

"Your mom was a powerful woman. She discovered a lot on her own. I didn't seriously believe until she came into my life. I was studying theology in school and the rest . . . well, you can say we had a little help from above." I perked up. I recalled how detailed my dreams were becoming. It helped me to think that I wasn't going to be fighting this alone.

"So here I am. Somewhere stuck in the middle, tuned in to Spirit talk radio. How am I supposed to hear from God if I can't even tune out everybody else?" He patted my leg as if to tell me not to worry.

"Both bloods are potent inside of you. You're almost like a double threat. But you are my son, so my blood is going to be dominant with you. You are a human man. Besides, Donyel broke a principle when he raped your grandmother so many years ago. He didn't let her choose to be with him. Choice is a major factor, the God-given power of the soul called human will. That is why I was able to get your mother. God allowed the gift of choice to be amplified with Andrea because choice was stolen from her mother. So she chose to leave Donyel, but his voice and the voice of the demons were so strong inside her head . . . that it was driving her crazy." His voice quivered and his hand was shaking. I could tell that this was something he had witnessed firsthand. I grabbed his hand to stop the shaking and I felt the same chill crawl up my spine.

Here I was peeking into my father's soul. I didn't try to do it, but evidently there was something I needed to see. I looked around and I saw my mother, beautiful and much younger. Her hair was long and wavy. I saw these memories through his eyes. In his hands there was a baby, and by my mother was a crib with another baby in it.

"Anthony, you have to burp Andy after you feed him or he's going to be crying all night." Was this me my dad was holding? This was the weirdest vision I've had yet. I was seeing myself as a child through my father's eyes. I was feeling what he was feeling. I felt how much he loved me and how proud he was.

"Sometimes I think Andrew knows what I'm thinking," he laughed.

My mother stopped smiling and walked over to him. "Why would you say something like that?" Her face was solemn and straight.

"I don't know. I just look at him and he stares me right in my eyes like he can see my soul." She looked down at the baby, me, in my daddy's arm. Worry filled her eyes.

"You don't think that they are like me, do you? I don't want them having to go through all this. Anthony, I want these boys to live normal lives." My dad took one hand and gently touched her face.

"Andrea, they will."

She shook her head and backed away from him.

"No, I have to make sure of it, Anthony, I can still hear him in my head. I can still hear his demons. Every time I go to sleep they come to me, telling me what they want to do with my children. I thought it was just a dream but it isn't. These demons want to take our children away! They want to change our children into something horrible!" My dad grabbed her close and hugged her with one arm while still holding me close to his heart.

"Andrea, I love you. I love Antonio and Andrew. This is not how I thought my life would end up but for some reason God has put me here for a purpose. I will do anything for you." She raised her head and looked up in his eyes. Her face was wet with tears.

"Anything, Anthony?"

"Yes. I love you."

"Then I have to go back to Heaven."

"Okay, we can go back . . ."

"Not we . . . me. I have to leave you here. Yesterday while you were gone a demon manifested and threw me against a wall. I think they can sense the children. As they get older they will only get stronger. I used my powers to destroy it but the more I use them the weaker in my soul I become to fight the darkness. I can't fight them forever."

"So you want to run? Andrea, I can't raise them by myself. These children are powerful. I can literally feel it with Andrew. They need you to explain this to them." He was panicking. He didn't want to lose Andrea. He didn't want to lose Andrea to Donyel. Even after they had conquered him it seemed unfair that he was still losing her.

"You're not losing me."

"Stop using that empathy thing. If I want you to know something I'll tell you."

"You're angry, Anthony, and that's okay. Look, Baby, I love you"—she looked him straight in the eyes—*"and I've always wanted the perfect marriage with the perfect life. But I know for a fact that God has a greater plan for these boys. I can't sit back and be selfish and let these nasty demons get them. I won't leave both of them with you. I figure that with three of us in the house, the triad energy of us all is too much and that's how the demons find us so fast. I'll take Andrew. His power is like mine. I'm not sure about Antonio, it may have skipped him. Antonio would be better raised by you."*

Dad shook his head. "Then what? What do we do? Do we act like none of this happened? Or do we prepare them for what may come?"

"Anthony, if they grow up normal and the demons don't seek them any more than usual then they can be normal. That's all I want. If you see any signs that they are gifted like an angel, then we must be prepared to tell them what happened."

I let go of his hand. I took a breath and my dad continued his thought. "That's why she left Dallas, to isolate herself from a world that was infested with spirits. She tried to run but there isn't anywhere you can run . . . I tried to tell her that." He looked at me; his thoughts were all over the place. "You really can't force a covenant. But Donyel is slightly more rebellious than his brothers. He wants his blood and his powers to stay with his family but it seems that his plan has been thwarted."

"But that means, that even if I do stay a Christian, then even my wife has to be Christian or Donyel could get my children." Dad nodded at me. It was a sad realization, but true. Donyel was our family's curse. He would follow us for generations. I thought about the dream with Donyel and the slaves and it dawned on me—he had been following us for more than a century.

"Donyel is bound for now but I don't know for how long. He is eternal. You and Antonio and your future children must all be protected. This fight has just begun. That is why you must tell your children of Donyel and who he is and where they come from. Write it in a journal, keep it safe."

I remembered Mom's journals and that I had to find them. I thought about the old chest in the attic that I couldn't open. I had to get those journals. This all was very deep and it was a large pill to swallow, but I'm glad I had him to explain it to me and to guide me.

"Hey, Dad?" He looked at me with his eyebrows up. I had caught him off guard when he heard me say "Dad." "Dad, I'm glad you're here. I really am. I just wanted you to know that." He smiled at me. His whole face lit up with that smile.

"I'm glad to have you with me, Andrew." It was then I felt what he was feeling without using any angelic gift at all.

I couldn't believe my eyes. All around me were pictures of Antonio on the walls. Trophies of his accomplishments decorated the mantel of the fireplace in the very spacious but modest apartment.

"You can check out the apartment if you like. There are some sodas in the fridge—I need to pack some more clothes to make our trip back."

"What about your job? Are they gonna let you off?"

"I'm a writer, Andy," he said with pride. "I started writing for a magazine here in town and now I write children's books. I live pretty well off the royalties."

"Really? I've never seen anything written by you. I would think that Mom would have collected your books." He smiled at me.

"I prefer to keep myself anonymous so I use a different name. A lot of writers do that."

"I've been thinking about writing a book one day. When I figure out what I want to write about, do you think you could help me write one?" I think he liked the fact that I wanted to do something he was into.

"I would love to." He patted my shoulder.

"So the ministry thing is in the past?"

"Well, I know there are some things God wants me to do and will get back to it . . . one day. But as it goes right now, for our safety I want to stay as mobile as possible."

"You say that as if you had some demonic attacks against you too." He stared blankly at me.

I changed the subject. "So are you from Dallas?"

"No, I'm actually from Baltimore. Came down here for school and met your mother and the rest is history. Speaking of which . . . I think I will call my parents and see if they are home. There's a couple of people that might want to see how you're doing." He excused himself to his bedroom. I didn't think about having another set of grandparents. Wow, now that would be interesting. I wonder what he told them about me? I bet they thought my mother ran off with me. I couldn't imagine him telling his parents about Donyel.

I was left alone in awe in this shrine to Antonio. It was obvious that he was special to Dad. Looking at the pictures, seeing Antonio was weird. He looked exactly like me and it was sort of eerie seeing the same face—my face in all those pictures. It's like one of those movies where the person gets amnesia and can't remember some life they supposedly lived but they see all the proof; that's how it was with me seeing these pictures of Antonio. Antonio was highly involved in sports and there were pictures of him posing in every uniform known to man. It must have been easy for him. Dad probably didn't realize that his strength was remarkable for his age until the recent years—that's when my powers started developing more.

I went to the kitchen and popped open a soda can. It was grape soda, dang, thought it was lemon-lime at first because it was in a green can. I really didn't like grape soda but it was something to drink and I didn't want to waste it. Besides, I was a guest. A guest in my father's apartment; now that's a weird feeling. I took a sip of the nasty soda. I also examined the pictures more. Antonio had my stunning good looks of course, but there were definitely some differences. Antonio had cut down his curly hair. His head was clean-shaven and smooth. He had pierced ears with metal hoops in each one of them. His eyes were fierce. Because he was athletic, his muscle tone was slightly bigger than my own but his body was still lanky and skinny. It was hard to believe that he could be as strong as Dad said. I walked through the house, past Dad's room and pushed open the next door—just a bathroom.

The last door was open a crack. It had to be Antonio's room. Maybe I could get a vibe for him and find him easier if I was in his room. I pushed the door fully open.

"Who the hell are you?" Antonio was stretched across his bed on his stomach, arms hanging over the side and legs hanging off the opposite side. His eyes were red and his face was pale. I stood there in shock. What was he doing home? We were looking for him and he had found us. But he looked as if he was drunk. Still getting no vibe from him, nothing at all.

"Hi, umm." I extended my hand and introduced myself. "I'm your twin brother, Andrew."

"Twin brother?" He looked up and squinted his eyes to get a better look. I could smell alcohol like his skin was sweating it. It only got stronger as I got closer to extend my hand in fellowship.

"My dad went and cloned me while he was gone." He chuckled quietly and cussed under his breath. "Well, ain't this just been a crazy time for me. I find out that my long-lost mother just died; now I find out that I got me a brother.

What other secrets does my dad have?" I shook my head at his comment. I grabbed his hand to shake it but still I couldn't get any vibe from him. What was the problem? Antonio pulled himself up on his knees on the bed and rubbed his head. Taking a breath, he took another look at me.

"Hmm, I see you like that nasty soda Dad bought; we can't be too much alike." He sat up and placed the can down. He just kept staring, which was beginning to make me uncomfortable. "Yep, we're identical. Ya' need a haircut though." He laughed but I didn't. I didn't like his look and I didn't want it. Antonio had an aggressive aura that made me feel slightly intimidated but I continued to hold my ground. Besides, he was my brother and I wanted this relationship to start off on the right foot.

"So, uhh, Aaron."

"Andrew," I corrected him.

"Whatever. What are you doing in my room?"

"Well your dad—I mean *our* dad was concerned about you since you ran away and he came and found me and figured that I could find you."

Antonio started laughing and fell sideways on the bed into the pillow. I wasn't sure if he intended on doing that because his butt was still in the air and he was lifting his leg to regain his upright position. I attempted to help him to his feet but he jerked his arm back, causing him to fall clumsily onto his back. With a glazy stare and a slurred tongue he looked up at me, trying to talk.

"What are you, a private investigator or something? How were you going to find me?"

"I was going to use my angelic gift. My power is a highly sensitive empathetic awareness."

"Your what? What the h*** are you talking about? Oh, gawd, my twin brother is a weirdo." Antonio rolled over and pulled the covers around him like a burrito, and before I knew it he was asleep. I felt a touch on my shoulder and I went into the hallway with my dad.

"He doesn't know, Dad? You didn't tell him about his angelic bloodline?" Dad pulled me by my arm into the living room and sat me down.

"I told you before that after I told him about his mother he ran off. I wanted to tell him more but I didn't get the chance. I didn't even get to tell him about you. I didn't plan on him being here and I wish you two could've met differently but that's besides the point now."

"So when are you going to explain this to him?"

"We'll wait till he wakes up. He's been drinking it seems," he said with shame. I was amazed that someone underage could get alcohol. But I was very naïve to a lot of things.

"I don't think you and Mom should've kept this secret from both of us. You can't expect us to be who you want us to be if you aren't who we thought you were. We expect our parents to be truthful, and all this time we've been living a lie." I sighed and gathered my thoughts. This was a frustrating situation because we would have to catch my brother up on what had gone down and educate him to who he was. There was no telling if he would take this news lightly. He stormed out before, there was a good chance he would do it again.

"Now that you guys are together our timing is imperative."

"What are you talking about?" I looked at Dad as he looked at me trying to figure the proper words to say.

"Donyel and his demons." His eyes got very serious, and I tried to be as attentive as possible. "The whole reason we separated you two was so that he wouldn't be able to detect where you were at any given moment. As children, to have your mother and both of you in the same house was too intense. Even if no one used their gift at all the demons found us. Your mother prayed to God to shield her powers from their sight. That was when your gifts were not developed. She prayed that you two wouldn't have gifts and be normal, but I guess God had another plan. As you guys grew older your gifts grew stronger. Maybe if we had taught you then you would not have used your gifts, but we were unsure on what to expect. That is why they tortured your mother every time you used your gift." He shook his head and it seemed that he could feel her pain as he talked. Maybe he could. "When you added the intensity of your powers plus her powers, it was like shooting a flare gun in the darkness of night. The demons could then detect the spiritual vibes you were sending out and trace where you were. Every time Andrea used her power in the past, she lost a part of her soul. Every time you used your power, a demon would sense that."

". . . and attack her. Then she would have to use her powers to fight it, which would in turn attract more." I wanted to kick myself. I knew what happened but now I was understanding.

Dad nodded. "The reason I think Antonio hasn't been spiritually hindered is because he's been with me and I don't have powers. Don't feel bad, Andrew. Whatever she did, she did to protect you."

"So what you're saying is, that now me and Antonio are here, Donyel will be able to detect us."

"The mind is the devil's playground." He tapped his forehead. "It's here he will attack first. He has a strong power of telepathy, and if he can sense you, he will attack you. I think it's only when you use your gifts, so just be careful."

Be careful? Good advice but how was I to be careful? Sure I had initiated my gift willingly a couple of times but sometimes it would pop up on its own. How could I be sure that I wouldn't accidentally sneeze and spark a signal for an all-out demonic attack on my brother and me? And how was I to protect myself from someone trying to get into my head?

I walked back to Antonio's room, and he was lying there silently asleep. Even though we didn't feel like brothers I felt a slight responsibility for him. Besides, when it came to this spiritual fight I knew a little more than he did. I sat down on the floor beside the bed and thought about what our relationship would be like. It was surreal to all of a sudden have a brother. All my life I had wanted a brother and here he was, a *twin* brother even. Okay, so he was drunk and slightly belligerent but he was still my blood. I yawned.

Dad walked in the doorway and looked at me. I saw a smile in his eyes. Maybe it was because he saw his two sons together after so long. I sensed how proud he was. Oops, better control that—can't be sensing people too much.

"You can sleep on the couch, if you want." He leaned against the doorway. I felt at ease in Antonio's room and I wasn't sure if I wanted to leave. It seemed that even he was sleeping more peacefully when I was there.

"Is it okay if I stay in here?" I looked up at him. He nodded and went to fetch me a blanket and some pillows that I arranged on the floor next to Antonio's bed.

"Okay, good night, we'll talk on what we should do from here in the morning." With a click of a switch Dad brought the silent darkness into the room, with nothing but the light from the nearby window filling the room with a dim visual. I turned on my side and closed my eyes, listening to the sound of Antonio breathing. At some point I must have fallen asleep.

It seemed as if I was only asleep for about five minutes. My eyes were still closed but I could see the sunlight through my eyelids. There was no way that it was daytime already. I couldn't recall dreaming or anything. I had an aching pain in my neck from being on the floor and that was the only evidence that I had spent some time asleep. I rolled over and cracked open my eyes, squinting and trying to focus. The shades were wide open and the sun lit up the room. Antonio was huddled under the sheets. From my angle he looked like a large quilted mountain. I sat up and stretched, groaning some in the process. My nose was stuffy from the cool draft on the floor. I sneezed and the quilted mountain moved and became a rolling plain. In the cave of the rolling plain two eyes peeked out at me. I smiled and I heard a groan.

"You're still here," Antonio mumbled under his covers.

"Yeah, I'm still here."

"So that wasn't a nightmare?" I wasn't sure if I should've been hurt by that comment or not but I tried to understand.

"Looks like you're stuck with me, bro."

I think he sighed, but it was really hard to tell with that humungous quilt over his head. Only thing I could see were his socks that peeked out at the other end of the bed.

"Antonio!" I jumped up at the authoritative voice. Dad was in the doorway. He sounded like a dad at that moment and his voice alone stuck a minor fear in my heart, but it wasn't me he was directing his comment to.

"Antonio, wake up boy."

"Quit yelling, Dad."

"Oh, I ain't yelling yet. Where have you been? Do you realize how worried I was about you? What if you were dead?"

"Then you would have found out later on just like I had to find out later about my mother."

"Antonio, watch yourself," Dad warned. Made me straighten up a little. "Antonio, you didn't even let me explain . . ."

"What do you want to explain to me, Dad? How you lied to me all these years?"

They argued around me and it was an awkward position for me. I was stuck in between and I felt like I should intervene. Antonio was still under the quilt like a turtle in his shell. I gestured to Dad that I would talk to him.

"I'm not through talking with you, Antonio. I'm gonna go fix you and your brother some breakfast." He walked out of the room. I could tell already that Antonio was not going to be an easy win.

"If it helps you feel any better, I know how you feel."

"It would make me feel better if you close those shades . . ." His head was probably aching from a hangover. I wrapped myself in the blanket that I had used and walked around to the window and pulled the window shades closed.

"Thank you, what's your name again? Alfred?"

"Andrew," I repeated. Was it that hard to remember?

"Sorry. Andrew." He laughed and pulled his quilt down. Maybe his laughter was a positive sign. "And you're my twin. Man, if this doesn't feel like a soap opera."

"Tell me about it." He sat there on the bed staring at me. He must've been just as amazed to see our resemblance as I had been.

"Where you from?"

"Excuse me?"

"You have a really country accent so I figure that you're not from the city."

What was he talking about? I didn't talk country. At least I didn't think I did. Compared with my friends, I spoke properly and I often took pride in the way I spoke. But evidently something had attached itself to my tongue and given me a southern "twang."

"Heaven."

"What?" He looked slightly confused, an understandable response.

"Heaven, Texas—that's the name of the town I'm from."

Antonio snickered but I kept a straight face. "Well ain't that something? Must be small. You the only black boy, huh? Bet you gotta be a good nigga so you don't get lynched. I bet Wal-Mart is like a mall to ya'll, huh!" I didn't quite appreciate him laughing at my town, even though Wal-Mart *was* like the weekend hangout. It was my town, I was the only one who should make fun of it, not some outsider from another city.

"No disrespect, man," Antonio said, releasing one last chuckle, which was really watering down his sincerity. "I see ya face getting all mad so I'm gonna leave you and ya hick town alone, Huckleberry Finn."

"Whatever, LL Fool J—at least I'm not a wannabe playa." Oops, my sarcasm had reared its ugly head and I had no power to stop it.

"Negro, I know you ain't talkin' to me! I will bust yo head, boy. Do you know that?"

I stood my ground. I didn't want him to think I was scared of him but I was—a little. He jumped out of his bed and threw the covers aside. He stood next to his bed shirtless with only his jeans on. He pulled them up from sagging around his boxers. He was as skinny as I was, but way more cut up and toned in muscle structure. With one hand he demonstrated his strength by lifting the entire bed with little more than his two fingers. The bed slammed down when he removed them. I tried not to be astonished. I prayed that he had inherited Dad's human blood to love God also, because he stared at me with all the fierceness he had in his pictures.

"So what, you're real strong doesn't mean you have anything inside that bald head of yours." Dang, there goes that mouth of mine again. I'm really gonna have to learn to shut up.

He walked slowly toward me. My heart was beating a thousand beats a second but my face didn't reflect any fear. I tried to control my breathing. He was almost in my face as he jumped to grab me. I closed my eyes as a reflex and tightened my fists. I heard an electric pop and afterward a scream and a thud on the floor. I opened my eyes and I was still standing. Antonio was on the floor, looking even more upset than before. I wasn't quite sure what happened. He picked himself off the floor in front of me and charged me again like an angry bull. I clenched my fists in front of me but this time I saw what stopped him from grabbing me. Every time he tried to hit me an invisible sphere surrounded me that flamed red when Antonio touched it. With an electric pulse it shot him back to the floor. I didn't know who was more scared—him or me. As I walked it moved with me, pushing things out of my way—clothes, chairs, even the little bits of dust on the floor. I could hear it around me whirling and encircling me like a dome, the bottom part of it underneath the floor.

"What are you?" he asked, now looking more scared than me.

"The same thing you are." I didn't know how to explain this. This was a new gift and I had been caught completely off guard. As I relaxed the sound faded and I knew the covering shield had ceased. Dad came through the door frantically.

"What are you boys doing in here?" The bed was slightly moved to one side and the jolt from the shield had moved a lot of things to one side of the room. It was not a pretty picture, not to mention that Antonio was flat on his butt on the floor. Dad looked surprised. He knew Antonio's strength, but I think he underestimated my capabilities for defending myself—heck, I had underestimated myself too.

"What happened, Andrew?" Dad looked at me, and I wasn't quite sure what to say. It looked as if we had been fighting throughout the whole room and I was the one who won.

"My—my powers . . ." I shrugged my shoulders, still confused to what had actually happened.

"What are you talking about powers?"

"What I told you last night, Antonio, we have angelic powers because we're part angel."

"What the h*** are you talking about?" He jumped to his feet and looked at Dad, who didn't say a word.

"Do you think you are that strong because you lifted weights?" I asked. "Look how thin you are. What position did you play in football?"

"Linebacker," he answered hesitantly.

"Why would they make anybody as skinny as you a linebacker? Your strength is not human, Antonio. If I'm weird then so are you."

"Neither of you are weird. You two are my sons," interjected Dad. I walked forward and Antonio jumped back. Dad laid his hand on Antonio's shoulder. He managed to stay calm throughout the ordeal and his voice was strong and reasonable. Where Antonio would upset me, Dad calmed me down just the same. His presence put me at ease. It was weird to feel this way and he hadn't been in my life that long but it was like there was some sort of instinctive nature within me to just give him respect.

"Antonio, Andrew, both of you come sit down in the living room. It's time that I told Antonio who he is."

~ chapter 21

I'm not sure how much time passed by. Dad clicked into a teacher mode and broke down things that we needed to know. He discussed Donyel, he discussed the family, the blood, the angels; I think we sat there for hours and yet I wasn't sure how Antonio was taking it all in. These things dealt with highly spiritual issues, and Antonio wasn't Christian and had avoided anything spiritual. If he couldn't see it, he didn't worry about it; that was who he was. It would be a challenge for him to adjust his entire way of thinking.

Dad told me that it would take my connection with God to get full control of my powers. Maybe the reason that Antonio's power was physical and not spiritual was that he had no spiritual link with God. Dad sat in a big cushioned armchair that gave him an appearance of a king. Antonio sat on the couch, closest to Dad, with me on the far right. From my vantage point I could observe all of Antonio's reactions.

Antonio shook his head in denial and walked over to the fireplace mantel and laid his head on it.

"You gotta be kidding, right?" His voice laughingly stuttered but I don't think he found anything funny about the situation. He looked up with his back to us.

"I'm an angel? So, if I'm an angel, why don't I have any wings?"

"We're not angels—we're only part angel. About a fourth to be exact, so it's not really that much, we're more human than angel." I was trying to make him feel better about the whole thing but I don't think he was really hearing me at all.

Dad walked over to Antonio and took him by the shoulders. "Antonio, I know this is a lot for you to handle at this time with your mom dying and now you find out about this. But remember this is a special gift, and God has a special calling for you to use these gifts . . ."

"And what if I don't accept?"

"What?"

"I didn't ask to be a freak. I didn't ask to fight some demon or whatever is out there and definitely didn't ask for a brother." Ouch. That hurt. Dad looked back at me to see if I was okay. I gave him the signal that I was fine.

"Look, Antonio. I don't care how you feel right now. This is who you are, this was who your mother was, she loved you, and your brother is about all you have left other than me. So I suggest you stop acting like a toddler and get your act straight. We are a family whether you like it or not and we need to stick together or we won't survive what's about to come."

"What's to come? Grandpa Donyel? Sounds like he is just itching for a family reunion too. I don't get why we're blocking him out. He's the angel, he knows more about who we are than we do." His voice cracked and I could tell he was getting emotional. It wasn't easy talking to a man like my father who didn't try hard to make you feel his words all through you. It was obvious he was a preacher by the way those words pierced your soul.

"Donyel doesn't care about you. He cares about what you can do for him. That's why I tell you that you need to be in Christ, Antonio." Dad was more stern with his words to Antonio than he was with me. I stared at Antonio. I could feel his feelings. *The harder Dad got, the more Antonio felt to do the opposite. Antonio didn't want anybody telling him what to do. I felt that Antonio loved God but he just didn't want to be a Christian because someone told him to. This, to him, wouldn't be sincere.*

"I ain't ready for all that. What does my religion got to do with this? I thought we were talking about family."

"Our family, the Bible, our spirituality, is who we are. It all connects." He picked up the Bible from the coffee table. "When all else fails you, the power in the history, the promises, the people, and the God in this one book will be the only thing that will pull you through." He sat the Bible back down gently like it was a baby. "You must know this or you won't even know yourself, and if you don't know yourself, then you will believe anything anybody tells you." Antonio didn't speak. Something Dad said had finally hit home. I bit my lip and looked back and forth at the two of them. They were still and quiet like two marble statues. Antonio dropped his head back and sighed.

"Dad, please, I'm not ready for all that yet." He moved from the mantel and walked back to his room. Almost verbally drained I could tell that Dad was frustrated. He wanted Antonio to have a spiritual awakening in every sense for the sake of survival, not for the sake of religion. There were forces in the world that we could not see and if we were caught off guard, that could mean our lives. I had seen and heard those demons. It was a scary thought, but I wasn't going to lose my brother. No, I wouldn't let anything happen. My gifts weren't all that powerful but at least I was getting the hang of them and I would stand by his side.

"Get ready to go—we're heading back to Karen's." I nodded, and Dad went to his room. I walked to Antonio's door and knocked softly.

"What?" Not exactly the cordial type of guy but I went inside anyway.

"Okay, Andrew, let's get something clear. When I say 'what' that doesn't mean come in." He was sitting on the edge of the bed. I ignored the comment, this time. Don't worry, I would have plenty of times in the near future to get him back with my wisecracks.

"Me and Mom would get in some pretty heated arguments too. I think it's just hereditary. I don't know if this is gonna help the situation any but before she died . . . yours was the last name she said."

Pure silence. I got up and walked back to the door; I didn't even turn back around to look at him. "Dad wants us to get ready—we're leaving." I closed the door behind me but the emotions were too strong in the house and once again I had that feeling. Still holding the doorknob and kneeling down in the hallway *I saw Antonio again. It was like I hadn't even left the room. I could feel his pain, his confusion. He sat there on the bed rubbing his bald head with his left hand. He was looking down and two tears dropped from his eyes, not even touching his cheek but just dropping to the floor as he blinked. I was trying to feel him more but as he closed his eyes I felt as if I were being pushed out of the room. A wind-like gust was pushing my soul away from his and I knew it had to be because he was blocking me out, maybe not intentionally but like the clouds in Courtney's mind I was confronted with some more weather-like emotions. Mental note: think about taking meteorology in college.*

The gust brought me back to myself and I was thrown to the floor. Antonio was powerful but he didn't even know it—and that was sad. I would let him have his moment.

Maybe Courtney could help him. She helped me. Yeah, she would be a positive friend for him also, but what about my friendship with Courtney? I was a hypocrite. I wanted Antonio to deal with his problems but I was just like him. I was running away from the problems too. I was preaching the sermon but not practicing it. I was talking the talk but not walking the walk. I needed to take a dose of my own medicine. I couldn't expect Antonio to do something I couldn't do. I would open up to Courtney because she wanted to help me.

Dad walked out with his overcoat on and bag in his hand. Seeing me on the floor perplexed him.

"What's wrong?" he asked me. I shook my head and stood up, passing by him on the way to the couch. He went to Antonio's room and whispered for him to come along and that it was time to go. I heard Antonio open the door.

"You ready? We gotta make a trip so pack for a few days."

"A few days? Fo' what?"

"I already told you, Antonio; from now on we are sticking together."

"Now you wanna stick together," he mumbled.

We made it back to Karen's house and waited in the front den. Karen walked up, hugged Dad, and froze with her eyes just stuck on Antonio.

"The other baby, my God," she whispered. Antonio stood behind Dad, sunshades on even though he was inside. I looked over to Antonio, who wasn't even trying to look at Karen when she hugged him. I was witnessing a family reunion of a family I had never known.

"Antonio and Andrew, my two godbabies together again." Godbabies, was there an ironic joke in there somewhere? It seemed as if Antonio really didn't care, and then his attention looked elsewhere. Courtney walked downstairs and made her way down the hall. She was wearing a wrap skirt with a simple earth-tone blouse. Why was everyone looking so nice today? Courtney stopped in the den and looked at Antonio and me. I wish I had a camera to capture the look on her face.

"My God, ya'll look so much alike," she whispered, but it was audible enough for my hearing.

"Except for the fact that I'm better looking," Antonio said as he offered his hand to Courtney. I was slow with the comebacks and wasn't sure how to respond to Antonio, who only gave me a sly grin as he peeked over his shoulder. I wasn't worried about his cheap dollar-store pickup lines. Courtney was far too smart for those and I was sure she would put him in his place.

"Charming too, well, mister . . ."

"Antonio, call me Antonio."

"Antonio, very nice to meet you." If I hadn't known any better I would have sworn Courtney had blushed (which is really hard to tell with black folks, mind you). Maybe she did like his pseudo-suave ways. I didn't care. Really, I didn't care. She wasn't my girlfriend. She could do what she wanted, so what?

"Will you be going to church with us this afternoon, Antonio?" Courtney asked, and I knew that his answer would surely mess things up for him. 'Cause heaven knows that any man that isn't spiritually minded wasn't going to get any play from her.

"Oh yes, I love me some chu'ch!" Time-out—offsides, did Antonio just say he loved church? Wasn't this the same

guy who told Dad he wasn't ready? Dad likewise had a surprised look on his face. This guy was pure game and I
couldn't believe Courtney was falling for it. She looked at
me and I tried to straighten up my face from the obvious
disgust I had for Antonio's dishonesty.

"Come on, gang, let's get in the car. I don't wanna be
late." Karen rushed everyone along while Courtney was
putting on the finishing touches of her lipstick in the hallway mirror. I guess she hadn't been paying attention to my
brother's flirtatious stares. But once again, I really, *seriously*,
didn't care if he liked her or not—honestly.

We all packed in the car. Karen was driving, with my
Dad on the passenger side. The rest of us sat in the backseat—with Courtney in the middle. Antonio kept whispering to Courtney and she kept laughing.

"It's really rude to whisper when other people are in the
car," I said. They both looked at me. It was only polite to
include me in whatever they were talking about. Okay,
maybe they had a lot in common being that they were both
from Dallas and I was from the country. But, like I said, I
really didn't care what they did. Courtney is a grown
woman and she's not my girlfriend.

"I'm sorry, Andrew. Antonio is so funny. He was just
telling me a joke about this pig and farmer and . . ." She
laughed in the middle of the joke. How could I even laugh
if she couldn't even tell it to me right? I hated when people
did that.

"I'm sorry"—still giggling—"okay, well never mind I
couldn't say the joke right. Antonio would have to tell you."

Antonio didn't even look at me. "Yeah, I'll tell him later
on." His eyes all lusting after Courtney. My brother is a pig.
But like I said, if Courtney likes that, I don't care (at all, not
in the least bit).

I felt uneasy being at church again even though Karen's church was way different. She went to a gigantic church in Dallas called the Potter's House. I was a little more than in awe to see such a humungous church. It looked more like a convention center than a church, honestly. But all the friendly faces and fellowship made up for the initial shock and bad past experiences that I had already had. All I could think about were my past few experiences at church. My mom's funeral, the preacher whom I had almost killed, and our embarrassment that led to the accident in the car. I sat through most of the service doodling on a piece of paper pretending I was taking notes. On it I drew little angels flying around with trumpets. I had been on my guard so much with the demonic spirits and any fallen angels I hadn't even thought about any good angels. Did I have a guardian angel? If I did, had my mother ever known of any good angels? Or were we exiled from communicating with such? I looked across the pew, and Courtney was sharing her Bible with Antonio.

I decided to ignore all distractions and focus on what the pastor was talking about. He wasn't the bishop of the church. He was some other dude whom I had never seen, never caught his name. He was a bald-headed man with a crazy smile. His face was animated with every word he said and I think that's what made me stop paying attention to Courtney and Antonio. He hunched over like a vulture picking over its prey every time he went back to his Bible to reference a certain scripture.

". . . all the people say amen!" He replied and in one unified voice the congregation said amen. I wasn't sure what everybody was saying amen about because I hadn't really been listening.

"Nowadays it seems that people have lost focus." The

young preacher's grin left his face and stared directly into
the audience, almost at me; I got slightly uncomfortable.
"There's nothing wrong with wanting to be blessed. There's
nothing wrong with wanting money because God wants to
bless you exceedingly, abundantly, and above all that you
can ask for and imagine."

"Amen!" A woman in the congregation hollered from
behind me, causing me to jump slightly.

"But the problem is," he continued, "that in this century,
most people don't get excited about the Lord unless there is
a dollar sign attached." The crowd mumbled. "Being blessed
from God goes beyond bling-bling and paying your bills.
There are people who have all that and still don't have the
peace of God. There are very rich people who are taking
drugs, drinking, and having sex with any and everybody that
comes their way. They are searching for peace and happiness
in tangible things. We as children of God should be different.

"In the book of Matthew, chapter six, verse thirty-three,
it says to seek ye first the kingdom of God and His righteousness and all these other things shall be added. God
knows you need things but the whole point is not the things
but it's Him. What God wants us to know is that everything
that we could ever need is in Him. That if we seek to do His
will, if we search to find out what His righteousness is then
He will take care of our needs. The Bible tells us that He
will supply our needs according to His riches and His *glory*.
The key word here is *his glory*. If it doesn't bring God glory
then why should He supply the need? In other words, if you
are doing something that doesn't benefit Him or bring the
attention to Him then why should He invest in it? If what
you are doing is for something that only brings glory to
yourself then you should supply the need yourself.

"Understand, people, that the blessing of God goes

beyond money. When a woman goes to her father and she has a man she wants to marry she asks for her father's blessing. Now if you are a father you will understand that when your daughter gets married you will be coughing up the money for the wedding." The congregation giggled a bit at this comment. "And even though Dad is paying for the wedding, it's symbolic of him giving his blessing that he is okay with his daughter marrying this certain man. When a daughter seeks her father's blessing, she is not seeking the money for the wedding. She is seeking her father's approval in her decision. She is seeking her father's support in her plan to be in this relationship. Finally, but not least, she is seeking her father's love and presence in her wedding. These things mean so much more to her than the money. Her dad paying for the wedding automatically comes if he is involved regardless, because what proud daddy would have his daughter looking bad on her special day?

"If an earthly dad thinks like this about his daughter, how much more does God think this over us? So when we come to church and we seek God's blessing, are we just screaming and crying cause we need a bill paid, or a new job? Or are we seeking His presence, His love, and His approval of our lives? Maybe you can't even ask God for His blessing because you know that your life wouldn't find approval in His eyes. You don't think you're a bad person but are you really good? The Bible says that only God is good and in order for us to be good we must be like Him. God made it so we could be like Him by becoming like us. Through His son, Jesus, he made it possible for us to be like Him—good. Without accepting His goodness, you are still a slave to sin and you are open territory for the demonic forces to wreak havoc in your life. Many of you want peace from the demons of this world, Jesus has that peace."

I looked over to Antonio, who seemed to be listening a little more attentively now. Man, I wanted him to give his life to Christ so bad, not just so that he could be in heavenly peace but so that he could get the earthly peace he so deserved. I understood why he was so angry, but he would never be happy until he learned to let that anger go and release it to God. I was so glad that my mom had taught me the basics of spirituality. She had prepared me for what was going to happen. When the Bible speaks of spiritual warfare I had no idea it would get this serious. Antonio got up and went to the bathroom before the altar call. I watched as a few people went to the front of the church for prayer. The emotions were deep in the room. A girl with bright red hair was in tears waiting for the preacher to touch her in prayer. I couldn't see her face but I was drawn to her spirit. By this time the entire congregation was up on their feet.

"I need a praying church right now," said the young pastor. Control, I thought in my mind. I felt that feeling creeping up on me, electrifying my spine and raising the hairs on my arms. I wasn't even touching the woman with the red hair but some inner desire of mine to know what plagued her mind caused a sort of knee-jerk reaction.

Amelia, that was her name. She had moved so many times to escape. Escape what? It was like I had seen a preview to a movie and I thirsted to know more. What was the matter? Why did she cry so much? I saw Amelia in her own mind, just a little girl. Little red pigtails and yellow ribbons adorned her hair. She lived in a small town much like Heaven but quite the opposite. Mr. Garrett was the eighth-grade teacher for the local private school and she often admired how perfect Mr. Garrett kept his clothes and his hair. He was a man in his thirties with wavy blond hair that he pulled back and a darker blond beard. He would smile and you could barely see the pearly whites underneath his mustache. He was the English teacher, reciting the wondrous tales of Odysseus and Beowulf—I recalled that tale often from my own education. I could feel the excitement she felt listening to him teach her. She had come to class early to make sure that he knew that she loved the class more than anything. There was nothing less than an "A" in the class as a grade.

Then one day Gary, her classmate, came to her after school. Gary was a skinny young man, slightly shorter with brown mousy hair and freckles all over his face. He never seemed to smile, and Amelia had always wondered how much more handsome he would be if he tried to smile once in a while.

"Amelia, hey, um, can I ask you a question?" This was quite unusual because generally Gary never really spoke to her—or anybody for that matter.

"Sure, Gary, what's up?" Gary looked in all sorts of directions other than in her eye.

"Well, I'm sorta flunking English and, well, I thought, actually Mr. Garrett thought it would be a good idea if you tutor me." The very thought that Mr. Garrett thought so highly of her delighted her to the utmost.

"Sure, where do you want to study at, your house or maybe my house?"

"Well, actually, Mr. Garrett said that we could use his classroom for one hour after school so I thought that would be best." So it was. One hour after school Amelia tutored Gary. This went on for a week or so and Mr. Garrett even joined them sometimes, bringing the kids snacks and drinks. If Amelia got stuck or was unsure, it was cool because she could always refer to Mr. Garrett, who was busily grading papers or filing past projects. Gary seemed to be very studious and would even stay after Amelia left. She could tell he was serious about his grade.

"Amelia," Mr. Garrett said to her on a rainy Friday, "you have done so well with Gary—far more than I could ever get across to him. I guess hearing something from your peers is so much different than hearing it from a teacher." Amelia smiled and blushed to her own surprise. She felt that even though she was only fourteen she was on some intellectual connection with Mr. Garrett.

"Hey, it's raining—I'll drop you kids off at home." They all jumped in Mr. Garrett's car, which to her looked like a teacher's car. All types of books and folders were in the back and on the car floor. Did this man rob a library or something? They reached Gary's house first. He seemed hesitant to get out of the car.

"You okay, Gary?" Amelia asked, looking back at him in the backseat. Gary had this horrid little stare on his face.

"I'll see you tomorrow, Gary," Mr. Garrett said. Gary put his head down and walked into the rainy weather to his front door, not even looking back.

"I can't figure him out," Amelia said, looking out the car window. Mr. Garrett continued his way slowly down the rainy road.

"Don't worry about him, Amelia. He's one of my special students. That's why I'm glad to have you in my class." He took his right hand and laid it on Amelia's knee.

"I don't know what I'd do if I didn't have my good students in class." His right hand eased up Amelia's thigh. Amelia sat frozen, in shock, not knowing what to say, not knowing what to do. He patted her thigh and moved his hand higher. Amelia couldn't hear what he was saying. She was closing her mind, attempting to wake up. This just couldn't be real. Her heart was racing.

"Please, Mr. Garrett, stop." She grabbed his hand. He

looked at her and pulled over at a playground. No one was around; Amelia wanted to scream but she was too scared.

"What's wrong, Amelia? You do like my class, don't you?" Amelia nodded. He unbuckled his seatbelt and with his right hand he violated her and he took her left hand and made her touch him. The beautiful eyes that Amelia once admired so much in Mr. Garrett were now dark and unfamiliar. I could hear the voices of so many. Were they children? No. They were demons, too many to decipher and they were hoarding and filling this man's mind. Everything went dark. She had closed her eyes, but I could still feel her in my very soul. She had closed her eyes to protect the little girl she had left and cried through these memories, the pain and betrayal of Mr. Garrett destroying her innocence. I felt the anger and the anguish as well as the shame and I wasn't even there.

"Don't tell anybody please," Gary told her one day at school. Amelia had gone to him because she hadn't had anyone else to talk to. Amelia looked at a teary-eyed Gary.

"He's done this to you too?" Gary's tears poured down his face.

"Please, I don't want anybody to know, please, Amelia. Can we pretend like it never happened?" Amelia didn't know what to say, but that's exactly what she did. Fortunately, she moved away, never to see Mr. Garrett or Gary again. But she took the demons with her. Amelia never tried to be the good girl in class again and she became socially recluse to men. Not a night went by that she didn't cry or have a nightmare and she never told anyone. But I knew.

Tears flowed down my face. I had never envisioned anything so clear and exact. Was it because God wanted me to see that certain part of her life?

"Andrew, you okay?" Courtney touched my shoulder.

My head was down and I couldn't shake the heaviness that was in my heart—Amelia's heaviness. I walked past Courtney and into the aisle. I stood behind Amelia and hugged her. She grabbed my arms.

"God knows what happened to you in the eighth grade." I spoke to her in her ear. "It's not your fault, and God wants to take all that pain away if you just give it to Him. God is good, and what that man did to you wasn't good." It was so simple but effective. She literally wailed from my arms to the floor, and the preacher came immediately and prayed for her. I felt a release from my heart like ice melting into steam. The young preacher stood up after praying for her and looked into my eyes, making me uncomfortable once again. His eyes were piercing and I wasn't sure what he saw in me. Maybe he wasn't sure either.

The congregation had assembled outside after the church service. I had returned to the sanctuary to speak with the young pastor.

"Excuse me, Reverend." He was just finishing up a conversation with an elderly lady. He grabbed my hand to shake it and smiled at me with that crazy smile. He looked through my eyes with his piercing eyes, causing me to be slightly apprehensive. I felt as if he was trying to figure me out.

"Hello, young man. How are you?"

"Fine, sir. I just wanted to tell you that I enjoyed the sermon and that I was really interested in what you had to say—especially about the demons and stuff."

He smiled. "Well they are a part of life, aren't they?"

"Yes, sir, I do have a question, if you could help me." His eyes lit up that I had a question. "Well, Pastor, umm, you spoke of demons. But how do we fight the fallen angels?"

"Wow, the fallen angels. Young man, it's not our job to fight the angels."

"What do you mean?"

"Well, God has given us power over the demons but only an angel can fight another angel. When we sing praises to God, we empower the heavenly angels to fight while the fallen angels detest any praises to God."

"Why is that?"

"You have a lot of questions. I'll be honest—I'm not sure. Maybe it's because the angels are made of pure praise. Angel means messenger or message. When God made them, He created them for the sole purpose to send a message."

"So only an angel can fight another angel. Thanks, Pastor." It was slowly making sense. People had certain functions and angels had certain functions. Then, there were people like me who crossed and mixed those functions—but to what extent? The pastor whistled back at me before I could walk down the aisle.

"Hey, son, I can see that God has some serious plans for you. Stay close to Him." I nodded at the pastor and continued to walk outside.

"Andrew." Courtney stood at the steps of the church, waiting on me. The wind lightly blew at her blouse and her hair was tightly bound in an African head wrap.

"I was worried about you. What happened there in church—and you better not give me a cop-out answer." She looked in my eyes and there was no way I could lie to her, nor did I desire to. I just didn't know how to explain how suddenly I had connected with this woman in church and how clear and exact was the vision of her life. I walked down a few steps and shook my head.

"Amelia. That was the name of the girl."

"Do you know her?" I asked.

"No. I'm not even sure how I knew her name. It just came to me when I touched you." Okay, as if things weren't already weird. Evidently, some bond Courtney and I had was still strong. I watched as Amelia walked to the parking lot. She said nothing to me and got in her car.

"Courtney, whatever God's doing with me, He's got total control of it 'cause I don't know what happened in there. All I know is that a lot of people need help in this world and there are a lot of demons out there." I could still feel the remnant of some of the pain Amelia had in her heart. I looked up in the sky and swallowed, trying hard to not let the feeling overwhelm me. Maybe Courtney felt it too.

"Dang, church boy, took you long enough, it's time to go!" Antonio said. I just wished God could fill me in on what His purpose was for my brother.

A brother? Yo, this is straight, wild man!" Mackenzie welcomed my brother to town. It was nice to have my dad and my brother in the house. Antonio nonchalantly shook Mack's hand, not really giving him any regard. As cool as Mack could be, possibly he was still too country for Antonio.

"Well, it's nice meeting you, Antonio. We're gonna have to kick it some time. Me and Drew will show you around town."

"Yeah, look forward to it." Of course I wasn't quite sure how honest those words were. Antonio looked around the house as if he really didn't want to touch anything.

"Do you want something to drink?" I attempted to be cordial. Family or not, this was his first time in my house and it was the proper thing to do. Antonio really paid me no mind and continued to explore the rest of the house (as if it were really all that big in the first place).

"I'll take a drink!"

I looked at Mack and smiled because he knew that there was some tension in the air, and here he was trying to lighten up the situation. I grabbed Mackenzie a soda as he whispered quietly, "Ya' brother is not really the social type, huh?"

I laughed under my breath and elbowed Mack in the stomach. He snickered and opened the fridge. He snatched some cold pizza and commenced to eating like one of those wild beasts on the Discovery Channel. It was old, but I let him eat it anyway.

Dad had retreated to Mom's room. The door was cracked open slightly. I peeked in, and there he was sitting on the edge of her bed.

"Oh, hey, Andy, come on in." He sniffed and put an old picture of her to the side. Was he crying? He had managed to stay strong, but inside he was a sensitive man. More sensitive than most men, I could tell.

"I guess I haven't been thinking about how this may have been affecting you," I said.

He looked up and smiled—a smile for me if anything. I admired how he tried to be strong, to be the image of fatherhood that I had desired but had never known. I admired him even more now to see his human side. His sensitivity was what he had passed on to me. The whole reason I was empathetic was because of him, the angel blood just intensified it a bit. As a child I remember being far too sensitive for my own good. The mere glare from adults could bring me to tears. I could feel their disapproval hammering my soul through their eyes. Their words whipped my heart and in no time tears would flow. I used to hate the fact that I couldn't stop crying or even hide how I felt from people. Now, as an adult, that sensitivity was intensified that people wouldn't be able to hide what they felt from me.

"Oh, Andy, com'ere son." He held his arms out and I sat beside him. He squeezed my shoulders in a side hug and I patted his chest.

"I love you, I want you to know that." Those words

jerked at my heart. I didn't know how to respond. He kissed my forehead, and I could feel in his heart how much he missed her, how he had wished things were different.

"Uhh, I hate to interrupt this sentimental moment but somebody is knocking at the door." Antonio stood in the doorway. I hadn't heard the door—must have zoned out for a second. As I walked away I took a look back at Dad. Antonio went back to the living room. I think to see Dad at such a weak state was scary for him. Antonio was always and continually trying to display his strength in some form.

Through the screen door I could see Tonya smiling. No Courtney to cause conflict, and I could figure out things for myself for a change. I joined her on the porch.

"Hey, Tonya." She smiled at me, and I couldn't help but notice how the sun shimmered down on her brown hair. She had that nice lip gloss that I love so much. Her hair was all pulled in a ponytail, but that only made me notice how lovely her face was.

"So, how was your trip?" She extended her left leg on the lower step, causing her to have to look up to me even more than she usually did. I sat down on the step and she joined me, sitting as ladylike as possible with the short skirt that she had on. Now we were at eye level but I somehow managed to avoid looking her in the eyes. I shied away from her eyes and stared out into the street to avoid letting her see that she could make me melt by the way she tilted her head when she talked.

"It was pretty interesting. I'm still trying to put some things together but I haven't forgotten about you."

"Andrew, don't worry about me, I'm here for you." She grinned. I glanced at her only briefly and I hoped that she didn't see my eyes dancing. Tonya was another crazy variable in this whole thing. Maybe I was totally misinterpreting her kindness for true romance. I was a hopeless romantic and I wanted so much to believe that she liked me more than as just a friend. I was searching my brain for the right thing to say, the cool statement that would seem just right. Anything—you know, like in the movies, when the guy says that one romantic line that gets the girl to kiss him.

"Well, well, looks like you two are starting to get along quite well." Mackenzie giggled through the opposite side of the screen door, still chewing some food. I tried to give him the eye (the "eye" was the universal signal to not interfere). He came outside and sat next to Tonya—evidently he didn't understand the signal.

She smiled at Mack. "Hey, Mack, how have you been?" A cordial statement nonetheless.

"Cool, Tonya, just trying to make sure my boy is a'ight, ya' know. Have you met his brother?" I could have strangled Mackenzie right then and there for mentioning Antonio.

"What brother?" She looked at me, confused. If this was a theatrical play, the director would be expecting me to have a line right about here, but once again I was lost for words. Honestly, I wasn't ready for Tonya to meet Antonio; *I* wasn't ready to meet Antonio. I just needed a way to buy some time.

"Well, he's in the house if you wanna meet him," Mackenzie said. Mental note—*kick Mack's butt.* I had to fake a smile when she looked at me. I must have appeared like a deer stuck in some headlights because Mackenzie looked at me and raised his eyebrows.

"Well, what are we waiting for then? Let's introduce everybody." I took her by the hand and helped her to her feet. When she was in the door, I socked Mackenzie in the arm real fast with my fist.

"What! What'd I do?" He grabbed his shoulder and

popped me back. It was amazing how she didn't see any of this. Antonio was in the kitchen looking for some food as Tonya came in. His eyes jumped immediately to Tonya but he still looked as if he was hungry. I groaned under my breath.

"Well, hello, and who are you?" He wiped off his hand and extended it. I was feeling like I was having a déjà vu moment.

"Antonio—Tonya . . . Tonya, meet Antonio, my brother." My voice was dry and lifeless. I was hoping that Antonio would take a hint but evidently my disapproval was not his concern.

"Are you two twins? Andrew, you have a twin?"

I cracked a smile, and Antonio slithered closer to his prey. "Yeah, we're twins; just as much a surprise to me as it is for Andrew. So we all decided to move here for the meantime and be here for each other since Mom died." He put his arm around my shoulder and I could feel how unnaturally strong he was as he lightly squeezed. He was blowing hot air once again, and I was hoping she would catch on.

"So you're going to be here a while? What about school for you?"

"Oh, I already graduated. I'm a child prodigy." He smirked. "So until Andrew graduates, we'll be here. But I'm from Dallas. Have you been to Dallas . . . I'm sorry, what is your name again?"

"Tonya." She smiled and I looked back at her. Why was she smiling so hard? When it came to females, Antonio was not afraid. I hated that I couldn't be the same. He was that guy in the movie that always said the right thing at the right time.

"Well, Tonya, maybe you could show me around town sometime." There you go, another perfect line and the perfect timing. Dad walked in and looked at the scene now playing out. Maybe he sensed trouble. He already told me that he wasn't sure about Tonya. But Tonya wasn't the problem; Antonio was. Antonio hadn't noticed, but when he saw me look across the room he turned his head past Tonya.

"Umm, sure, I guess so. Well, I gotta get my mom's car back to her. Andrew, I will talk to you later. Antonio, it was nice meeting you." Mack opened the door for her and she walked out. Mack had that look on his face and in his eyes like he wanted to talk to me outside too. How was it that I could understand his nonverbal signals and he couldn't do the same?

"Dad, I'll be back later."

He nodded at me. "Call me on my cell if you need me." I walked out on the porch. Tonya was just getting in her car. Mack nudged me.

"Say something to her, man."

"Hey, Tonya, I'll call ya, okay?" She closed her car door and smiled and waved at me. Antonio was messing up everything I had been working for, and I was starting to regret I knew him. It was almost like he was doing it on purpose just to spite me.

"How you gonna let ya brother ease up on Tonya like that?" I looked at Mack.

"How you just gonna volunteer to introduce them when me and Tonya are just about to hit it off?"

"Oh, so you mad at me again?"

"Naw." I took a breath. "Just mad at myself, I guess; trying to get used to this brother situation."

"So are you gonna explain how all this happened? I mean, dang, you have been really keeping me in the dark."

I knew that. Mack was always around but he knew the least about what was going on. But the problem was not whether I could trust Mack because I knew I could trust him. It was just that I wasn't sure if I wanted to involve him in this. Being part angel was who I was and it wasn't going to go away like a cold. At some point he would find out. I just didn't want him to get hurt. I wanted to protect him from anything unseen. I wished he had been far more spiritual minded as that would make explaining things to him so much better. But Mack wasn't like me or Courtney. "What you see is what you get" was his philosophy.

"Dude, I promise to explain everything to you later."

"Later? How much later do I have to wait, man? Come on, why did your mom not tell you that you had a brother—and a twin at that?"

"It's too soon right now to talk about this but like I said, I promise that I will run down everything with you. All this is very confusing and when I figure some things out I will fill you in."

"Every time you leave to figure something out, you come back with a new family member." I laughed. "Andrew, I've known you too long. I'm ya boy. If there is something you can't figure out then talk to me, man."

I did seriously need a friend and Mack had been on my side from the very beginning. He was more my family than anybody else right now and I felt like I was betraying him to keep a part of myself from him.

"Let's get away from here. I'll tell you everything but not here." We jumped in the car.

"Where to?" Mack asked, turning the key in the ignition.

"I don't care, go to the lake." Lake Papa Pete was the perfect place for me to think and get away from it all.

When we arrived at the lake there were a few people already picnicking and fishing. The breeze felt good by the lake, and I remembered how I used to come out every day after school to do my homework. The lake just seemed to stimulate my thoughts and ease my soul. When everything else was rocky I found peace at the lake. Mack sat on the hood of the car looking out to the water and I joined him.

"Beautiful, ain't it?" Mack said.

I took a breath, inhaling the breeze and exhaling it slowly—releasing some of the stress that life had dumped on me these past few days.

"Yeah, it's real nice out here. Man, you remember when we were little and we used to play pirate ship out here?"

"Yeah, except we didn't have a ship. We would bury all your toys out in this field."

"A couple of my toy cars are still buried out here somewhere. We need to get a metal detector and see if we can find them."

Enough stalling, I needed to tell him what had happened these past few days. "Mack, I really don't know how to explain what's been going on."

"Well, you can start with where this twin brother came into the picture."

"Well, you know about as much as I know about that. Antonio has been living with my dad while I was living with my mom."

"So, why didn't they tell you that you had a brother?"

I had never really seen him this serious. His eyes were concerned and he had asked the question that weighed on my mind when I had found out. "They were trying to protect us."

"From what?"

"My grandfather Donyel."

"Your grandfather? What's he got to do with this, and

why would they protect you from him? Is he a kingpin or something?"

"Something like that." Times like this I wondered if it was better to give the info slow or just rip the Band-Aid off real fast.

I decided real fast. "My grandfather is an angel." I don't think it hit him right because he still looked at me like he hadn't heard me. "Mackenzie, I said that my grandfather is an angel."

"Andrew, will you stop playing around and tell me what's been going on."

"I just told you. Donyel is an angel, a fallen angel. He raped my grandmother and my mother was born as a Nephilim and when she . . ."

"Nefer what? Boy, what's wrong with you?" He touched my forehead to see if I had a fever.

"Will you stop it?!" I pulled his hand off my forehead. "I'm serious. I'm part angel and I have special gifts. So does Antonio."

"An angel . . ." He laughed, "Then where are your wings?"

Okay, I had no idea how to answer this question. Every image of angels people had ever seen involved wings, and I had never seen an angel so I couldn't ask why this was such a stereotype.

"Look, Mack, that's not the issue. The issue is that Donyel has been looking for us because Antonio and I can continue his bloodline, so he needs us to be on his side. But as long as I am a Christian I pose a threat to Donyel."

"So, Donyel is a demon?"

"No, demons are different. He's an angel—just a bad angel."

"And you are a good angel."

"No, I'm human. I just have some angel blood."

". . . which gives you powers."

"Right!"

"So what are your powers? Can you fly or something?"

"Well, umm, no. I can sorta read people's minds. Well, not really read their mind but read their heart."

"Okay, read mine."

"It's not that easy; it comes and goes. It kinda does it on its own or when I'm excited."

"Boy, quit lying to me!" He jumped off the hood of the car and got back in the car.

"I am so serious, Mack. Why would I lie to you? That's why my parents kept all these secrets, that's why they kept me and Antonio apart, and that's why I want you to know because you're my only friend, and I'm not even sure what's going on but I need you to believe me right now." The words rushed out of my mouth like verbal laxative relieving me of this emotional constipation. I sighed. I stood outside the car as he sat with the car door open. He looked up at me, and I was hoping he would see my sincerity.

"Man, I need a cigarette." Mack patted his pockets. I stood there wishing that I could get my gift working so I could show him something but nothing seemed to be happening. I thought that maybe the problem was that I was tired.

"Please believe me."

"Get in the car. I don't know what to believe. But what I do know is that you're having some major family issues and you're like family to me so—whatever you're going through . . . I'm gonna be here until you figure it out."

"Thanks." I smiled. That's all I could expect from Mackenzie. He was a natural skeptic and I didn't expect him to believe me at first. He always thought I was slightly weird and maybe he just wrote me off as having another weird moment. Whatever was going on in his head, I was appreciative that he had my back.

"Andrew, quit standing there smiling and get yo ass in the car!" (We'll work on his spirituality at a later date.)

~ chapter 23

It would seem that during the next month things had gotten back to normal; whatever that was exactly I wasn't sure. Most kids in my generation were dealing with the fact they were mixed. I was mixed, but being part white wasn't my issue—being part angel was. Graduation was only a month away and I needed to focus. I wanted to be as normal as possible. I resumed my job at the store and attempted to go to school, despite my father's recommendation that I get a tutor and stay in the house. I hadn't had any prophetic dreams in a while and I hadn't heard any demonic voices from beyond, so I was beginning to worry a little less.

Dad stayed on edge, and he would never tell me his personal experience with demons. At times I saw how he and Mom were alike. Maybe it was his overprotective parental nature. On the other hand, Antonio was adjusting with no problem. When he became bored he would take the car and drive back to Dallas and not return until the next day. This of course would make Dad flip. At all times he wanted us to be ready. With all of us together, as Dad would say, "It was just a matter of time."

But Antonio didn't know what or why he needed to be

ready. Antonio hadn't seen what I or Dad had seen. His mind was totally in the now. We never seemed to bond on anything. He rarely spoke to me when he was around the house and constantly stayed on the phone. Dad bought another bed and split my room so Antonio could sleep in there—but he never spoke to me, he just slept there. At times he would pick me up from school, but the loud music on the car's sound system was a sign that he didn't want to talk. I wasn't sure what it would take for us to be together as true brothers. It seemed every time I looked up he was doing something to bring us further apart.

"What up, Andrew?" Antonio was standing at my checkout line with his arm around Tonya. I looked at him, perplexed, trying to understand what exactly was going on. I looked at Tonya and she really didn't look at me—just pretended like she was reading a magazine. He gave me a sly smirk and I kept my face straight.

"Whatsup, Tonya?" I asked, trying to get some response from her, but she just gave me a tiny wave—what a cop-out.

"Tell Dad I ain't coming home for dinner. Okay?"

"Yeah . . . sure." I wanted to ask him why but once again I was being the town chicken. I started checking out my next customer but watched them as they walked out the store. I could see out the window as Leonard came up to them. He seemed to be a little upset that Antonio had his arm around Tonya. My first thought was that Leonard thought my brother was me. This was not going to be a pretty picture. But hey, Antonio didn't need me babysitting him.

"That'll be five dollars and ninety-five cents, ma'am," I told my customer. I packaged the groceries up and just as I was about to spray down my register with some cleaner I heard a crash. I turned to see Leonard grabbing my brother by the collar and holding him against the store window. They had knocked over the watermelon display at the front of the store.

"This doesn't look good," I said to myself and I ran outside.

"Andrew, stop them before somebody gets hurt!" Tonya screamed. I stood there trying to decide who to stop first as I watched the anger build in Antonio's eyes. If I didn't know any better I would have thought his eyes changed color, almost crystal-like. Leonard glanced up at me and was startled a bit.

"There's two of you?" It was a long enough distraction for Antonio to gather his balance against the wall. He grabbed Leonard's arms and picked him up. Leonard was dangling in the air, shocked at the moment that his feet weren't touching the ground. In his anger, Antonio flung him against a nearby soda machine, denting the plastic front of the machine.

"Leo!" Tonya ran to him and lifted his head up. I grabbed Antonio by the arm, and he looked at me with so much evil in his eyes.

"Calm down," I told him and he regained his senses. "What are you doing? You want everybody to ask questions?" I reprimanded him. He was still upset and his shirt was all mangled.

"I don't know that son of a bi—"

"Antonio, please calm down!" I grabbed him by both of his shoulders and I looked into his eyes. Then for the first time in some weeks I had that feeling. The hairs on my arms stood up and I saw through Antonio's eyes.

Antonio had driven up to the school. It wasn't even time for school to be out and there in the distance coming from the school I saw Tonya, her cleavage slightly exposed with a tight black shirt on. Her hair flowed behind her as she hurried to the car and jumped in. I couldn't hear what she was saying— it was all muffled. I could see that she had grabbed Antonio's hand, and they drove some distance until they arrived at her house. Still holding hands, she led him to the door and inside the house. Her mother was gone and it was only a few minutes past twelve. Maybe she had invited him to lunch. She grabbed him around the neck and he grabbed her around the waist and he pushed the door closed with his foot. I felt what Antonio felt, and when she kissed him I felt both pleasure and anger. The anger, however, was my own. They fell back on the couch and she straddled him down, pulling her shirt off, exposing her bra. I felt through his hands as he caressed her stomach and kissed her neck. I felt all the heat of passion. I could taste her saliva in my mouth and I could smell her erotic aroma. And it angered me. I let go of his shoulders.

"You slept with her?" Antonio looked at me, stunned. I didn't want to see any more of his soul. I glanced past him at Tonya, still holding Leonard; she was staring at us as if she knew what I had said, but she was way too distant to have known what I said.

"Why did you do it?"

"She ain't your girlfriend, so don't worry about it." He was right. I had no claim to her at all. But it still made me mad. He had everything I wanted, and I wasn't sure if I was really mad at him at all. I looked at him and he gave me a cold stare. Screw it, if he didn't care—I didn't care.

"Dude, I don't even wanna bother with you anymore," I said.

"You act like I give a damn." He punched me verbally in my face. I wanted to cry but not in front of him—not at this moment. I certainly wasn't going to let a brother I *just* met hurt me. He walked away from me and told Tonya to follow him. His power of suggestion must be remarkable because she left Leonard and got into the car with Antonio. Maybe Antonio was Donyel incarnate. Maybe my enemy wasn't Donyel; maybe it was my own brother. Ever since I had met him he had been nothing but bad. Others came from inside the store to help Leonard and put ice on his head. I walked back in the store.

"Oh, my God! What happened out there?" Lydia asked, attempting to stay calm as most managers do but you can tell they are frantic. She was a heavyset white woman with a double chin, a country accent, and thin, curly blond hair. She had bright red round glasses that made her look like Sally Jessy Raphael and every day, rain or shine, she wore a navy blue sweater with a red scarf—even though our store really had no set uniform. She had come from the back of the store and was still holding a box that she was using to stock some shelves. The grocery store I worked for wasn't all that big. It had about eight aisles and four cash registers. In a small town like this the news of this fight would be known by the end of the night—each with his own version of what happened.

"It was a fight, but everything is cool. Just Leonard being a knucklehead again and this time he got called on it."

"Ohh. Tell Leonard he's paying for those watermelons he knocked over." I smiled at the thought that Leonard finally got a dose of his own medicine, but I was still upset that Antonio was the bringer of vengeance. I prayed that this fight would get written off as another one of Leonard's episodes. He got in fights often and I wanted to keep Antonio out of it.

When I got home, Dad was waiting for me in the living room.

"Where's your brother?"

"Um, he said that he wouldn't be eating here tonight." Dad didn't even comment. Antonio's absence was something that bothered him but he wasn't the type of guy to pressure Antonio. Besides, Antonio was a man himself. Mack busted through the door not too long after me.

". . . Heard that Leonard and Antonio got in a brawl."

"What!" Dad hollered. Wow, news had traveled faster than I had thought. I looked over to Mack, trying to give him those signals to not say anything—but I forgot that he didn't catch them once before and he didn't catch them this time.

"Yeah, Antonio and Leonard Freeman got in a fight at the store. Andrew, you saw it, right?" Mack pointed at me. All I could do was glare at him. Dad turned completely around and faced me, waiting for some explanation.

"Well, Andrew? Is this true?"

"Yeah, Dad. Antonio threw Leonard into a soda machine."

"Really? I heard that Antonio took a six-pack of soda and knocked him out," Mack said. Dad stared at me like I did it or something.

"No!!! That's just town rumors. None of that happened, Dad, trust me."

Dad rubbed his forehead in an effort to relax himself and sat back down on the couch.

"What's wrong with Mr. Turner?"

I pushed against Mack to encourage him to leave.

"Just talk to me later, you've caused enough trouble."

"What? See I'm tired of you blaming me all the time."

"Go!" I told Mack and he left, not speaking another harmful word. Mental note: *Teach Mack those nonverbal signals.*

"Why didn't you stop him?" Now Dad was yelling at me. It wasn't my fault that Antonio was so hotheaded.

"I did! I was just a minute too late before he threw Leonard. It wasn't really his fault, Leonard jumped him fir—"

"I don't care. I don't want you guys displaying your gifts in public!"

"Why are you telling me this? I know this! Antonio, the son *you* raised is the one acting like a fool outside. I can't even get close to him 'cause he acts like he hates me."

"He doesn't hate you."

"Then why does he never want to talk to me? Why is he stealing Tonya from me? Why does he look at me like I'm his enemy?" Dad stood at attention and turned his ear toward me.

"What did you say?"

"I said why does he look at me like . . ."

"No, I mean before that."

"Tonya?"

"Yeah, is Antonio dating Tonya, the same girl I told you I wasn't sure about?"

"Yeah, but what does she have to do . . ."

"I knew that girl was trouble." My mind was closed to the suggestion that Tonya was the cause for all this. The problem was Antonio, and I was determined to get Dad to understand this.

"Andrew, in order for you to be able to develop right and for you to understand your calling, you and your brother have to be of one accord, mentally and spiritually. You guys are twins, you have a natural bond, and once you make it spiritual then there's no devil anywhere that can hurt you guys."

"What are you saying?"

"The devils want to keep you guys apart. This is your brother and you have to keep trying to bond with him."

"I tried. You're talking with the wrong twin." He looked directly in my eyes and gave me that father stare.

"I'm talking to the right twin. Now please, despite how he acts, try harder . . . remember he is your brother."

Remember he is my brother, words that would always echo in my head. I dismissed myself to my room and flopped on my bed. I saw pictures of myself and pictures of Antonio, but not one picture of us together. We had so many years apart, practically most of our lives, and yet I had always had a void in my heart for him. Somehow I knew he had to have that same void in his heart for me. I thought that he was probably with Tonya right now and I became angry again. I closed my eyes.

"If we can't have you, we will have him." I jumped up from the bed and looked around. Nothing. But it was something. The voices—the demons—they were all around all the time and they were after Antonio. I proved to be strong, but now they were going after my brother, who was weaker. Dad was right—I couldn't give up. I lost Mom; I wouldn't lose Antonio. I got out of bed and ran from my room and out the front door.

"Where are you going?" Dad yelled.

"I'm going to go find Antonio."

~ chapter 24

I only knew of one place he would be so I went there. Tonya lived a pretty good distance from us but I walked the entire way. I stood there outside looking up at her house. I had to make amends with him. If he was here, I would have to learn to accept his relationship with Tonya. It was the manly thing to do. It was getting dark and I wasn't planning on staying outside forever. The closer I got the uneasier I became. I almost felt like I was being watched—but it was just my shadow, I think. I was being silly. I walked to the porch and rang the doorbell. Tonya answered, looking very surprised to see me.

"Andrew! What . . . are you doing here?" She looked like the cat that swallowed the canary.

"I need to talk to my brother." I held my peace. I felt like I just wanted to scream knowing that he was here, in her house, doing God knows what. He came to the door and he was looking far different from when I first met him. Of course he was drunk when I first met him, but yet there was something different. Nothing physical had changed but when he looked at me his eyes seemed darker. Tonya was hanging off his arm, and if I didn't know any better I would have thought that they were joined at the hip.

"Uh, can I talk to you alone?" He motioned for her to go back inside and she followed suit. Once again I was amazed at how docile and obedient she had become to him in such a short time. Seeing them together was like dreaming of myself with her except when I saw them . . . I knew that wasn't me on that porch.

"Look, we don't need to be against each other, Antonio. We're brothers and I want us to be friends."

"I have plenty of friends, Andrew. I didn't ask for a brother, nothing personal but I'm not into all this sentimental stuff. I've lasted this long by myself and I'll keep surviving on my own." I walked eye level with him and we were perfectly the same size. I stood there staring at him.

"Being on your own is all good but right now we need each other."

"I don't need you!" He shoved me backward.

"Yes, you do! You need me . . . just as much as I need you!"

"Yeah, for your demon hunting? You need me because you don't want to get hurt. You need me to protect your ass from getting attacked from our devil granddaddy. Well, let me tell you something, Andrew. I don't really believe in all this mumbo jumbo so I don't think it can really affect me, can it? So why don't you and Dad take your crazy superstitions and bother somebody else." His eyes were even darker than I remembered. He wasn't talking—this couldn't be Antonio talking. What happened to him? I was speechless.

"Just because you don't believe doesn't mean it's not real, Antonio. Look, you are my twin. I have always wanted a brother. Antonio, all demons aside and whatever else is out there, we have a bond." I wanted to cry and as I looked into his eyes, I felt my heart hurting. "I know you have to feel that bond like I do. Please, can we be brothers?" The darkness in his eyes began washing away. His eyes quivered. He didn't speak and turned around to walk back in the house. I had said my piece and I didn't know what else to say. I walked back down the stairs and back into the street.

"Hey, Andrew." I turned around. Antonio stood there in the doorway. He was fighting the urge to come down and go home with me. I wanted him to understand my intentions, my heart, and to know what it really meant to have a brother.

"I know I never asked for a brother . . . but, umm, that doesn't mean I never wanted one." He stared at me so blank, so empty. I reciprocated his statement with a smile and I couldn't help but drop a tear—I had fought all too long. He turned back toward Tonya's house and went in and closed the door. My brother wasn't far from me. There were some walls up but I knew it wouldn't be long before they would come down. The walk home didn't seem as long because my brother's last words stayed with me, giving me an inkling of some type of hope. But it would take more than my hope to protect him from the demons; it would take God Himself.

I was in the school cafeteria early the next morning studying when Tonya confronted me. She had on a Heaven High School sweater with two big H's on the front. Our mascot was the Archangel. I never noticed until now that everything here in Heaven centered on angels. She took her tray and sat across the table from me.

"Hey, how are ya doing, cuzzin?" she said, sipping a small cup of orange juice. I hated eating breakfast here. The portions were always way too small for growing boys like myself. The only reason I came in here was to study in a quiet area. I really didn't want to talk to Tonya. All my feelings were just tearing me up inside.

"I'm cool. How have things been with you?"

"Nice. You haven't called me in some time." What was this girl expecting from me? She was dating my brother and now she was concerned that I wasn't calling her? Was she leading me on or was I truly being a butthead about all this?

"Well, um, I've been busy trying to get caught up on my schoolwork so I haven't really had the time. You know me, always studying."

"Oh, which reminds me." She passed me some old notes of mine. I smiled that she remembered (even though I really didn't need the notes anymore).

"Thank you. So how are you and my brother getting along?" I didn't even look up but kept writing in my spiral. I really wasn't sure what I was writing but I didn't want to give her the pleasure of thinking that I was all that interested in her response.

"Your brother is real sweet. I'm sorry that you guys don't get along like you should."

"Who says we don't get along?"

"Well, I overheard you guys arguing last night on the porch and you seemed real upset that he was at my house." I glanced up.

"Well, we were just having some family issues but things are getting better now. Besides, I'm still getting to know him."

"Yeah, he told me that he lived with your dad when your parents were divorced."

"Well they really weren't divorced."

"Then why did they separate for so long?"

I really wanted to change the subject. I was getting uncomfortable and I didn't want to let on that I was hiding something. I shrugged my shoulders. Just as she looked as if she was going to ask another question I intentionally elbowed my juice over to get the attention off my family situation.

"Oh, crap! Hey, can you get me some napkins, Tonya?" Tonya jumped up to help me clean the mess. Mack entered the cafeteria.

"What up, buddy?" he said, grabbing food off Tonya's plate and sticking it in his mouth.

"Mack, stop eating my food!" she yelled, coming back to the table with some napkins.

"Hey, I didn't see any names on this food." Mack was always stuffing his face. He was the type of guy who was always eating but never seemed to gain weight. I had no idea where all that food went. If I called him on the phone, he was eating. If he came to my house, he wanted something to eat, and if we went out to kick it, we went to go eat something. Tonya popped Mack on the shoulder and grabbed her tray.

"Hey, call me later, okay?" I nodded to her. Mack looked back at me and grinned.

"Playa, playa!! You trying to get her back, huh?"

"No. She just came over here talking to me about last night."

"What happened last night?"

"I went over to her house to find Antonio."

"Was he over there?"

"Yeah."

"Were they having sex?"

"What? Mack, come on, man!"

"Well . . . were they?"

"No, no they were not having sex." Mack gave me a skeptical look, and I just tried to ignore his rude comments. At some point you just can't even worry about people and what they do, but you have to accept them for their flaws and that they might not change. This was the case with Mack.

"So, who are you taking to the prom?" I hadn't even thought about the prom and I certainly didn't want to go by myself. I had invested so much time in Tonya that I had totally forgotten about the prom. If I asked a girl I didn't know there was a good chance she'd say no. I knew a lot of girls, but Tonya was the only one I was interested in. Of course she would probably have Antonio take her. I shrugged my shoulders.

"Come on now, Andrew, I know you gonna take ol' girl."

"Who, Tonya? Maybe you have forgotten, she's with Antonio now." He smiled and patted my shoulder.

"Nope. I'm talking about Courtney."

Courtney wasn't a bad idea. Courtney was cool, but I wasn't sure if she would want to accompany me to my prom. I would have to be as charming as I knew how to be to convince her. I just knew that she would try to find some excuse to not go since she was so much more mature and she was a college student.

"That girl likes you, and I really think that you should see if she will kick it with you."

"Man, you're trippin'. There's no way that she's gonna go to the prom with me." Mackenzie looked at me and shook his head. Why was he looking at me like that? Was I being a chicken? I hadn't even given the girl a chance and I had already written her off. If I kept this up I would always be single.

"Stop looking at me like that!" I threw a ball of paper at his forehead, and it didn't seem to faze his frozen stare of disappointment.

"Okay, okay!" I had given in once again to peer pressure. "I'll call her tonight. But if she rejects me, then you're gonna have to hear me whine about it for the next few months."

"It's not like you don't whine about things now."

"Ha-ha." My sarcasm was nothing compared to the look on my face at his comment. I looked at my watch and it was ten minutes before the first bell, so I prepared to put my books in my backpack.

"So who are you taking to the prom, Mack?"

"I'm not taking anyone."

"Wait a minute. If you're going alone then why are you pressuring me to find a date?"

"I need to be on major pimp patrol during the prom, hence the name Mack. Besides, I don't need you slowing my game down that night, so it would be better if you had a date."

"Gee thanks for thinking about my well-being."

"That's what friends are for!" He smiled and grabbed his books and left the cafeteria.

I let out a breath. There was way too much drama going on my senior year, and I really just wanted to graduate like a normal kid. But what was going to happen after graduation? With all that was happening, I wasn't sure if I was ready for the responsibility that was before me.

I remember when Mr. Crowley, my English teacher, had a lecture about freedom, but more specifically about our new freedom from high school into the big world. He had told the class that with much freedom comes much responsibility and that there were two different types of freedom. There is good freedom and bad freedom. Now this kind of threw me for a loop because I always thought that any freedom was good. But he went on talking about how in this country we have freedom of speech and that's good, but sometimes that means that we have to allow people like the KKK to display their hate and that's bad. In another instance, there's celebrities who use their freedom to be rather sexually liberal. So that freedom of empowerment gets other young girls and even guys thinking that sex appeal is more important than other factors of a person's total package.

The whole point was that, the more freedom one obtains the more responsible one *should* become, but that's not necessarily the case with all people. His lecture that good freedom can only be produced through responsibility will always stay with me.

The bell rang. I grabbed my bag and threw it over my shoulder and watched as the dark clouds outside made the clear windows appear tinted. As I pushed my way through the hallway I was amazed at how so many people kept talking in the hallways and still made it to class on time. By contrast, I would leave right as the bell rang, and after going to my locker and pushing my way back through the hall I would just make it by the tardy bell. But then again, sometimes I didn't think I was too aggressive in getting through the hall. I wasn't too aggressive overall. I had to push my way through and get to where I wanted to go.

I was going to call Courtney without a shadow of a doubt.

chapter 25

I was psyching myself up, standing in front of the mirror listening to some smooth music on the radio. You would have thought I was going on a date. It was just a phone call. I knew that Courtney was nothing like Tonya. But subconsciously, I was comparing the two because Courtney was still a girl and there was a chance that I would mess things up with her too. Come on, Andrew, stop doubting. My problem was that I was always second guessing myself.

Antonio startled me when he came into the room. He didn't even say anything; he had been up so late the night before the only thing he could think about was sleep. He jumped in his bed and rolled the sheets around him with his clothes still on, with the exception of his shoes, which he flopped off. I quietly grabbed my cell phone from my pocket and went to the living room. Not because he was asleep but because I didn't want him to know my business. Sleep or not, people could still hear.

Dad was in the living room reading a paper so I made my way to the kitchen. He didn't even budge from his spot on the couch, just groaning occasionally in response to whatever he was reading about. I dialed her number.

"Hello?"

"May I speak to Courtney?"

"This is she."

"Hey, Courtney, this is Andrew . . . how are ya?" Small talk was always a good thing before you drop the bomb.

"I'm doing okay, Andrew, how have you been? Are you getting along with your brother?"

"He's dating Tonya now."

"The girl ya dad didn't like?"

"She's not the problem, it's Antonio. But I talked to him so I think he's coming around."

"That's good. Don't let a girl come between brothers." One additional thing about Courtney was that she was really good for words of inspiration. I had almost forgotten what I had called her for. We had spoken ourselves into a tangent and now I had to tell why I had called this evening. I sighed.

"You okay?" she asked me. Maybe I sighed too hard.

"Yeah, I'm cool. Hey, I was wondering if you could be my . . . my uh . . . date."

"Your date?"

"Yeah . . . to the prom." It seemed the more nervous I got the more fragmented my sentences became.

"Did you say the prom? I'm so surprised you would ask me to your prom."

"Okay I'll take that as a no." I prepared to hang up.

"Andrew, I didn't say no." I decided to not hang up.

"So what are you saying?"

"Well I tell ya what. Let me check my schedule and make sure I have some free time and I would love to accompany you to the prom." I actually smiled, and I'm glad that she couldn't see because my whole focus was to stay cool.

"Okay, well, prom is next weekend and I know this is short notice so forgive me." I was trying to be cool but deep down inside I was very excited that I had managed to get a prom date and really didn't have to beg.

"Andrew, I've been really feeling weird lately." Oh crap, I hope she wasn't having any emotional issues. I needed to stop avoiding this. I liked Courtney and I didn't know what was wrong with me. If I looked at the big picture, she was way more stable and reliable than Tonya. Courtney was stimulating to my soul. Tonya, however, was stimulating to my body. Be that I was seventeen, it was obvious which side of me I was listening to.

"What's wrong?"

"Well, ever since you touched me—ever since I heard you inside my heart, I've been having different dreams."

"Are you sure it has anything to do with me?"

"It has to. Andrew, I've been having dreams every now and then about the future. Last night I had a dream that I was at your prom but something wasn't right."

"Like what?"

"I don't know . . . I'm really unsure about that part. I just didn't feel right." Now she was scaring me. The last thing I needed was something screwing up at my prom. But maybe she was just imagining things. My gift couldn't have possibly overflowed into her—could it? Maybe she had a gift of prophecy already and my gift stimulated hers. Whatever happened, I didn't want to think about how creditable her vision was. We would just have to wait and see. Besides, she could've just eaten before she had that dream.

"Are you sure you didn't eat something like a chili dog before you went to bed?"

"Andrew, I'm serious!"

"I'm serious too. Well, look, let's not freak out until something happens. But just in case, we'll stay on our guard."

"Yeah. Too bad we don't know for what, though."
Courtney had taken the words right out of my mouth. I was
trying not to let her know how nervous her dream had now
made me but it did. After we said good-bye I tried to gather
my thoughts. Dad looked over at me in the kitchen and joined
me. He refilled his cup of coffee and sat down at the table.

"Who were you talking with?"

"Courtney. I was calling her about the prom."

"Well, I couldn't think of a better person for you to take.
You guys are so much alike."

"It would seem so," I said under my breath. He looked
at me suspiciously, and I grinned my comment off. Didn't
want my dad knowing that my gift had caused some problems. What was I going to do?

I went back to the room, and Antonio was barely moving. He groaned and rolled over, resembling something like
a burrito. I walked across the room and turned the ther-
mostat up. This guy must love living in an igloo. The
thought of something bad happening at my prom kept dis-
turbing me. All this alarm had started because of demons.
All this frantic watching over my back had started because
of my grandfather Donyel.

Ignorance is bliss. All my life I was unaware that this
threat had existed and I was left to think my life was just
fine. I guess that was what Mom wanted. She wanted my
life to be normal. I couldn't be upset with her for holding a
secret from me. I walked to my door and peeked out into
the hall, seeing Dad sipping his coffee at the table. I
couldn't be mad at him either. They both had sacrificed
being together so that Antonio and I could be normal. Now
it was time for me—for us to learn how to protect ourselves.

Thinking of fallen angels made me wonder again if I
had a guardian angel. Maybe I didn't. I thought I would

have heard from one by now or at least seen one. I sat on the bed and looked over to Antonio who, by now, was snoring away. I bowed my head. Everything was stirring and I had absolutely no peace. I remembered Mama. I remembered how she used to sneak up behind me and hug my neck when I stayed up all night studying. I remember the smell of her perfume. I remembered how she would sing so melodically in church. You could hear her voice over everyone else there. I missed her.

I hadn't prayed in some time and wasn't sure what to tell God. I closed my eyes and tried to forget about everything around me and focus on the greatest eternal being who knew what I was supposed to be doing.

"Father, God, it's me, Andrew. I'm sure you have been keeping up to what's been going on in my life and, well, I'm really confused to what my purpose is. I feel like sometimes I can't handle what you have given me. I know it says in the Bible that you wouldn't give us more than we can bear but to me this seems like a lot. God, why can't I be normal?" And in an instant I heard a peaceful whisper in my heart,

"What is normal?"

"I mean, why can't I be like everyone else?"

"Everyone is different. Everyone is made in a unique way. You are special and exist for a reason."

"But what if I mess up? What if I don't fulfill the purpose that's meant for me?"

"You can do all things through Christ, who strengthens you. God is faithful. He has faith in you. Have faith in God." I opened my eyes and realized that I was getting answers. They weren't loud and they weren't annoying like the demons but it was something my heart was hearing. Had the God of the universe heard my prayer? Was He reaching out to me as I was trying to reach out for Him? A tear rolled

down my cheek as I thought that God had enough time to be mindful of my affairs. But time belonged to Him. He owned time. If He didn't have time He could make some more. I had heard once that the angels were the ones who carried the prayers to the Lord. I had read in another book that our prayers themselves became angels. I wasn't sure. There was so much about this world I wasn't sure of.

I knew that this world was vast, and the more I found out the less I felt like I knew. I lay down, and from my bed I could see out the window into the vast night sky. Sometimes I got upset how we as people concentrated on some of the most elementary heavenly principles. People in the world only reference the Bible to quit having sex, drinking alcohol, and to gain worldly riches. Was this happiness? I mean, true happiness? I rolled over to my side and thought about the peace that came over me when I was praying. I didn't have everything I wanted, but to know that God wanted me to do something special brought me joy.

I wanted to know more about God. I wanted to know more about who I was and where I came from. I wanted to know what type of man I was to become. I truly wanted to know who God really was.

"All things in their season," popped in my heart. I smiled because I knew God had heard my heart. He was watching me. I wasn't alone. He and all His angels were watching over my life and my family. Whatever was out there trying to hurt me I knew I had protection. I looked around the room and wondered about the things that I couldn't see. I shivered at the thought of all the things I may have done that God may not have been pleased with and how He had seen those things also. I cringed at the thought and wondered how He could still love me. God must be an amazing being. That was the whole reason why He had sent Jesus,

because He wanted to understand us and wanted to pay for our sins. To conquer death one must die in the place of the one sentenced to die. Jesus had died for men so that men could be redeemed spiritually to God. Simple really. It was like a light had gone off in my head and I was born again. Yeah, I had always been Christian, but being born again was something I was doing mentally every day. I was seeing things in a new light. I loved this feeling when I prayed. I didn't want to lose the youthful freshness of having communed with God, and yet I didn't want to be immature and be stagnant in learning about Him. God was more than abstinence and finances. There were deep things—deep, creative things about Him that I wanted to weave within myself because truly I didn't understand who I was and why I was here (on the planet).

Antonio rolled over and groaned some more, looking like he was struggling in a dream. I wrapped myself in a blanket and sat on the floor beside his bed. I lay my head on the edge of his bed, just barely touching Antonio's forehead with my own.

"God, hear my prayer tonight and grant this request." A tear rolled down the corner of my eye and I let it fall. "Give my brother peace in his heart and help him to see how much You love him."

Prayers are not magical spells. Don't let anyone fool you. You can't tell God what to do. Sometimes prayers get answered and sometimes they don't, for whatever particular reason. Only God knows and sees the big picture. I've heard that sometimes God will give you what you want when you don't even ask. I've heard of times when God will give you things that you really don't need just to show you that you really don't like a certain something—thus the term "be careful what you pray for." But that doesn't work with everyone. Sometimes people pray themselves blue and never get something because they just aren't ready for that thing to happen. But then sometimes prayers are delayed for the pure simple issue of faith.

I wasn't quite sure what the issue was with me and my prayer for my brother, but I do know that it seemed he was getting worse. Over the next few days, he was arguing much more and giving Dad a really hard time. Now remember that my brother and I are quite tall and my dad is no competition when it comes to stature. Antonio also has that strength thing on his side. But in my view, it's all about respect, something it seemed that Antonio was lacking. He would leave late in the night and take the car. Dad would be both mad and scared—not really sure if Antonio was all right. Fear would grip him occasionally, as Dad would think that Donyel had come back and taken him. I would tell him that I didn't feel that Donyel was anywhere near and that I would probably feel something if he did.

But I'm the biggest hypocrite. I was calming Dad down and I was just as worried that something bad might happen to Antonio, too. He wouldn't listen to the voice of reason, and I could tell he was not running away from me and Dad . . . he was running away from God. One night when Dad was long asleep, Antonio came in smelling of cheap liquor. He didn't go to sleep—he just sat down on the bed.

"Hey, boy. What choo doing?"

"I'm trying to sleep."

"I ain't talked to you in a while." I was trying to sleep and I had a test in school and now this Negro wanted to talk? Can you say perfect timing? I wanted to blow him off as he had done to me so many times in the past but I decided to entertain my brother. Besides I welcomed any time he was willing to give me (pretty pathetic).

"What do you wanna talk about, Tonio?"

"I'm drunk," he said in his slurred speech and he smiled at me.

"Yeah, I noticed that."

"I ain't ever seen you drink? Why don't you come kick it with me sometime?"

"I don't drink, Antonio."

He laughed at me. With his head bobbing side to side and his eyes glazed over he leaned forward so much I thought he was going to fall off his bed. "Why not? Come on, man. How are we going to be brothers if you don't ever kick it with me?"

It hurt my heart to think that to ensure or build our

brotherly bond I would have to come down to his level, rather than him coming up to my mine. I was upset and I almost considered it. I mean, really—he had never invited me to do anything with him and I wanted to have that bond with him. But I really didn't want to compromise myself in the process. However, I didn't want to alienate him and make him think that I was better than him. What is the right answer? Maybe there is none. Either way I have to learn a lesson. For me the test wasn't in the morning, it was right now.

"Antonio, I'm a Christian. That's a full-time commitment. You know that. If I get drunk, that may be the time the devils may try to attack me and those I love."

"Awww, there you go again." I could smell his breath. It wasn't beer but it was something hard. I don't know why I was talking to him—it wasn't like he would remember anyhow.

"You always talking about Jesus and God, Andrew. If He is so good, then why does He let stuff happen to good people?" The classic question most asked, and I knew he was referring to Mama. I didn't know what the right answer was but I just spoke from my heart. I sat up on my side with my elbow supporting my weight on my pillow.

"Antonio, there are demons and devils that do these things, not God. Sure God is in full control and nothing goes on without Him seeing it, but the only thing He allows is free will. Free will is a crazy thing. People have free will to love or hate, speak or keep silent, give life or kill. Sometimes it seems that things are chaotic but all things are in His control, and ultimately whatever happens is going to be judged one day. So if someone uses their free will to do something that God didn't will, God will judge accordingly. God has a perfect plan that will give us life and give it to us more abundantly, that's what the Bible says. But He loves us so much that He's not going to force His plan on us. He wants us to love Him enough to decide, on our own, to be on His side."

He was quiet. It shocked me. My words came out as smooth and as sweet as honey. I surprised myself because usually I was the type of guy who was lost for words. He smiled at me, and it seemed that he was sobering up slightly.

"You should be a preacha."

I smiled at him. "Naw, I'm not really the preacher type." I laughed at him.

He got up from the bed and walked to the door. "Get some sleep, you got school."

"Where are you going, Antonio?"

"I'm just going to be on the porch. I'm not tired yet." He closed the door behind him, and I laid on my back, looking up at the ceiling. Had I gotten through to him? I smiled to myself.

"Thank you, Jesus." It felt good. I can't even explain in words how I was feeling but whatever it was, it felt good.

⌐ chapter 27

The weekend had arrived, and it was the Saturday before prom. I was excited about that but some residual thoughts had once again taken over my brain, distracting me. I rummaged through different drawers looking for a key—a key to the infamous chest in the attic. I had almost forgotten about it. I looked through some of the boxes we used to pack Mom's stuff, thinking that maybe the key had gotten packed. In my searching I found some recent journals but nothing of her beginnings. The journals I had were post-Donyel and I was determined to find a little tidbit of something to help me along the way.

I went into my mom's room. Dad had left for the moment and I had the house to myself. He had many of her pictures out and spread across the dresser. I wondered if he was getting any sleep at all. In the far corner he had his laptop plugged into a wall socket and sitting nicely on a TV tray. His clothes were still in a large suitcase at the end of the bed, and I was wondering why he hadn't used any of the drawers. Karen had already removed all of Mama's clothing during the funeral preparations, but maybe he didn't feel okay placing his things in there yet. I opened one drawer. I knew it was empty but I just had to look in it. I sighed.

I looked into the mirror at my reflection for a moment. I had to smile more—my eyes were getting that sad appearance. I leaned forward at my reflection.

"Come on, smile, Andrew. Things are going to get better," I tried to reassure myself. I thought about the mirror in my dreams and how Donyel looked. I couldn't help but feel slightly scared. I wasn't ready—that was the pure truth. A box caught my eye in the reflection. It was under the bed, peeking out only slightly. I turned around and sat on the floor. I slid the box into my lap. It was a metal box used to put things in for safekeeping just in case of a fire. I wasn't quite sure if it belonged to Dad and he had brought it or if this was something of Mom's. The only way to find out would be to open it, I guess.

I pried open the rusty latches on the front and opened the grayish metal box. On the top were about five fifty-dollar savings bonds, then some old bills, a birth certificate, and . . . buried underneath it all something more precious to me than all of that. No, not the key—which would have been good to find also—but a photo. It was old and appeared worn from the weather. It was faded and the corners were bent. It had been folded in half at one time. But regardless of its condition it didn't depreciate the value of the image captured on this four-inch square.

On the face of this photo was a picture of us—all of us. Mom and Dad were outside a red car on a bright sunny day. I knew it was sunny by the way the sun bounced off the hood and how they both squinted so hard to keep their eyes open. My mother was posing for the picture and sitting on the hood, holding either me or Antonio. Dad was standing with his foot against the bumper, looking off at something as he was holding the other twin. I wondered what he was looking at. His eyes were stern and serious in the picture.

His neck looked tense. He gripped the baby close to his chest and the face wasn't even visible. At least with Mom, the face of the baby could be seen.

"What are you looking at?" Dad had walked in. I jumped. Mom used to say that you didn't jump unless you were doing something you weren't supposed to be doing. But in this case it was merely because I didn't know he was home.

"Just a photo. When did you get home?"

"Just a minute ago—you didn't hear me come in?"

"No." He shook his head and looked at me.

"You have to be more aware of your surroundings." I looked at the picture and noticed the young man who couldn't have been a few years older than I am now who was very aware of his surroundings.

"When did you take this picture?" I held the photo out toward him. He took it in his hands and looked at it in the light of the room.

"Where did you find this?" he asked, sitting on the edge of the bed.

"It was in this box under the bed." He sat there, silent for a moment. Man, I wanted to know what was going through his mind at that very moment—but I managed to control my urge. He looked at me, knowing I wanted to know the story.

"That's before we went our separate ways," he whispered as his voice barely left his lips. I could tell that it was bringing back so many memories for him. He handed me back the picture.

"You keep it."

"That's okay if you want the pic—"

"I have plenty of memories right here." He pointed at his head. My dad was like an old war veteran and I wasn't sure how I could relate to him on his past. I was just waiting on him to vent his soul to me. He got up and went to the kitchen. I knew where Antonio got his social skills now. I looked back at the picture of my family. I thought about all the hell my parents had been through. It was time-out for being scared. I had to make sure that whoever Donyel was, he wasn't going to haunt my family forever.

Courtney arrived at the house a couple of days before the "big" night. She came up on the porch and knocked on the screen door. She should have just walked in, as familiar as she was with our family. I was sound asleep on the couch, enjoying the breeze coming through the door. Dad was mowing the lawn in the backyard so he didn't hear anything.

"Is anybody home?" She attempted to peek inside. I rose up slightly with a sleepy frown. My eyes were crusty from the short time I had been asleep and I could still feel the heaviness on my body. I managed to get myself up. My eyes were still focusing as I walked toward the door.

"Wake up, boy," she said as I opened the door. She dragged behind her a garment bag and a small suitcase, which of course I helped her with.

"The couch pulls out to a bed so you can use that if you want."

"Woo, you look tired." It was amazing how people made these observations as soon as you woke up.

"Where's your brother?"

"I don't know. I'm not really worried about it." She stood next to me as I sat back down on the couch and lifted my chin so that I could see her eyes.

"It bothers you that he is with her, doesn't it?"

"Of course not." I gave her an offbeat look. She looked back at me with skepticism. "Okay maybe just a little bit. I mean, dang, how else am I supposed to feel?" She shook her head and shrugged her shoulders.

"I understand how you feel. Sometimes it's hard to be totally honest with yourself about your feelings." I wasn't sure what she meant by that. Just then Dad came in from the backyard.

"Courtney! Hey, how was your trip down here?" He gave her a big hug and sat her down at the kitchen table while he searched the cabinet for a cup to get her something to drink.

"Just fine, Mr. Turner." Dad poured some orange juice into a blue cup and placed it in front of her. She smiled at him and looked back at me.

"I brought my old prom dress—is that okay?" That was a question which in any case you better agree or else.

"Sure, go ahead." It wasn't like I had a certain color scheme going. Antonio walked in the house and stopped in his tracks.

"Well, Courtney, good to see you again." He smiled at her that slick smile that I wished so hard was mine. I thought I had a goofy smile. When I would smile, all my teeth and gums would show.

"Hey, Antonio!" Courtney looked up and then continued to hang up her dress. Her voice was happy—I didn't recall her saying my name so happily. I was purely jealous.

"So what brings you to this small town? Couldn't resist being away from me too long?"

"Uh, no, not quite, Antonio. I'm going to be Andrew's date to the prom." I can't express how those words made me feel and how those words made Antonio's whole demeanor change.

"Andrew, huh," he said, glancing quickly in my direction and then back at Courtney.

"Yeah, aren't you taking Tonya to the prom?" she asked, sipping from her cup. This time Dad glanced up at Antonio. Antonio turned away and grinned at me.

"Yeah, we'll be there." I kept my composure and tried not to react.

He started to leave the room and stopped in the doorway. "Be sure to save me a dance, okay?" I watched him as he continued to the bedroom.

Courtney came over to me with her cup in hand, rubbing my shoulder. "I know he makes you mad but you have to chill out, for real, Andrew," she whispered in my ear.

"It makes no sense. Sometimes it seems he's trying to provoke me."

"Probably so." She took another sip. Her eyes caught a thought and she quickly set her cup aside.

"I want you to see my dress and tell me what you think." Once again—a no-win female test, because if I said anything bad she would never talk to me again. So my best bet was to say it looked nice no matter what. I didn't care if the dress looked like ogres made it—I was going to say it looked nice. She unzipped the garment bag, and I prepared my "Oh, that's nice" smile. She glanced at me.

"I feel what you're thinking, Andrew. You don't want to see my dress." I sat startled for a moment.

"Huh, what are you talking about? Of course I want to see it. How do you know what I'm thinking?"

"I told you, over the phone, remember. When you touched me something happened." This was weird, but it was almost like I had somebody who really understood me.

"Can you do this with anybody? I mean, like, can you hear other people inside?"

"No, just you." She smiled. "But I still have dreams, and those seem to be about anything. My mom lost her keys, and in my dream I saw them under the couch and when I looked to see—there they were."

"Wow, you're scaring me."

"Please, I wasn't the one floating in the middle of a room."

"Okay, okay, you got me. I'm sorry, this is all my fault. Now I've infected you." Courtney put down the garment bag and looked directly at me. Her eyes were so beautiful. She was kneeling and took her left hand and slowly gripped my right. Her mind was searching for the right words to say but instead she didn't say anything—with her lips at least.

"What I have now, I've always had ever since I was little. Andrew, you just woke up a part of myself that I had forgotten about. I haven't known you long but it seems that every time I'm with you, you help me to see sides of myself that I didn't know that I had. You stirred up my gift inside. You didn't infect me, you affected me, and for that I am grateful. Whatever happens from here on out, you won't go through it alone."

I let go of her hand and I was in awe. It seemed like weird things were happening every time Courtney and I were together. She wasn't part angel but her human spiritual gift had been something like mine. When she was with me I acted like an amplifier, but how? I had accidentally poured myself into her, and something in her received a part of my self, my soul. My thoughts overwhelmed me. Courtney was different from the others I had touched. Like a puzzle, something inside her had interlocked with something inside of me. I saw in her eyes that same light growing in her but this time no clouds. I touched her face with the tips of my fingers, feeling the pulses electrifying my skin.

She was more than my friend; Courtney was my soul mate. I had finally found someone like me. Her lips pressed gently against my lips and my heart pounded in my chest. For a moment I was lost in myself. Her lips were moist, and I could think of nothing else but her.

"She will die, too. Everyone you love will die." A voice like a breeze flew over me. I jumped back.

"What's wrong?" Courtney looked at me, bewildered. She thought she had done something wrong and I didn't want her to feel that. There were demons constantly around and I couldn't see them. They existed in some other plane and I didn't know how to fight them. How would I protect her? They were after me; I didn't care what happened to me but I didn't want other people getting hurt on my account. She followed me to the couch.

"I'm okay, nothing's wrong." She looked at me.

"You're not telling me something. You're blocking me out. You're scared about something—what is it?" I could see hurt in her eyes. I bowed my head. I wasn't sure what to say. Dad walked into the living room.

"Hey, kiddos, how about a pizza tonight? What type of pizza do you like, Courtney?" Dad was smiling and drying his hands. He was unaware of what had just transpired. Courtney was still looking at me.

"Whatever. It really doesn't matter to me." Her voice was cold and slightly hurt. She was the type of girl that was very tender inside, willing to love full-heartedly, but all that was encased in the shell of a very tough warrior, and she had retreated back into the comfort zone of that shell. She got up and went to the bathroom. I looked back at Dad, who was feeling like something had happened and was trying to figure it out.

I went outside and Dad followed me, but I couldn't hear what he said. I started walking, walking faster—then run-

ning. I had to release this pressure in my mind. I felt like I
was running against the wind. But I kept running harder
and harder. My heart raced alongside with me and my legs
burned, but I ran even harder. I was angry. I was determined to win, to not lose. I was running and I didn't know
to what. I ran until I could run no more. I found myself at
my mother's gravesite, where her ashes were buried.

Her tombstone was so new and shiny, with her name
carved so elegantly on the pink stone. On either side of the
stone were carved two praying angels. I dropped to my knees
and my chest heaved in and out. I beat the ground with my
fist, again and again. Why did she leave me like this? Why
didn't she teach me? I lay facedown in the dirt and cried. I
didn't care that I could taste the earth, and I didn't care that
the bugs and ants were biting me. I just needed to let go. I
hated that I cried so much. I hated that feeling. I pulled
myself up and hugged the tombstone. It was cold and gave
me no comfort but I laid my head on it anyway.

"I heard about your mother." I looked up and saw an
old man—the old man I had met some time before with the
matted dreadlocks—Frank. He looked much more sober
but he was still tattered looking. I wiped my face.

"Hey, Frank. How have you been?" Maybe he would help
me get my mind off my problems. He didn't let me though.

"Staying at the shelter now, like you told me, getting on
my feet slowly. You seem upset, Andrew. Is it because of
your mama?"

"Sorta. It's a long story. How did you hear about it?"

"I saw the funeral and this is a small town. An old bum
like myself is bound to hear people talking. People don't pay
me no mind. It's like I'm invisible to society." It saddened
me to hear something like that but it was true. Frank had a

life that was invisible to everyone because of who he was. All my friends, those who were close, seemed to all have an outcast aura about themselves.

"I saw you hitting the ground. Having a tantrum never solved anything." My complexion flushed with embarrassment. He sat next to me and smiled.

"Aren't you the same young man who so boldly told me to look toward God to help me in my time of need?" Ouch. Frank had just hit me with a dose of my own medicine. But he was right, instead of getting angry at the world for what life was dishing out to me I needed to seek the counsel of God, who was in control. I laughed at myself and that Frank had opened my eyes.

"You're right, Frank. I do need to pray." I sighed. "Do you believe in destiny?" Frank smiled and his eyes lit up. I had forgotten that he was homeless, and I was as comfortable as if he were an uncle or something.

"Oh yeah. I believe in destiny. We all have choices. We all have free will. But in life there is that one thing or many things that you just can't get around. No matter what decision or road you take, you will end up at this point B." He drew this in the dirt to illustrate.

"Some people have big destinies. Life pushes them toward a certain goal, and God puts an itch in their soul to not be happy unless they get it done. These people may try to do small things, but it's the small things they fail at. They have to do the big things. They have to be the presidents, the pastors, the leaders, the movers, the shakers because it is their destiny. But just because someone has a small destiny doesn't make them unimportant. These people are not known as much, but without them the people with big destinies couldn't get where they need to go. These are the people who are the workers, the helpers, the soldiers, the encouragers." I looked at him when he said the encouragers. "We all need one another."

"Yeah, we do." I hugged him and he hugged me back. I prayed with Frank and thanked God that once again He showed me that He had my back. The sun had set and night was upon us.

Prom night. What more can I say? I was nervous for more than one reason. I was looking in the full-length mirror behind my door in my room, getting ready. Courtney was with Karen, who came in early that morning to help. She was getting ready in my mom's room. Dad was in the living room with a camera. Antonio had managed to elude the camera by getting dressed at Tonya's house. Courtney had braided back all my curly hair so it was neatly down on my head. I had on my tuxedo pants, and my jacket was on the bed. I sprayed some cologne on my bare chest before buttoning my shirt. Dad came in to help me with my tie and cuff links, and I could tell that he was absorbing every moment of it. He was glad that he hadn't missed this pivotal time in my life. But I was sad that Mom had. I shook the feeling off. I was going to try to be happy no matter what. But I had to remember to stay on my guard for . . . whatever.

I went into the hall and knocked on my mom's bedroom door. Courtney opened it and she looked . . . incredible. She still hadn't spoken to me, but I couldn't hide that I thought she was so beautiful. Her hair was wrapped in a beautiful white African kente cloth, and she had on a long white dress that wrapped itself around her, leaving her shoulders bare and her cleavage squeezed together. On her neck she had a necklace made of iridescent stones. She wore stub earrings that matched the necklace. Around her shoulders she held on to a lace shawl. Her brown skin looked so smooth and soft, and I wanted to touch her. She tried not to look at me but I could tell that she was hiding her feelings.

"You look great." I smiled and took her hand.

"Thank you." She smiled, still not looking up. Karen was smiling as always with that cute gap in her teeth. She was trying not to cry. In truth, it looked like we were getting married. Then we went through the horror of what seemed like a hundred pictures, which one could have put into a flip book and started an animated movie of us walking from the porch to the car. Finally we left the parents at home to their home videos and used-up film and proceeded to the school gymnasium, where the annual Heaven High School prom was held.

I was so nervous in the car on the way there. We drove her car because, well, basically it was much nicer. I had given the excuse that her car was more economical when it came to gas. But it wasn't like everything wasn't a hop, skip, and jump in Heaven, Texas. I was driving so slow. I didn't want anything bad to happen. She would glance at me every so often. Courtney was feeling like she was more than a friend, and I was getting that uncomfortable feeling like I would feel with Tonya. I tried to keep my cool head though. My hands were sweating and I dared not try to grab hers. All through the streets in other cars I could see my classmates with their prom gear on, heading in the same direction.

"Want to hear the radio?" I fiddled with the tuner and the stations she had programmed all came up static. I should have remembered that this was the country and only the country music stations came in clear as a bell around these parts. I hope she didn't hold that against me. I must have been sweating because I could smell my cologne in my nostrils.

"Do you like Tim McGraw? All we have is country music on the radio," I asked. She smiled and nodded and turned it up.

"Tim McGraw is cool. Country music doesn't bother me—plus I like this duet song he does with his wife, um, what's her name?"

"Faith Hill. Yeah, this song is pretty." Wow. Courtney was really a cool female. Maybe my issue was that when I found somebody who was so perfect for me I got really scared because I figured they wouldn't want me.

When we got to the prom, people were shocked to see that I had grabbed an "outsider" as my date. Courtney was beautiful and she had a very urban look compared with the local townspeople. She didn't care that they stared; she welcomed it. She held my arm and held her head up like a queen, and I stood next to her, impressed at the way she carried herself. The gymnasium didn't even look the same. It was amazing what a few balloons, streamers, and mood lights could do.

Mackenzie strolled up behind us with his date. I didn't know her name but had seen her around, some girl with stringy dishwater-blond hair down to her shoulders and a very revealing dress. She was known around school as being pretty "easy." Mack patted my shoulder and winked at me when I looked at her. I shook my head. I grabbed his arm and whispered in his ear.

"I thought you were coming solo tonight?"

He leaned back in my direction to reply, his breath smelling like winter fresh mints. "She gave me an offer I couldn't refuse."

"I got two words for you Mack—venereal disease." He looked at me and snickered.

"Just a date, Drew, just a date, that's all. I already know. Hey, Courtney." Courtney looked at Mack who, I must admit, was looking very debonair also.

"Oh my gosh, Mack, you are finally living up to your name." He blushed. I smiled to see my friend look as red as a strawberry. I saw my brother in the distance with Tonya. His suit was similar to mine but he had adorned himself with more jewelry. Tonya was in a sleek and sexy blue dress with a slit up the side. The back was cut out and it accented the curvature of her spine down to her round posterior. Her hair was pulled up and she had curled it so some of the curls dangled down over her forehead. She had caught me staring and our eyes connected. She smiled and waved. I smiled back and looked at Courtney, who was still talking to Mack.

"Hey, do you want to dance?" I asked Courtney, who still really hadn't said anything to me. She looked at me, finally, and I took her by the hand before she could answer. The song by Evanescence called "Bring Me to Life" was playing. I had heard that song on the radio and had related to it. It was alternative rock, but something about that song had spoken to me. We danced face-to-face. It wasn't romantic—it was ministering—not like the way church does, but the way that makes you think. The song was saying things we couldn't say. I held her closer and whispered in her ear.

"I'm sorry. I was just scared; scared that something would happen to you."

"Nothing's going to happen to me. I'm here. We're friends and I'm always going to be here for you, Andrew." I didn't cringe when she said "friends." Something about the way she said it made me feel good. At that moment it seemed that having her as a friend wasn't as bad as I

thought. It was better. I was hugging her without even trying as we danced. I closed my eyes. I wanted so bad to say
something that would express what I was feeling. I wanted
to share this good feeling she had brought into my world. I
had been looking for some special girl and hadn't realized
that Courtney was the one girl who stood by my side when
I was still figuring things out. She was the girl who helped
me figure it out. I couldn't get my lips to move. I didn't want
to stop dancing with her. I wanted to let her know how
much she meant to me. I wanted to share my heart so bad
with her.

"I love you." My heart spoke, and she pulled back and
looked at me. I was shocked at my inability to hold it in. I
didn't say it audibly but I felt it, and she had heard my
heart. She smiled because it didn't need to be said—at least
not now, but it was good that it was felt. This time I kissed
her, like in the movies; I did it with that perfect timing.

"Woooohooo, you two lovebirds!" Mack said, dancing
next to us. We looked to our side at Mack, and Courtney
buried her head in my chest.

"Maybe the bad that you saw in your dream was just us
fighting," I told her.

"Maybe. Then again maybe it was just a silly dream. I'll
be back. Let me go fix my makeup." She left holding my
hand, not wanting to let go. I watched her leave the gym
and go down the hall to the girls' room. Mack nudged me
and smiled.

"You got the bug, man!" I rolled my eyes at Mack but I
knew he was right. It felt good to be honest with my feelings about Courtney. Antonio was alone at the punch bowl
so I went to speak with him. Tonya was gone, and this
would be a good time for me to at least be fraternal (and to
make sure he wasn't spiking the punch).

"Hey, Tony." He looked back at me. I hadn't given him a nickname before so I thought I'd try it out once to see his response.

"Hey *Andy*," he responded back, sarcastically, but I didn't mind.

"Where's Tonya?"

"In the bathroom. Courtney looks real nice."

"So does Tonya." There was a crazy, awkward silence as neither of us knew what else to talk about. I was trying hard to not talk about the weather. So I decided to be blunt.

"So have you been thinking about the stuff we talked about the other night?"

"Let's not start talking about religion—we're at a prom."

"I'm not talking nor have I ever talked religion, Antonio. All this stuff we're going through deals with a relationship—a relationship with God."

"Yeah, okay I know this An—" Tonya interrupted us and grabbed Antonio's arm. "I wanna dance, baby."

Courtney came behind me and pulled me aside. "Andrew, I gotta talk to you." I was upset that timing was against me right when I was talking to my brother. But as I looked at Courtney I could tell that something was bothering her.

"When I was in the ladies' room . . . Tonya." She looked over my shoulder at Tonya, who was seductively dancing with my brother.

"What about Tonya?"

"Something is not right about her. I was in the bathroom fixing my makeup and she came in. She didn't say much to me, just kinda stuck her nose up at me and smiled, and I guess when we kissed you had my gifts stirring again . . ."

"What is it, Courtney?"

"I looked in the mirror and I saw this darkness in her

eyes. I almost dropped my compact, but I think she's not . . .
she's not . . . right." I didn't know what to believe. What was
Courtney trying to tell me?

"I've known Tonya for years."

"But do you really *know* her? Your dad didn't feel right
about her either—maybe this is why."

"You think she is a demon or something? If that's true,
why haven't I picked up on it already?"

"I don't know what to say, Andrew. Please, I'm not lying.
Maybe she is why I had that dream." There was some des-
peration in Courtney's voice, asking me to believe her. I
looked at her—there was so much truth in her eyes. But
maybe she had misinterpreted something. Maybe she was
just jealous or maybe . . . I truly had blinded myself.
Another song had started and Antonio and Tonya came to
join us. Courtney hadn't spoken a word and was still looking back at me.

"Hey, what's up, Courtney?" Antonio asked. "You don't
mind if I dance with your date, do you, Andrew?" I glanced
at Courtney and she looked nervous for me as Antonio
pulled her on the dance floor. Tonya stood next to me and I
wasn't sure what to think. I had known this girl all my life.
Tonya was so beautiful and so kind to me. I had to open my
mind to think that there could be something she wasn't
telling me just in case.

"Hey, Tonya, can we talk privately?"

"Sure." She smiled and took me by the arm and I led
her outside. It was quieter outside but I could still hear the
echo of music from the gym. But at least this way I could
talk and hear at the same time.

"What's on your mind, cuzzin?"

"Well, actually, I wanted to know the same about you."
She looked at me suspiciously.

"What do you mean?" I wasn't sure what to ask. I went with my gut.

"Why are you with my brother? I thought you liked me for a moment. Why the sudden change?" She was shocked at my up-front approach, as was I.

"Andrew, your brother swept me away. He's very charming, and handsome, but so are you. He doesn't have the same mind as you. You are so pure, so innocent. There's so much about you I can't figure out, Andrew Turner."

"What are you trying to say, Tonya?" I was getting uncomfortable. I wasn't sure if she was trying to play a game with me or not. Either way she had been with my brother and I didn't want to get in a game that could hurt him. I wanted to know the truth.

"What I'm saying is . . . I was with Antonio to get your attention. I've always liked you, Andrew, and I haven't stopped." She grabbed my collar and pulled me down and embraced my lips. It caught me off guard, but as our lips touched my mind wandered and that feeling electrified through my body. I closed my eyes.

I saw Tonya, her body as beautiful as ever and she was dressed in a silky black dress, her hair falling down on her shoulders. But her eyes, dark like Courtney had told me. She looked angry. Donyel's face flashed in the darkness. I asked the one question I desired to ask.

"Who are you?"

"The man you call Grandfather, I also call the same, cousin." *The darkness whirled around her like snakes or weeds from the seed of evil, and Tonya . . . was the blossom.* I pulled away.

"How? What the . . ." She looked at me, knowing that I had found out. I had seen her for who she was, another Nephilim grandchild like myself. But I didn't know that

Donyel had any more. If she was my cousin, why was she having sex with Antonio?

"You bastard!"

I pulled away too late, and Antonio had witnessed the whole kiss. I looked at him as his anger built up.

"Kill him," I heard. It wasn't demons. It was Tonya. She was a Nephilim but she had inherited the seed of evil from Donyel. *She* was his offspring. Antonio and I merely had inherited our power.

"Good thinking, Andrew. Too bad it won't help you. Antonio, get Andrew, what type of brother is he? He doesn't love you—I love you. He tries to steal everything away from you, your mother, your father, and now Tonya. He is evil." I could hear everything she was telling him. Antonio thought these thoughts were his and his anger flooded his good sense. He charged me like a bull.

"Antonio, no!!!!" I yelled to him, but to no avail. He grabbed me by my shirt and picked me up with one hand. His strength was incredible and even stronger now that he was angry. He flung me like a rag doll into a thicket of bushes. The branches scratched my face but I wasn't hurt. I didn't catch my breath well enough before he grabbed the back of my collar and started pulling it tightly, choking the air from me. I was losing consciousness as I heard Courtney scream. She jumped on Antonio's back and hit his head with her fist.

"Stop, you'll kill him!" He flung her to the ground with no effort. Tonya stood at a safe distance, focusing her eyes into Antonio's soul. Antonio picked me up once again and flung me this time against the nearby Dumpster. I hit the pavement hard. I picked myself off the ground and saw blood on my hand. My head was hurting, and I couldn't stand up straight because my leg was hurt. I didn't see

Antonio approach me before a fist popped across my face, knocking me back down. I felt my right eye throb. He must have held back because I knew he had the ability to kill me with one punch. He wasn't totally gone. I struggled against him, but he started squeezing my throat again. He was angry, and his face had no emotion but his eyes were crying. I was losing my wits. I was scared and I was losing the power to fight back.

"We fight not against flesh and blood but spirits, principalities, and powers in high places." I remembered what Dad had told me before about not fighting with my physical strength and how I was much stronger than Antonio spiritually. That was the only thought flashing through my mind. Mack had just come out to see where we were and grabbed Courtney up off the ground. Mack saw Antonio and tackled him down with all his weight. It bought only a few seconds.

"Courtney, it's Tonya. She's in his mind!" I tried my best to yell but I couldn't catch my breath between my coughing. Fortunately, she had heard me. Antonio flung off Mack, sending him flying through the air and against a tree, knocking him out.

"Mack!" Courtney yelled.

"Go!" I yelled back. Courtney took off her shoes and ran for Tonya, who was too focused to notice. Courtney slammed her to the ground. It was good enough to stop Tonya's influence over Antonio's mind, but now I had to deal with his anger. He was back up and breathing heavily. I could tell his mind was slightly free as he didn't have that "lost" look in his eye.

"Antonio, stop! Please, I'm your brother. I didn't kiss her. She kissed me. She's trying to put us against each other. Please, I love you. I'm not trying to take anything from you . . . I'm not trying to hurt you!"

"Shut up!" He slapped me, knocking me back down. I tasted the blood in my mouth. It put stars in my eyes and it took me some time to refocus.

"No . . . I won't. I love you, Antonio." I picked myself up off the ground. "I won't let the devils in hell take you or any-body else I love away from me." This time I walked up to him. He was confused that I approached him. He just stood there. I felt his heart blocked in this wall. Tonya had helped him isolate himself from me. She had fed his hurt and she did it for a reason.

"Don't listen to him, Tony!" Tonya yelled, but Courtney slapped her and held her face down with her knee in her back, which I think she was enjoying. I kept my focus on my brother. He was at a crossroad, and my life depended on him making the right decision. His fists were balled. I thought for a moment that I was being foolish to approach him. I'm sure he thought the same.

"I'm not going to fight you. I love you, Antonio, and I'll die if that'll show you. You are my brother. Look at me! We're twins. I'm sorry that Mama died. I'm sorry because I know you didn't ask for all this. But I refuse to be sorry that I'm your brother. No matter what, you know I'm going to be here and that won't change." I was in his face by this time and I could see tears welling up. I could see the wall around his heart cracking. Tears blurred my eyes as well. I took a chance. I hugged him. I trusted him. You can't have a rela-tionship with God or man unless you trust. You can't trust unless you love—can't do any of that without faith. I hugged him and felt as helpless as a mouse in the presence of a lion. I was at his mercy. Being vulnerable is scary, but as I laid my head on his shoulder and wrapped my arms around him I felt a tear hit my neck—not my own. For about a minute it was like hugging that cold tombstone in the graveyard, but then the stone melted. I felt his heart-beat, and his arms gently wrapped around me. I closed my eyes and saw his soul.

I saw the pain and the loneliness—the darkness. I saw and felt how cold it was without having Mom in his life. I saw how he was much like me but he learned to hold his emotions in. Somewhere he relied on his ever-growing strength as a crutch, and it gave him power and made him an outcast at the same time. I felt his desire to fit in. Antonio was the type of guy who didn't think anybody understood him because he was so alone. I had felt the same way. Then, sud-denly, I didn't feel alone anymore. I gave him the light of my memories. I let him see Mom at her finest moments—the time when she sang in the choir, when she volunteered with the kids in the neighborhood. All the bits of wisdom she had ever told me growing up—I gave to Antonio as if they were his in the first place. My memories were becoming his memories. My memories were like fireflies lighting up the darkness in his mind, and soon his heart was filled with them. I let go and looked him in the eyes, which were red from crying.

"I'm sorry, Andrew," he said with a raspy voice. I accepted his apology. I was sore all over, but it felt good to hear that. Mack came to. I helped him get up, and he looked at Antonio.

"Sorry, man. I didn't hurt you, did I?" What else could he say? He dusted off Mack, who was slightly disgruntled. Courtney left Tonya on the ground.

"Are you guys okay now?" She straightened her dress and picked up her shoes off the ground. I put one arm around her and the other around Antonio. He smiled at me.

"So I was right about Tonya," Courtney said.

"She's not a demon, she's one of Donyel's grandchildren too. She's part Nephilim," I said weakly, holding my side. Antonio looked shocked.

"Did you say she's related to Donyel? That means she's our . . ."

"Cousin, yeah, pretty gross, huh?" Antonio looked as if he were getting sick. He looked at her on the ground, still not registering that she was part Nephilim.

"Why didn't you tell me?" he shouted at Tonya.

"Because, it was my job to purify the bloodline and stop the curse," she said.

"What?" Antonio was lost that I wasn't the only one talking weird.

Tonya pulled herself off the ground and grinned. Her hair was messed up and her dress was ruined from being ripped when Courtney body-slammed her. She dusted herself off.

"I had to purify the blood of our angelic line and continue the great legacy. I needed to get pregnant by the same blood and destroy those who were not born of his seed but of his power. I was after Andrew at first but he was hard to get to because of dear old Mama. So I sent my demons after her to torture her."

"You did that! I thought . . ."

". . . that it was your fault, Andrew?" She giggled softly, mocking me. "I know, that way when you had your wimpy guilt trip I would comfort you. Do you think you are the only one with gifts? You have your empath gift, your brother has his strength, but what man can resist the amplified seduction power of a succubus? I don't have lust, I *am* lust—but don't you just love it?" She winked and I looked away, guilty that I had been such an idiot.

"You couldn't detect me because you chose not to. Your mother would have known, however, so I had to get rid of her. Unlike you, I don't have angelic powers. It took me some time to learn the craft from my mother." She smiled. I wasn't sure what types of things she could do as a witch.

She snapped her fingers and a fiery spark popped. I tried not to show fear. "But as you can see I'm quite experienced now. It was hard getting to your mind 'cause you're Christian; your brother . . ." Antonio looked at me. He hadn't known how easy of a target he had made himself by avoiding a relationship with God.

"Your brother was perfect. So much hurt and hate. He was a perfect match to fulfill Grandfather's plan. Antonio, Antonio . . . you were all too easy. But I didn't count on your little heifer catching on." Courtney looked as if she was about to jump at her again but I held her arm.

"But enough of these mind games. If I can't have you at least I can destroy you as he would have me do." She stood back and the wind caught up. Courtney grabbed my arm and Mack looked scared. Antonio held his arm against his eyes to keep the dust particles from blinding him.

"Stay behind me!" I yelled at everyone. Courtney held on to her dress and did as I said, pulling Mack along with her. Antonio was at my other side. I wasn't sure what I was going to do.

"God, I need you to do something!" I yelled. She began to conjure every demon she knew by name, and I saw many apparitions jumping into her. Her body jerked with each possession.

"What is she saying?" Mack yelled.

"I don't know. Everybody, this would be a good time to pray." I felt Courtney grip my hand and I heard her praying in the name of Jesus.

I turned to my other side and there was Antonio with his mouth open. "God, I'm sorry. Help us please." I grabbed his hand. I wasn't afraid anymore. Tonya's face was cold and stiff as stone and her eyes were darkened—she looked like she was a different person completely.

"It's time for the twins to die," they said inside of her. An orb of fire gathered in her hands and she flung it at us.

The fire exploded around us but didn't burn us. An invisible shield surrounded us and stopped it. The shield burned red when it was hit but faded invisible again.

"There's a shield around us!" Courtney said.

"It's our combined shields of faith." I had read about it in Ephesians chapter six ever since Antonio had run into mine last time. With everyone connected, I used my angelic blood along with my God-given human spiritual gifts to intensify it. Tonya stood shocked that the fire had not consumed us. She looked at her hands and built herself another orb, bigger than the first, bigger than her.

"This time you will die," the demons said inside of her.

"Don't be afraid! Have faith!" I yelled.

"Jesus, help us!" Antonio screamed. Then I saw Frank walk from behind the building.

"No! Frank! Get out of the way!" He looked up at me and waved. I didn't want him to get hurt, not because of me. Tonya looked at me, having heard my fear and aimed toward him.

"Nooo!" I yelled. She blew a fiery kiss good-bye at Frank. The blast hit Frank, and all I saw was a standing body of fire. I broke loose of Antonio's and Courtney's hands and charged toward Tonya. She didn't even flinch and grabbed me by the neck and lifted me up in the sky. I was too angry. I kicked and struggled. All I had learned about fighting spiritually drowned in my rage. Antonio was about to jump her but she faced him, knowing his actions.

"Do it and you will see your brother's neck squashed like a grape," they said inside of her. Antonio stood still, not knowing what to do, feeling all the more guilty. I felt the pressure in my neck and began to struggle for my life. The

veins in my forehead rose and I couldn't even close my eyes.
I pulled at her steel-like fingers but her grip was too tight. I
grew weaker, slowly losing consciousness. I couldn't talk. I
was just thinking that I was the fool. If I hadn't been so
infatuated I would have known about Tonya. I had been
deceived but I didn't want to die, not like this.

"Well, cuzzin, I guess this is . . . the end."

Courtney gasped and wasn't paying any more attention
to the possessed Tonya. I turned to see what she was looking at; to the best of my ability and in the corner of my eye
I could see the burning Frank moving toward Tonya. He
was still moving, slowly—but very alive. His eyes were
fierce. As his flesh burned off beams of light broke through.
The light made her drop me. As I fell to the ground, I scooted back and Courtney helped me to my feet. The fire had
not killed him but merely removed his skin—or his covering. Frank wasn't human at all. Frank was an angel.

The light from his appearance was blinding, and he
seemed to illuminate even more as he walked closer. He
was beautiful. He was the same Frank, except he was
younger, stronger. His hair was locked and long and his
skin was shimmering like old gold. His eyes were filled with
fire, and when he spoke his voice was like the wind blowing against all the spirits inside Tonya.

"May all the confusion you have brought to this family
be returned to you a hundredfold!" he said to them inside
of her. Tonya screamed and hit the ground in convulsions,
foaming at the mouth. We were behind him, and he turned
his head only to see our reaction. Everyone was speechless.
All this time, Frank was an angel.

He didn't speak, but his eyes burned into my soul like a
passing breeze.

"I am Shariel, one of your guardians. I shielded my identity

from you for this reason: It was my job, Andrew, to watch you and stir up your gift when you had proven you were ready. When you prayed for me no matter who I was, you passed the first test. Your heart for God has shown you to be a man of God. Your destiny will be fulfilled, young prince. You are a brother to men and angels, and God has a purpose for you and Antonio's existence."

"What if I had not passed the first test?"

"I would have had to destroy you." My mouth stayed open. I couldn't close it. Antonio's as well. *"Stay faithful, young warriors. There are new devils arising already to attack you. Just remember this one thing: This battle is not yours, it is the Lord's."* Mack stood behind us, silent, and Courtney was in tears. I wasn't sure if they had heard what I had heard. Shariel smiled again (that smile that I remembered), and he faded away—disappearing into nothing. We all stood there, silent. Courtney, Antonio, Mackenzie, and myself, sitting there outside the gymnasium while Tonya lay on the ground, foaming, still convulsing and incoherent to what had happened.

"Okay, I'm going to church now fa' real," Mackenzie said.

Well, I finally made it to graduation day. I didn't think I ever would. I had more distractions than an average teenager, but all in all I think I pulled away with more. Dad and Karen weren't too keen on hearing what had happened at the prom, but they both understood that it was time to pass the baton to the next generation.

I haven't seen Shariel (or Frank) since that last confrontation. However, it made me realize that angels are all around us, good and bad, and that I wasn't alone. I figure that sometime in the future I will probably run into him again. I had so many questions for him, every time I see an old homeless man I take a double look to see if it is him or not. Only God knows.

Courtney and I talked about our relationship.

"So you're a graduate. Congratulations." She gave me a big hug, and I know that she felt that same spark. I looked at her but she turned her eyes away. The one thing I ever wanted was a woman to look at me and tell me she loved me. Maybe I'm just a hopeless romantic. I thought Courtney would look in my eyes.

"Courtney, I want to thank you for being here for me. I

don't think I would have made it through this whole ordeal without you."

"Yeah, well, Andrew, you opened up a whole new world for me. When I say you're really different from any guy, I really mean it." She half-heartedly laughed. I pulled her chin up, wanting to kiss her, but all I could get my lips to do was formulate words.

"Courtney, I-I lov—" She placed her fingers on my lips.

"Shhh. Not right now, Andrew. I wanted to tell you that I'm leaving. I'm leaving Texas. I need to get away. So much has happened and it's really changed my life. I just don't know what to think about it."

"But what about us?" I felt my eyes burn. She looked back down and placed her head on my chest.

"Andrew, you know how I feel. That will never change. I don't think I will ever find anybody that can replace what you have given me." She had decided to go to school outside of Texas to think about some things. I think that seeing all the stuff with Tonya and Frank kind of spooked her and she was still trying to figure everything out. We promised to keep in contact though. Courtney is really special to me, and I learned that maybe I need to focus on different aspects of women who really matter. She would stay in my prayers. Being apart would keep her gift from acting crazy because I stirred her up—in more ways than one—so this was better, for the meantime, so she could concentrate on her education. But I hope she realizes, wherever she goes, that spiritual warfare exists everywhere. I stood in the crowd of graduates as she walked off.

I decided to not go to college (not yet at least). It was more important that I spend time bonding with Antonio. Whatever plans that were going to be made were going to be made together. Just like Dad said, we needed to stick together from here on out. Besides, Donyel was still out there and there was no telling how he would try to attack next. He used Tonya, and who knew if we had any other cousins.

Tonya was admitted to a psychiatric ward and was rumored around town to have had a seizure and gone crazy. She doesn't speak, she doesn't even respond to anyone. Just sits as a vegetable in a room, shaking. I visit sometimes, and it looks like she's scared, like she can see something I can't. Who knows? Maybe this is all for the better—that way she can't tell anybody our secret.

"Whatup my brooootha!" Mack yelled out at me from his car.

Mackenzie started going back to church and is now a born-again Christian. He's still the same Mack, just a radical Christian version.

I walked over to the car. "Hey, Big Mack!" He still had his cap on, and it seemed he was jamming to some Kirk Franklin.

"I see you listening to some gospel music now."

"Yeah, I'm going to have to get down with the flava for my savior." I couldn't help but smile at the fresh spiritual glow I could see around Mack. I wondered if it was just my gift that allowed me to see such a glow.

"Man, Mack, here we are." I looked at him and remembered when we were just boys running around the playground. "Looks like you're about to make that big college move to California. You know you will always be in my prayers."

"I better stay in your prayers! If we have this many crazy things going on in Heaven, who knows what I might run up against in college!" He chuckled and then he got the most serious look I had ever seen on his face. *He looked at*

*me knowing that for the first time we were going to be sepa-
rated.* Today was an emotional time, and even Mack was
getting teary-eyed.

"Hey, stop looking like that, Andrew. You got ya brother
now. You don't need me around," he said, trying to make
me feel better. I knelt down by the car and looked up to
him, which is something I rarely had to do.

"Mack, you will always be my brother. No matter what
anybody says or where you are . . . you *are* my brother." I
gripped his fist and hugged him through the car window. He
held that hug tight—speechless. All this made me understand
the love of Christ when it came to a "friend that sticks closer
than a brother." All that had made him believe that there's
more to Christianity than just going to church—there's this
unseen war being fought every day. I've never seen someone
studying the Bible so much. Mack said he's going to study
theology in college, which I think is great since in high
school his major was lunch. I started my trek home.

Everything was getting somewhat back to normal. We
all had grown and benefited from it. Antonio even started
to get serious about his relationship with God, which was
really cool. He began reading his Bible, and it just seemed
that things really appeared to be working out. Our brotherly
bond seemed to be even more powerful now that we were
on one accord. I knew my mom would have been proud.
When I got home, I went straight to her room and stared at
her pictures.

"Andrew!" Antonio called me from the other room. I
went into the living room to see what he wanted. He stood
by the couch with a small box wrapped with a bow. "Here."

"What's this?"

"Your graduation gift. You have given me so much and

I didn't wanna fail in giving you something special from me." I took the box and opened it. It was a silver necklace and on it was a silver key.

"Dad had given it to me on my graduation and said that Mom had given it to him. He told me that it means that nothing will be held from you if you seek after it hard enough." I took the necklace in my hand and let the key dangle in front of my face.

"Hey, wait a minute . . . did you say Mom gave it to Dad?"

"Yeah, why?" I almost tripped running to the hallway. Antonio followed me.

"What's wrong, Andrew?"

"Nothing, nothing at all. Everything's right for a change!" I pulled down the ladder and climbed up to the attic. I tugged on the string that lit the single lightbulb and pulled the old chest that I was so determined to open before to the middle of the floor and into the light. Antonio was behind me.

"What's that?" I smiled at him as he looked in wonderment.

"Answers." The key fit perfectly. I turned the key and the lock fell off. I took a breath as I opened the box, revealing dozens of small books. I started laughing and crying all at the same time. It was like I had found a million dollars. We had found Mom's missing journals. Antonio and I read through each one, learning what Mom had took her whole life to discover, understanding why Dad was so cautious, and, better yet, learning more about Donyel and who he was. But like Mom said, it's a long story and I would have to write a whole book about it . . . which may not be a bad idea.

reading group guide questions

~ chapter 1

Early on in his story, Andrew tells us, "I mean, I'm a Christian, but not as much as I could be." What did he mean by that? Could you make a similar confession? Why or why not? What would it look like for you to be as much of a Christian as you could be? Explain.

~ chapter 2

Scripture is clear that God speaks to us through dreams. (See Joseph's story in Genesis 37: 40–41 as just one example.) This story suggests that our dreams—which often seem like nightmares—may also reveal something about darker spiritual realities. Have you ever sensed a spiritual revelation through your dreams? In what way?

~ chapter 3

"Our family isn't as simple as you would want it to be, Andy," his mother told him. Isn't that true for most of us? (Granted, none of ours is as complicated as Andrew's would prove to be!) Scripture is rich in stories about what we would call today "dysfunctional" families—whom God still used in powerful ways. (See 1 and 2 Samuel for the stories about King David and his family—a royal mess, indeed!) How have you seen God at work in and through your own family's dysfunction?

～ chapter 4

Why was Andrew's mother so upset by his semi-humorous statement about the hellish "friend zone" and girls being the devil? Would such a statement upset you (in the absence of Andrea's extenuating circumstance)? Why or why not?

～ chapter 5

"I love God, but . . ." Andrew was wrestling with some tough questions—about his life, his family, and God's role in all of it. When have you wrestled with such questions, and how do you manage to hold on to your faith through the questioning? (See Genesis 32:22–32 and Mark 9:14–27, especially verse 24.)

～ chapter 6

All families have secrets, Andrew has already acknowledged. He is learning that his may have more than most. What experience have you had with family secrets, as a child and as an adult? Why do we keep secrets—and what are the pros and cons of them? Consider this question in light of Genesis 29:29 and John 8:32.

～ chapter 7

Courtney and Andrew have an animated discussion about reconciling biblical history with what science is discovering. Throughout history, Christians have engaged in such discussions—among ourselves and with "secular" scientists and historians. Even among Bible-believing Christians, there are a wide variety of approaches and theories to such debates. Do these debates, discussions, and theories interest you? Why or why not?

~ chapter 8

Ignorance and knowledge, secrets and truth . . . Andrew wasn't sure which he wanted. The not knowing was almost driving him crazy—but he feared *knowing* would push him over the edge altogether. When have you shared that kind of uncertainty—wanting to know but fearing it at the same time? Have you ever experienced that fear in relation to knowing the things of God? Why or why not?

~ chapter 9

In the movie *A Few Good Men,* Jack Nicholson declares, "The truth? You can't *handle* the truth!" Andrew is still wondering about that. He feels a bit like the mythological Pandora, who opened the box that released all the deepest and darkest mysteries into the world. Of course, keeping the truth in a box doesn't keep it from being real. As an adult, how do you balance a young person's need to know the truth about his or her past with that child's ability to understand and respond constructively to that knowledge?

~ chapter 10

The Nephilim are first mentioned in Genesis 6:4, and the reference is pretty obscure. An entire Christian mythology has developed around them, usually describing them as a race of giants (see Numbers 33:22). In this novel, the Nephilim are portrayed as the offspring of fallen angels— not exactly demons themselves but damned all the same. Hearkening back to the question of biblical history and reconciling it with fact—how do you reconcile the sparse biblical account with this fictional novel?

～ chapter 11

Courtney was shocked that the pastor at the church had not even tried to help Andrew and his mother when she fell into convulsions at the funeral. What was your reaction? If your church were to face such a situation, how would your church leaders (and you yourself) respond? How can Jesus' ministry to those possessed by evil spirits be a model? (For starters, see Mark 1:21–28; 5:1–20; and 9:14–29.)

～ chapter 12

"How do I know God's will in my life?" Andrew demanded. He recognized that most of us *want* to do God's will—but we tend to get sidetracked by our own desires and agendas. How *can* we discern God's voice (audible or not) from all the other voices in our head? Prayer is a good starting place, as Karen suggests (Psalm 40:8, 143:5–10). Meditating daily on scripture, such as a section of Psalm 119, is also a powerful tool for seeking God's will.

～ chapter 13

"But maybe I choose to be who I want to be," Andrew reflected fearfully. Despite his mother's assurances that his soul was redeemed through his father's blood, Andrew had been forcefully made aware that he had conflicting desires and a powerful gift that could be used for good or evil. Some new Christians believe (naïvely) that salvation is the end of all temptation. Scripture makes it clear that we continue to wrestle daily with sinful desires (see Romans 7:15–25). How do you experience and respond to this everyday struggle?

～ chapter 14

Alluding to Jesus' parable that we know a tree by its fruit, Courtney points out that some trees need fertilizer before they can be fruitful. And fertilizer is some nasty stuff—the waste and decay of once living things. How have you experienced God's ability to "use crap to make fruit" in your life?

～ chapter 15

Andrew was so full of grief, confusion, and fear that his emotions exploded in temper at his best friend. It's a common reaction to intense and traumatic experiences. It's also a good reason for learning how to deal with your emotions before they get to the flash point. How can we minister to people like Andrew? When we are in his shoes ourselves, how can we accept the ministry of others?

～ chapter 16

Andrew listened to Tonya talk, and a lot of what she said made sense. But something about her ideas also felt wrong. The fact is, no living human being knows exactly what life after death looks like, so even among Christians, our beliefs will differ. Sift through her beliefs and try to sort out what you agree and disagree with, and why.

∼ chapter 17

Now Andrew knew the full story—about his mother, his father, *and* the identical twin he hadn't known existed. He finally received what he had been asking for—knowledge, truth, *and* a more adventurous life. And, for the first time, he realized just how much he needed God. The question was, would God be able to save his family through the days to come? Can God save you and yours? (See Romans 8:28–39 and Jude 17–25.)

∼ chapter 18

"You don't have to be part angel for your world to turn upside down," Courtney told Andrew. The Bible is full of stories about people's lives turned topsy-turvy . . . Hagar, Joseph, David, Job, Daniel, Esther, to name just a few. Consider the stories of Mary (Luke 1:26–56) and Joseph (Matthew 1:18–25, 2:13–23) as one case study, told from two sides, and explore what lessons might be learned from how they responded to having their lives turned upside down.

∼ chapter 19

What do you think about Anthony's explanation about the missing tribes of Israel and the covenant blood being disseminated throughout the world, allowing all people to participate in the covenant? How much of this is biblical history—and how much is biblical fiction? What works in a good book may not be good theology once we return to the real world—so how do you distinguish between biblical truth and myth? (For example, compare Anthony's theory with Paul's teaching in Romans, especially texts such as chapters 2, 4, and 11.)

⁓ chapter 20

Andrew had high hopes for meeting his twin. He figured, not only would he finally have the brother he had always wanted, but he wouldn't be alone in the strange predicament in which he had found himself. The meeting was disappointing, to say the least. We hear about it from Andrew's perspective. What do you think Antonio was thinking and feeling?

⁓ chapter 21

Throughout the book, Andrew has acknowledged his lack of control over his angelic gift of empathy. In this chapter, he is finally able to put it to use in a ministering way. Scripture tells us that we each possess different gifts (Romans 12:4–8; 1 Corinthians 12:27–31, 13:1–14:5), and each gift is powerful in its own right. But the raw talent God instills in each human being can be used for good or ill. What is your gift, and how do you try to cultivate it for God's good purposes and for ministry to others? (See Ephesians 4:1–16.)

⁓ chapter 22

Andrew's friendship with Mack goes way back. It's a relief to share with Mack what's been happening in his family. Even though Mack isn't a Christian (or perhaps *because* he isn't), he can't really understand or accept what Andrew tells him—but he accepts Andrew himself and vows to have his buddy's back, no matter what. In times of crisis, a good friend who shares your faith is invaluable—but have you ever experienced a time when a nonbelieving friend is even more accepting, nonjudgmental, and loyal than a fellow believer? Explain.

～ chapter 23

Repeatedly, Andrew's sensitivity to emotion—his own and others—has kept him on the brink of breaking down. Tears threaten often, but he chokes them back more often than not. By contrast, Antonio is the stronger, more aggressive (and angrier) twin. Their father observes that Andrew's sensitivity is a spiritual gift; Antonio's strength is a physical one. When you meet a man, which gift draws you more—sensitivity (which is rarely considered "manly") or strength? Why?

～ chapter 24

Good freedom can only be produced through responsibility, Andrew recalled a teacher saying. What does that mean to you? How does it relate to Paul's teaching about freedom in Galatians 5:1 and 13–18?

～ chapter 25

More than once, Andrew has asserted just what he tells Courtney: "[Tonya's] not the problem, it's Antonio." Why is he inclined to believe nothing bad about Tonya—even though there are multiple signs (including the instincts of his own father and Courtney herself) that Tonya could indeed be part of the problem?

～ chapter 26

"Prayers are not magical spells," Andrew observes. After all, his mother had prayed that he and Antonio would be spared any angelic inheritance. And now, when Andrew was praying desperately for peace in his twin's life, Antonio seemed to be falling deeper into turmoil. How have you experienced such apparently negative answers to prayer? Why do you think we get these negative responses—in Andrew's life and in your own?

～ chapter 27

In the course of the novel, Andrew has gone from being a dreamy, oversensitive, vulnerable boy who feels alone in a hostile world after his mother dies to being a focused, sensitized, compassionate young man who is determined to protect his newfound family from demonic attack—or whatever else comes. What effects that kind of change in a person? (See Romans 8:38–39, 12:1–2, Ephesians 6:10–18, and Philippians 4:12–13.)

～ chapter 28

"I took a chance. I hugged him. I trusted him." In what ways did Andrew's willingness to embrace Antonio represent a decision to trust his brother? How are trust, faith, and love all tied together in making relationships possible? How have you experienced the same kind of risk that Andrew took in hugging Antonio—and, for that matter, in sharing his love for Courtney?

～ chapter 29

Andrew's story is fiction, of course, and while it may be challenging at times to sort out the truth from the fiction in some parts of the story, Andrew's reflections about Frank (aka Shariel) are consistent with scripture. What experiences have you had that make you believe that "angels are all around us, good and bad"? (See Ephesians 6:12 and Hebrews 1:14, 13:2.)